Maskmaker

JANE JOHNSON is a writer – for adults and for children – and also works remotely as Fiction Publishing Director for HarperCollins Publishers UK.

For many years she was responsible for the publishing of the works of J.R.R. Tolkien, and as Jude Fisher she wrote the bestselling visual companions which accompanied Peter Jackson's movie trilogy of *The Lord of the Rings*.

She is also a trained lecturer and holds a master's degree in Old Icelandic. When not writing and publishing, she likes to rock climb, and it was in 2005, while researching a novel and climbing in Morocco, that she met her husband. Now they split their time between the UK and Morocco, and share their life with Jane's Norwegian Forest Cat, Thorfinna Hairy-Trousers: or Finn, for short.

Her most recent books are *The Tenth Gift* and *The Salt Road*, for adults, and she is working on a new adventure novel for children. Her previous books for children include *The Secret Country*, *The Shadow World* and *Dragon's Fire*.

Maskmaker

Jane Johnson

First published in the UK in 2010 by Marion Lloyd Books
An imprint of Scholastic Ltd
Euston House, 24 Eversholt Street
London, NW1 1DB, UK
Registered office: Westfield Road, Southam, Warwickshire, CV47 0RA

ISBN 978 1407 10687 8

A CIP catalogue record for this book is available from the British Library.

Printed by Bookmarque Ltd, Croydon, Surrey
Papers used by Scholastic Children's Books are made from wood grown in sustainable forests.

1 3 5 7 9 10 8 6 4 2

www.scholastic.co.uk/zone

For William

CONTENTS

PROLOGUE

Snowy wings spread wide, the owl flew whisper-soft through the night. Below it lay the dark expanse of Churnock Woods, the trunks of the beech trees stretching silver towards the moon. Below them lay the Delving Caves, which reached their great hollow roots down into the depths of the earth. The owl lived in the woods; but the one who commanded his loyalty dwelled far below in the dark caverns, amongst columns of twisted rock, the sedimentary icicles of age-old limestone.

On it flew like a phantom, aware of the prey it passed – the vole crouching in the lee of a hedge, the field mouse on the edge of the meadow path – but undistracted from its mission. There would be time to feed later; there were still many hours before the sun showed its face over the hills to the east. It ghosted over the Downs, where stone circles marked the passage of ancient peoples and their mysterious worship; over copses and valleys, rivers and streams.

It flew over Jaggard's Farm, taking in without interest the machinery left rusting in the paddock, the tangle of empty chicken coops and the uncut fields. The farmer was in the dark kingdom now; the owl knew, for it had helped to deliver him there.

On the edge of the town known as Cawstocke, the owl circled. The built-up areas were always the hardest to negotiate. Usually, it was the cats and the feral dogs which patrolled the town; but the number of cats willing to bear the dangerous burden had dwindled, and the dogs were engaged in their own turf wars. Dreams floated up towards the owl through the darkness, and the night-bird felt each one as it passed. In a block of flats just beyond the industrial estate, where the units were now more empty than used, a young man dreamed repeatedly of a car crash in which his legs were trapped and he could not escape the wreckage before fire started to lick at him; in the flat below, a girl ran through a corridor of closed doors pursued by someone intent on harming her. None of the doors would open.

In a cul-de-sac of expensive houses near the park, Douglas Grant paced up and down his front room, woken from restless slumber by a dream so disturbing he dared not go back to sleep. A monster had visited him, of that he was sure; but more than that he did not want to remember.

A few moments later, his son, Andy, cried out, as if the nightmare had travelled the few metres down the corridor and visited him as well.

The owl's mission did not lie here. It flew on, over Victoria Gardens, over Porchester Terrace with its smart Edwardian villas and their imposing bow windows and well-tended gardens, towards the poorer end of town.

The owl remembered, with its long ancestral memory, when there had been no houses here, none at all, when the whole area had been forested; then when it had been first settled by people who came from the east, driven out of their territory by tribal wars. They had brought their own ways and worship with them: sun dances and sacrifice, erecting stone circles and enacting rituals; and they were soon followed by others who brought maypoles and mask-making. People just kept on coming, wave after wave of them, a great noisy tide of humanity. And with them came the house-building, and then the train, and at last the cars, roaring over the ground, polluting the air, poisoning everything.

It was time for it all to stop, for peaceful night to fall for ever across Cawstocke and this whole once-lovely area, for the land to return once more to the creatures of darkness.

The owl now found the place it had been seeking. It noted with satisfaction the way two feral dogs trailed quietly away through the waste ground on the edge of the housing estate, heads down and exhausted. More nightmares successfully delivered.

It glided over the tallest block and concentrated on the sleeping inhabitants.

John Jones, builder's merchant, his debts rising as the demand for new houses dropped away, dreamed of falling into one of his own cement mixers. Round and round he went, crying out soundlessly, like a man trapped in a washing machine. All around, people passed without a glance as the thick grey sludge covered him over and began, second by second, to set into a rock-hard overcoat in which he could move neither finger nor toe.

Philippa Gough watched her daughter Gillian going down for the third time in a wide black lake, just out of reach of the hand Philippa held out to save her. She reached forward an inch more, and found herself falling, falling, towards the black water.

At last the owl found its target and sent on its way its heavy but invisible burden. . .

Cadence Wave turned over beneath her duvet, and a moment later was kissing a boy, though only in her sleep. He was tall and handsome and had the blackest, wickedest eyes she'd ever seen. She didn't know his name; it didn't seem to matter. He was good at kissing, and she was sixteen, and they were dancing with their arms around each other. After an unknowable time in which the music changed, drawing her slowly into its dark rhythms, she pulled back to look at him and found herself embracing a monster with fire in its mouth and eyes. . .

Troubled, the owl turned its flat white face towards the window of the flat. It could sense immediately that it had failed, for in the room next to the silently screaming girl, her younger brother lay untroubled, his sleep as sweet and peaceful as ever, a smile twitching his lips as if someone had just told him a joke.

The owl had been looking forward to a night of carefree hunting, of small, warm creatures struggling in its talons; of their blood running down its beak. Now, its thoughts were mired in dread as it turned for the distant woods and the shadow of its employer.

1 JAMIE WAVE

Dreams.

Everyone dreams, they say, even babies and dogs. Often you can just catch hold of a wisp of a dream – a lucid, shining fragment that stays with you when you surface from sleep: a leaf turning in a breeze, the cry of a strange bird; a car passing silently, its wheels a foot above the ground. Sometimes dreams can become so vivid, so intoxicatingly real, that you can remember them long after waking up. And some dreams can seem more real – and far more enticing – than your own life. These are the dangerous ones. They insinuate themselves like false friends. Like a will-o'-the-wisp, a flickering flame hovering over boggy ground, they will lead you away into strange dark places and then abandon you to your fate.

Cawstocke was in the grip of a plague of dreams.

*

One day Jamie Wave arrived at school to find everyone chattering excitedly.

"What's going on?"

"We're comparing dreams," said Jinny Briggs, a twinkle-eyed girl with hair the colour of the orange heart of a flame. "We all had really good dreams last night. Johnny was in a band, singing to hundreds of people in a club—"

Everyone laughed again, since Johnny's voice was rasping and awful. The music teacher, Mr Doherty, chastised them for laughing at him. "Leave him alone, his voice is breaking," he would say, and someone was bound to chorus back, "I think it's already broken, sir!"

"And Linda dreamed she was swimming in the sea at night."

"Yeah, that's proper skinny-dipping!" someone sniggered. Linda was painfully thin.

Linda pretended not to hear this. "It was gorgeous," she sighed. "The water was all silver and sparkly, and there were dolphins leaping in and out of the waves."

"I was a pirate, all dressed in black," said Jack Cole. "I had sword fights and climbed the ship's rigging with a cutlass between my teeth." This was hard to imagine, because Jack looked as unlike a pirate as you could imagine: he was, if you were being honest, a bit fat, and he was hopeless at sport. No one could imagine him climbing the rigging: he could barely get off the ground on the ropes in the school gym but would hang there, flailing and wailing like a fly trapped in a spider's web.

Wayne had dreamed of finding buried treasure in a big, dark cave, and Tessa had been transformed into a cat. "I always wondered what Minkie did when Mum shut him out at night. Well, now I know. It was great: I spent the whole night running around with him and his mates. We chased some mice and knocked over Mrs O'Shea's bin, and sang to the moon."

Pete topped that. He had *been* to the moon.

"How did you do that?" asked Jamie Wave, curious. Jamie was curious about everything: he saw wonders in the world where other people only saw the ordinary. But flying to the moon was certainly not ordinary; it sounded exciting. Except that you would have to fly through the night and Jamie was afraid of the dark; not that he would ever admit it to anyone but his mum. "Were you in a rocket ship, or a flying saucer or something?"

"I just . . . flew," grinned Pete. "I put my arms out and soared into the air. First of all I zoomed around the room; then I flew out of the window and all around the estate, looking in through people's windows. And then I flew all the way up to the moon!"

"A dream like that's wasted on you, you manky little

runt!" a posh voice interrupted. "If I'd had your dream I'd have flown up to look through Cadence Wave's window and watched her getting undressed."

It was Michael Rose, the class bully. He belonged to a gang of older boys who liked to pick on anyone they regarded as different to themselves. They picked on Pete because his dad was in prison, they picked on Tessa because her frayed uniform had belonged to her older sister, and from time to time they picked on Jamie because, well, Jamie didn't really understand why they picked on him.

Jamie was about to open his mouth to object to this disrespect to his sister, but it was Jinny Briggs who fixed Michael Rose with a steely gaze and said, "Oh, do grow up." She turned to Jamie. "What about you, Jamie, what did you dream about?"

"Yeah, Benefits Boy, what did *you* dream about?" mimicked Michael Rose. He turned to his mate, Mouth. "Probably getting his skin whitened, eh? Like Michael Jackson?"

Mouth, whom nobody called by his real name of Freddie for fear of being thumped, had a face like a weasel, little mean black eyes and wide lips like a pair of chipolata sausages. "Nah. He dreamed he had a dad!" joked Mouth. "And his dad was the King Under the Hill!"

The King Under the Hill was a shadowy figure in local folk tales who stole children from their beds or lured them into his caves in order to populate his fairy kingdom. People often touched wood when his name was mentioned: if you didn't he might get you.

No one said anything; they all knew that Jamie Wave's dad had disappeared and that no one knew where he'd gone.

"Don't pay any attention to them," Jinny said, smiling kindly at Jamie. "They're just ignorant." And she glared at Mouth and Michael Rose, her cool blue eyes sparking defiance. The two bullies glared back, then sloped off.

For such a tiny girl, Jinny was very brave, Jamie thought.

Jinny smiled at him. "Tell me what you dreamed about last night, Jamie Wave."

"Nothing."

"You can't dream of nothing!"

Jamie grinned at his best friend. "I didn't dream."

"What, you mean you can't remember what your dream was about?"

"No, I just didn't dream. I don't really dream at all."

"You must dream: everyone dreams."

"Not me." He gave a shrug. "Why, what did you dream about, Jinny?"

Jinny was just about to answer when the school bell rang for the start of lessons and everyone started to pile into the classroom and they were swept along in the tide.

"I dreamed of you, Jamie Wave," Jinny said quietly. But her words were lost in the din.

At morning break, Jamie Wave was minding his own business out in the playground when someone came up behind him and kicked him in the back of the knee so that it buckled and he fell down like a complete idiot.

"Hey, Benefits Boy, what you got for us today?"

When he looked up it was to find Mouth and Michael Rose staring down at him.

"Get his bag," said Mouth.

"Here."

They unzipped it and upended it so that its contents spilled over the tarmac. Mouth kicked the books and pens away so that they ended up in a puddle. Then he snatched up Jamie's battered CD player.

"Hey!" cried Jamie. "You can't have that." It had been a gift from his mother to celebrate his winning a scholarship for Cawstocke's only private school. "Sorry it's not an iPod, love," his mum had said with a wry smile. And he'd laughed because she hadn't known an iPod was no use unless you had a computer, which they didn't.

Mouth levered the CD player open and examined the disc inside. "Ugh, Blue Flamingos – they're rubbish!"

"No!" Jamie scrambled to his feet, but he was too slow.

Mouth sent the CD spinning across the playground like a flying saucer, a rainbow of colours reflecting off its silver surfaces. Grimly, Jamie scooped up his school bag and looked for his books. One of them had fallen in a puddle, its red cover darker by the moment as it soaked up the muddy water; he'd have to copy out his English essay again. His beloved sketch book had fallen face down. Jamie had brought it in because it was art with Miss Lambent this afternoon and they were working on a project that he'd been making sketches for all week. If they opened it they'd make fun of them or tear out the pages. His knees began to tremble. He was such a coward! Why was he such a coward? He gritted his teeth. "No!"

Mouth leered at him. "What did you say, Benefits Boy?"

"Give me my stuff back."

"What'll you give us in return?"

Jamie thought fast. He had nothing to give them. "I . . . er . . . I'll make you laugh."

Michael Rose snorted. "Looking at your ugly face makes *me* laugh."

"Shut up." Mouth stepped in front of his lieutenant. "Go on, then, Benefits Boy. Make me laugh."

Jamie cleared his throat and out popped the first joke that came into his head, which was a pity because it wasn't one of the better ones. Jamie had hundreds of jokes stashed away in his head: jokes and riddles and wordplay and other pointless bits of nonsense. It was probably why he didn't dream: imagination needed room to roam, and his brain was full to bursting, like an attic stuffed with boxes and bags of old rubbish.

"Two p-parrots are sitting on a perch. One turns to the other and says, 'It really smells fishy around here.'"

Mouth looked expectant. "Go on, then," he said at last. "What's the punchline?"

"Sitting on a perch," Jamie said. "It's a sort of fish."

They didn't laugh.

Michael Rose made as if to stamp on the CD player. Jamie gabbled: "OK, OK, what do you call a fish with no eyes?"

They eyed him as if suspicious that he was trying to make them look stupid. But they didn't need his help to do that: they were really good at looking stupid all on their own.

"Go on then," said Mouth at last. "What do you call a fish with no eyes?"

"Fsh."

It took a while but then Mouth's lips twitched. "That's quite clever, that is. A fish with no *i*'s. But I'm not laughing, Benefits Boy, just smiling. Smash it, Rosy."

Jamie trawled desperately through his array of jokes. "There are t-two g-goldfish in a tank."

"What did he say?" Michael Rose frowned.

"Something about g-g-g-goldfish in a tank," Mouth said cruelly.

"Two goldfish in a tank," Jamie repeated, swallowing his stutter. "One of the goldfish turns to the other and says, 'You got any idea how to drive this thing?'"

For a brief moment puzzle-lines appeared between Mouth's eyebrows, then his lips quirked into a smile, and then he was laughing, throwing his head back and guffawing with all his might. He punched Michael Rose on the arm. "A tank," he said, grinning and gripping an imaginary steering wheel. "A fish driving a tank! Geddit?"

"Oh, yeah." Michael didn't look as if he'd got it at all.

"Brilliant!" Mouth shoved Jamie matily on the shoulder. "You're lucky, Benefits Boy: you made me laugh. Just as well or we'd have had to beat you up, right, Rosy?"

For a moment, Michael Rose looked disappointed. Then he yawned. "Yeah, right."

And they walked off to pick on someone else.

2 MISS LAMBENT

"Today," said Miss Lambent, "we are going to make masks."

She walked around the class, handing out white cotton aprons.

A scuffle soon broke out at the back of the art room where she had passed, two boys slapping each other with their aprons, using them like whips.

Miss Lambent turned. "Now then, Alan, Michael," she said quietly. Miss Lambent never shouted. Under the gaze of her golden eyes they stopped horsing around immediately and meekly put their aprons on over their shirts.

Everything about Miss Lambent was golden: her skin, which was as translucent as porcelain; her hair, which was as long and pale as sunlight; her eyes as tawny as caramel. She was slim and graceful, like a willow. But she looked strong, Jamie thought, as if like a tree she could endure anything, live for hundreds of years through storm and flood and fire. It was impossible to tell her age. *Ageless* was the word that came into his mind when he thought about her. Others might have called her beautiful. All Jamie knew was that when she smiled at him, or encouraged him to tell the class a joke at the end of the lesson, he wanted to please her. He didn't feel this way about any of the other teachers at school.

Mr Martin had a tendency to look down his long nose at him and sniff loudly, as if implying that he smelled of old cheese. Mr Reynolds always asked him the most difficult questions, even though he was hopeless at maths, and then when he got the answer wrong would sigh and roll his eyes as if dealing with an idiot. Mrs Hobb would stare at him, then look away sharply. And Mrs Willis made him stand up and recite in class, even though she knew it made him stutter.

"Masks," said Miss Lambent, sitting on the desk at the front of the art class. "Who can tell me about masks?"

Helen Russell put her hand up. Helen Russell always knew everything. Jinny Briggs raised her hand too; so did Jamie.

"Jinny?"

"People wear masks to hide behind," Jinny said.

"And why might they do that? Jamie?"

"Because they don't want people to know who they are, like a disguise; or because it makes them feel braver if no one can see their face?"

Miss Lambent tilted her head. "That's a very interesting answer, Jamie. Who might want to hide their face?"

"A bank robber!" offered Andy Grant.

"The Elephant Man!" Michael Rose twisted his features into a grotesque expression and waved an arm in front of his face like a trunk.

"The Phantom of the Opera!"

"A plastic surgery patient." This from Linda Myhill, who was said to be already planning her first facelift at the age of twelve.

"Someone at a masked ball."

"Someone pretending to be someone else."

"Someone really ugly. . ."

"Jamie Wave!"

"Now, why would you say that, Angela?" Miss Lambent said sharply. "It's hurtful and untrue. It's usually people who are ugly on the inside who accuse others of being ugly on the outside."

And she fixed Angela Horne with her toffee-gold eyes until Angela went pink. Miss Lambent peered intently at her victim.

"Are you wearing make-up, Angela?"

"Yes, Miss Lambent." She had turned beetroot-red.

The teacher watched her for a few long seconds. Then to the rest of the class she said, "Make-up is a sort of mask too, isn't it? Something to hide behind. Cosmetics can hide all sorts of ugliness. They can transform the plainest face into something that gives the appearance of beauty. Or, for that matter, make a beautiful face hideous. Masks are ambiguous things, you see. Who can tell me the meaning of the word 'ambiguous'?"

There was silence. Everyone had an inkling of what it meant, but it was hard to put into words and no one wanted to get it wrong, especially when Miss Lambent was in this sort of mood.

At last, Jamie put his hand up. "S-something that can be appear to be good, but be bad? Or the other way round."

"Listen, everyone. Jamie Wave knows something important about the world: that it is not always what it seems. Appearances can be deceptive. It can be difficult to tell good from bad, particularly if people try to hide their real selves. If people wear masks, how can you know who they *really* are?"

Her eyes flicked from one pupil to the next, resting for a moment on Gillian Gough (known because of her initials as Pony) before moving on to Michael Rose, whose mouth hung open as if he was catching flies. They settled on Jamie once more and her voice was softer as she said, "But masks can also make you feel safer, and they can protect you from danger. A gas mask can save you from poisonous gas, and a welder wears a steel mask to save his eyes from dangerous sparks. And some masks act as shields against . . . all sorts of perils.

"Last week I set you the task of drawing a mask that represents someone or something you admire or aspire to. This week we're going to make some of those masks, so let's see what you've come up with."

Tessa McIntosh had drawn a moon in profile, a graceful crescent with a curved smile, "Because Mum says the moon watches over us while we sleep."

Jack Cole had sketched a famous footballer, "Because I want to be like him, rich and successful."

"And married to a supermodel!" added Wayne Hunt.

Jinny had drawn a rose with a face in it. "Because my grandmother grows roses and they make her smile, even though she's ill and hardly sleeps any more."

Andy Grant had drawn a monster. It had fangs and snakes for hair and horrible scribbles for eyes. "Why did you draw this, then, Andy?"

"Dunno, miss."

She scrutinized him for a few long moments. "Did you have a nightmare, perhaps?"

He looked surprised, then gave a barely perceptible nod. Miss Lambent folded his sketch and put it to one side. "No need to encourage the dark things of the night to visit us in the daytime."

Jamie Wave had drawn a tiger. He had spent a long time on his sketch. His tiger had a broad rusty-orange muzzle and black stripes that radiated from the centre of its wide forehead, outlined its piercing golden eyes and ran down into the long white fur of its cheeks. He wanted to be like a tiger, fearless and proud, but to say so was to admit how afraid and weak he felt and that was an invitation to more bullying. "Because they're so good at hunting and looking after themselves. They're brilliant hunters because their stripes act as camouflage in the jungle so you can hardly see them. And they're brave and loyal and will defend their cubs to the death," he said when asked why he'd chosen it.

Miss Lambent looked at him, then she looked at the tiger. Then she winked at him, and Jamie was sure that she had seen everything he was and all he wished he could be.

3 MAKING MASKS

Miss Lambent picked out six designs for the class to work on, and Jamie's tiger was one of them. Everyone was divided into teams to make the chosen masks. Jamie found himself working with Jinny and – to his dismay – Michael Rose.

They cut up lengths of plaster bandage into little strips. Then they filled a bowl with water and placed the strips of plaster into it to soak. Because it was Jamie's design, he had to be the one to have the mask modelled on his face. He sat on a chair while Jinny put a shower cap over his short, wiry black hair to keep the plaster out of it. She giggled. He looked very silly, like her gran when the hairdresser came round to redo her perm. Then Jamie rubbed Vaseline over his face, to stop the mask from sticking to his skin.

"Shut your eyes," Michael Rose ordered. "If you dare."

Jamie closed his eyes. The first strips of wet bandage were slapped on to his forehead, feeling cold and clammy, like a dead man's fingers. More went on to his cheeks and chin. A big bit flopped over his mouth. It tasted like a mixture of chalk and antiseptic, and he spat it out. "Yuk!"

"Not like that. You've got to leave holes for the mouth and nose and eyes," Jinny said impatiently.

He could feel the gentle pressure of her hands as she pressed the strips of plaster on to his face. After a few minutes of this, Jamie found himself transported back in time to when his sister, Cadence, had used him as a guinea pig for one of her organic face masks. It was supposed to leave your skin flawlessly smooth, but instead had left him covered in ugly swollen blotches. "How was I to know you were allergic to strawberries?" she had wailed. Jamie had shrugged: up to that point he hadn't known either, and neither had his parents.

His mother had had a blue fit, insisting he should be rushed straight to hospital, but his dad had tried to calm her down, saying wasn't it better to wash everything off and wait half an hour to see whether the blotches went down? They had got into one of their terrible rows, and his mother was yelling at his father how he'd changed and not for the better. "You're not the man I married!" she'd wailed, and then burst into tears.

That had been a couple of months before his dad had

disappeared, for good. The trouble was, Jamie knew it was his fault that his father had left. "Dad never wanted another child," Cadence told him cruelly one day. "It was easier when there was just me. He can't afford you, especially now he's not working down the mine." Their father had worked at the silver mine for the last dozen or so years: down in the dark depths of the earth, leaving before sunrise every morning and coming home only as darkness fell. When the mine had closed, like so many other businesses did around Cawstocke, Thomas Wave couldn't stand hanging around the house. He slept all day and started going out alone at night. That caused their mum to be angry and upset, and after a series of interminable rows Jamie's dad had left altogether.

Cadence was beautiful – everyone said so – as blonde and statuesque as Jamie was dark and small. They hardly looked like brother and sister at all. Mrs Wave explained that it sometimes happened that one child took their genes from the mother and the other from the father. Jamie loved his sister but she could be mean, and lately she'd got more snappy and aloof. He could remember when they had been close, when they hadn't fought like their parents, when they'd played and joked and had fun. But now it was as if someone had taken his real sister away and substituted her with a horrible simulacrum.

"Mmmmph!" Suddenly he couldn't breathe. His eyes fluttered open, to find Michael Rose grinning at him evilly.

Jinny pushed Michael away. "You've just stuffed a load of plaster up his nose! Are you trying to kill him or what?"

Michael stuck his chin out belligerently. "Even a weed like Jamie Wave wouldn't die of *that*."

Soon the mask began to set, and as it did it became hot and uncomfortable, pinching his skin, pressing against his nostrils, squeezing his cheeks. What if it stuck to him for ever, he thought in sudden panic. What if he could never get it off? But he was sure that Miss Lambent would never let anything bad happen to any of her pupils.

As he thought this, she appeared in front of him, as if by magic. The hairs rose on the back of his neck. "That's coming along nicely. Well done."

Then she was gone and Michael Rose thrust his face at Jamie. "Think you're safe in there behind that tiger mask, do you? Don't worry, I'll get you later, Benefits Boy."

Jinny stared at him. "That's a horrible thing to say."

"He's council house scum," Michael Rose declared with the disdain of one whose family was rolling in money. His father had closed the mine where Jamie's father and so many others used to work, instead transferring the business to Eastern Europe, where labour costs were lower.

"Money means nothing," Jinny said angrily. "It's who you are that matters: not what you've got."

"We don't want his kind here," Michael said. "Monkeys with scholarships. Everyone else has to pay to come to this place: why should beggars like him be able to come for free?"

"Better a beggar than a total moron like you!"

At this, Michael raised a hand to thump Jinny. Without thinking, Jamie launched himself at Michael, thrusting his masked face at him. A roar swelled up inside him. Then it escaped, growing in volume until it filled the classroom with a wall of sound.

Everyone stopped what they were doing, their eyes wide with surprise and fear. Someone screamed and Tessa McIntosh burst into tears. "Don't let it get me!" she wailed, as if there was a real tiger in the room.

Jamie Wave stood as still as a stone. He could hear the echo of the roar reverberating around his skull. Had that enormous roar come out of his own mouth? It didn't seem possible. Adrenaline raced through him, making his heart race. For a moment he wanted to leap and pounce and bite.

Then Miss Lambent was at his side. She lifted the mask carefully away from his face and looked at him with her golden gaze. Then she smiled. "Go to the cloakroom, Jamie, and wash your face." She turned to Michael Rose. "You are a bigot and a snob, Michael Rose," she said to him, her face hard and angry.

Then she turned away. Behind her, Michael Rose stuck two fingers up to her retreating back.

Without turning around, Miss Lambent said softly, "Bad things happen to people like you, Michael: you had better change your ways."

4 TIGERS

"Knock knock."

There was a long, heavy silence on the other side of his sister's bedroom door. Jamie Wave leaned in closer, resting his cheek against the wood panelling.

"Cadence?"

Still nothing.

He opened the door a crack and repeated, "Knock knock. . ."

There was a weary sigh; then his sister responded dutifully, "Who's there?"

Jamie grinned. "Police."

A pause.

"Police who?"

"Police let me in, it's cold out here."

Cadence groaned. "Lame, lame, lame, little bro. What a horrible way to wake up. What time is it, anyway?"

"Gone eight."

"Urrgh. Why didn't you wake me earlier?"

There was a flurry of movement, the rustle of a duvet, feet hitting the floor, and then the door was flung open. Cadence Wave stood there, her blonde hair like a haystack, her face all creased from the pillow, mascara smudged beneath her eyes.

Jamie regarded her critically. "You look like a panda."

Cadence pushed him out of the way. "What on earth would *you* know about it? What would you know about *anything*?"

In the kitchen he searched for something to eat for breakfast. The cornflakes box was empty, and there was no bread. Nor was there any milk or juice. In the end he discovered two stale Rich Tea biscuits, a can of fizzy drink and an apple with a soft, ripe bruise. It was hardly the world's most nutritious breakfast but it could have been worse.

Cadence stomped in, her hair all wet from the shower, ran the hot tap for a minute, stuck a mug under it and made herself a cup of instant black coffee.

"Knock knock."

"Not again. Who's there?"

"Buddha."

"Buddha who?"

Jamie grinned from ear to ear. "Buddha me some toast."

"Crikey O'Reilly," Cadence groaned, an odd phrase she had picked up from their father. "They get worse."

Jamie shrugged. "Sorry." He gazed at his sister. Clean now, Cadence's face revealed that the darkness around her eyes was from shadows beneath the skin, not from smeared make-up after all. He pushed his plate towards her. "Here, you can share my breakfast if you like."

She gave him a wan smile. "No thanks, not hungry." She reached across the table and snagged the packet of cigarettes their mother had left there the night before. "Model's breakfast," she declared, lighting up.

Jamie wrinkled his nose. "Knock knock."

"Oh, not again. Who's there?"

"Mrs Rosberg."

Mrs Rosberg was their neighbour, a stick-thin woman who boasted that she used to be a model, but who now had skin like a corpse's – pale, loose and deeply incised with gullies and wrinkles, especially around her mouth. Jamie leaned his elbow on the table in an eerily exact image of their neighbour, puckered his lips as if smoking a cigarette and regarded his sister with crossed eyes.

Cadence laughed, despite herself. "OK, point taken." She put the cigarette down.

"She's got a mouth like a cat's bum."

"Gross!" Cadence shrieked. "But she's ancient. I've got

no intention of living *that* long. Not around here, anyhow. No wonder people leave: it's so depressing."

Jamie looked at her, alarmed. "You won't leave, will you, Cadence?"

She looked away. "There has to be something better than Cawstocke. Sometimes, I dream. . ." She sighed and pushed herself away from the table. "Who am I kidding?"

Today was the day they were going to decorate their masks. The masks were all lined up on the window sill. Jamie didn't have to look at the name on the back of his to know it immediately. There was something about it, something alive, as if it had been sitting there all this time taking on a character of its own. He remembered the roar that had come out of him so unexpectedly when he thought Michael Rose was going to hit Jinny, and he shivered.

"It looks very fierce," Jinny said, turning it over in her hands a bit gingerly, as if it might bite her.

"Don't be soft," sneered Michael Rose. "It looks like next door's moggy. Geriatric old thing that's scared of its own shadow. Someone should put it out of its misery. Perhaps I will."

Jamie ignored him. He had brought a length of fake fur that his mum had let him cut off one of her old scarves. "Your dad gave it me for a birthday, but I never liked it much anyway," she'd lied. Then she had gone to her room for a lie-down. She did that a lot nowadays. "This is for my tiger's mane," he told Jinny. "And these are for its whiskers. . ." Some fuse-wire which he had cut into whisker-sized lengths.

They painted the tiger's face in shades of orange and black and white. They coloured its nose a dark, dusky pink, and Michael drew in between its black lips the tips of sharp white teeth. Then they stuck the wires into its muzzle and glued the fringe of white fake fur around its head. Jamie added black stripes with a wide marker pen and Jinny cut out a pair of little round ears from cardboard and added those amidst the fur; and there it was, gazing up at them blankly.

"Try it on, Jinny," Jamie suggested, but it was Michael who snatched it roughly – so roughly that one of its ears fell off.

"Hey!" cried Jinny. "Be careful!"

"Be careful yourself, you ginger mutant!"

Gritting her teeth, Jinny laid hands on the tiger mask and pulled. Michael Rose held on for a moment, then pushed it at her so hard that she fell over backwards and the mask flew out into the air. Without even knowing what he was doing, Jamie leapt for it and jammed it on his head.

All at once it was as if the classroom rushed away from

him, as if he were suddenly seeing it through the wrong end of a telescope, making it tiny and distant. A hot damp heat enveloped him: he let his mouth hang open to pant for air, and abruptly the smells of paint and glue were replaced by the scents of wet earth and jungle vegetation and a powerfully sweet iron-tang that made him feel ravenously hungry, more hungry than he had ever been in his life. And there in front of him was something fawn and spotted. It was a small, pretty deer, but the word *prey* came into his head. He felt his muscles bunch, his jaws open wide: wider than any human mouth could open. And then he was leaping and his teeth were fastened on something warm and soft, something that writhed and twisted beneath him.

The part of him that was still Jamie Wave heard the screams; but they seemed a long, long way away. . .

5 BLOOD

"Jamie, get up!"

He lifted his head from the tantalizing scent of the deer. As his grip loosened on its throat it wriggled away from him and fled. Two legs! There were two-legs here, the pale animals that walked upright. Human beings.

The tiger-who-was-Jamie twitched his nostrils.

One of them was close to him: too close, reaching out. The cerulean sky glimpsed through the canopy tilted sharply as the mask slipped sideways, and all of a sudden his sense of power and confidence fell away with it. The smells of the jungle were replaced, abruptly, by the smells of the classroom, though for two or three hallucinatory seconds they seemed far more pungent and distinct than usual. He could make out the paints and the clay and the glue, the rolls of paper in the cupboard, even the water in the sink at the back of the room. Now he became aware of Jinny's peach shampoo, the cheesiness of Pete Flynn's trainers; and closest of all Miss Lambent. To his tiger-self she smelled like a tree with a rotten core, eaten by termites, something long dead and decayed to dust. Then the mask fell from him and suddenly he was Jamie Wave again, standing in the middle of the art room with everyone staring at him. Michael Rose had his hands to his throat as if he had been bitten, though there was no sign of a wound. He looked scared to death and for a brief moment Jamie felt a tiny zing of satisfaction.

"What was all that about, Jamie?" Miss Lambent asked, picking up the tiger mask. In her hands it looked like the harmless piece of plaster and fake fur it really was. Some of the paint appeared to have run through the hole for the mouth and stained the white plaster on the other side a bright red, and suddenly Jamie realized that his mouth was full of blood. Had he bitten himself? Or (and this possibility seemed far worse) *someone else*?

Miss Lambent's eyes were very bright. She looked . . . odd, excited even. "Are you all right, Michael?" she asked.

Michael Rose nodded slowly. He watched Jamie warily, rocking on the balls of his feet as if getting ready to run. The other members of his class stood at a distance, looking pale and scared.

Miss Lambent turned to Jamie. "I think you'd better come with me, young man," she said solemnly. To the rest of the class she said, "There's only five minutes to the bell, so clear up your areas. When the bell goes, make sure you leave quietly, and have a nice weekend. Don't have nightmares."

Then she led Jamie out of the classroom.

Jamie felt the blood in his mouth. It tasted hot and metallic. He thought he might be sick. Miss Lambent marched him purposefully along the corridor, past the cloakrooms, heading for the staffroom. Was she taking him to see Mr Jellicoe, the headmaster? Would he be punished, even expelled? What had he done?

Worry knotted his stomach. He snatched a glance at Miss Lambent. She didn't look particularly angry: in fact, as if she had felt his eyes on her, she turned her toffee-coloured gaze upon him. "I'm taking you to the sick bay," she said gently.

In the sick bay she sat him down on the couch, wetted some paper towels at the sink and blotted them around his mouth. "Dear me," she said brightly. "What a lot of blood. Does it hurt?"

Actually it didn't hurt at all. Could you bite your tongue so hard that it bled that much and didn't hurt? It seemed unlikely. "No, miss." He paused. "Is Michael Rose OK?"

Miss Lambent smiled. "Apart from being a bully, a bigot

and an ignoramus? Yes, Michael is fine. It's you I'm worried about. Let me have a look at your mouth."

Obediently, he tilted his head back and let her look.

"That's very strange," she said after a while. "I can't see anything wrong with you at all." But she looked not puzzled but somehow . . . triumphant as she said this. "Tell me what happened when you put on the mask, Jamie," she said softly. "Because I don't think this is your blood. I'm not even sure it's human."

6 AN INVITATION

Jamie told Miss Lambent all he could remember about putting on the mask, about the heat and the smell of the jungle, and the poor, struggling deer. "I k-know it sounds mad . . ."

Miss Lambent leaned towards him. "I don't think it sounds mad at all. I think, Jamie Wave, that you have a very special gift. One besides telling jokes." She blotted his face with some fresh paper towels and this time they came away clean. "There," she said. "That's better. Have you ever worn a mask before? Try to remember."

Jamie wrinkled his forehead. He had been to fancy dress parties as a little boy, but largely as cowboys and firemen and Bob the Builder, so all he'd worn were costumes and plastic hats, never masks. For Halloween, he'd worn a sheet a few times and pretended to be a ghost, and once had allowed Cadence to put a long orange wig and a tall witch's hat on him, and blacken his teeth with a crayon; but he couldn't ever remember wearing a mask. He shook his head.

"I want you to have this," she said, reaching into the pocket out of which she had taken the handkerchief and drawing out a small white card.

He turned it over, and read:

The Maskmaker
27 May Street
Cawstocke

"The area's a bit run-down nowadays, but the shop has been there for a long time. A very long time. It was one of the first shops in Cawstocke. I rarely invite anyone to it. Will you come to my maskmaker's shop, Jamie?"

"W-when?" Something about this invitation made him suddenly nervous.

"Tomorrow?"

Saturday was the day the whole family used to go shopping to the big supermarket in the modern mall on the other side of town, but lately his mother never seemed to be able to rouse herself sufficiently to make such a major foray.

"At what time?"

"I shall be there all day, just until it gets dark."

Jamie wasn't at all sure he wanted to go there. Something

about the idea of seeing a teacher out of school hours was weird: it would be like seeing a rhinoceros in the street, or finding a crocodile in the bathtub. And after the strangeness of the tiger mask, he wasn't sure he wanted anything more to do with masks ever again.

He felt her eyes upon him. She was waiting for his answer. He looked up nervously, all sorts of doubts running through his mind, culminating in a sort of dark and nameless panic.

"OK. I'll come tomorrow afternoon. Before it gets dark." He didn't want to be out after the sun had gone down. Ever since his dad had left he'd been scared of the dark: it was as if his father had held back the night, made it a safe place to be, and now that he was gone there was no one to do that. He slept with a night light in his room, even though Cadence teased him about it.

"Yes, come well before dark," Miss Lambent echoed. She gazed at him intently.

Just like that, the pact was made. Something had changed in the world – something tiny, something subtle, and yet something huge – as if a decision had been taken and great events hinged upon it.

Miss Lambent smiled at him, her eyes like lamps. "That's perfect. See you tomorrow, Jamie Wave."

*

The next morning Jamie knocked on Cadence's door, and then at his mum's door, to ask if they wanted a cup of tea, but there was no reply from either of them.

It was probably just as well, because in the kitchen everything was in disarray. It was always in disarray, but maybe it had hit critical mass. Unwashed dishes were piled up all around the draining board. Used cups and mugs made unsteady towers. Pans sat in a bowl of scummy water in the sink, as if his mother or sister had had the impulse to do something about them, and had then run out of steam. There were empty pizza boxes and choked ashtrays on the table, old newspaper on the floor, and the bin was overflowing and smelly. He hadn't realized how bad things had got. He should, he knew, try to do something about it, but the task was enormous: he felt overwhelmed.

One small step at a time, said a little voice in his head. It was something his mum had kept saying to herself when his dad had disappeared. *We've got to take it one small step at a time*, delivered with a brave smile that had soon wobbled.

Jamie rolled up his sleeves.

"You are an angel."

His mother was leaning against the jamb of the kitchen door, watching him. How long she had been there he did not know: the sounds of the clinking of the dishes and the swirl of the water had masked her arrival. She looked wan and exhausted.

"Shall we go out?" he suggested, drying his hands on his jeans. "Get some fresh air, maybe to the park or something?"

His mother yawned. "I'm too tired."

Jamie sighed. He'd done his best. "Do you mind if I go out then?"

Mrs Wave looked puzzled. "What day is it? Shouldn't you be at school?"

"It's Saturday," Jamie replied slowly. He hated it when she got like this. "It's the weekend." He watched her face fall. Weekends were when they spent time together as a family, sitting together on the sofa, watching old films, playing games.

Suddenly she reached out and grabbed him by the wrist, holding it so hard he gasped. "Don't leave, Jamie. Promise you'll never leave me."

Later that afternoon, while his mother dozed on the sofa, Jamie slipped out of the flat and took the bus into town. But the bus didn't go anywhere near May Street, for that part of town was not much used any more. Jamie had to walk past the shopping centre and the war memorial, up the continuation of the high street with its junk shops, everything-for-a-pound store, key cutters and cobblers. What had once been the Grand Cinema had become a bingo hall; but even that had closed down, its once-bright posters faded and tattered, and a padlocked chain was across its main door.

May Street was the next on the right. It was a grim-looking street, dark and dank, as if it had swallowed every ray of sunlight that had filtered through the gloom. Jamie almost turned back, but he could feel the card Miss Lambent had given him like a lead weight in his pocket and knew he had to go on. He took the card out and stared at it for the hundredth time, though he knew perfectly well what it said.

"Number twenty-seven. . .'

None of the boarded-up shops had numbers on them, as if they were too embarrassed to admit to belonging here. He kept on walking, his footsteps echoing off the cobbles. He passed abandoned cars, two of them burned out, rusting tin cans, and drifts of old newspaper gone pulpy from last night's rain. He skirted a large puddle and stopped suddenly, convinced that someone was watching him. All the little hairs on the back of his neck rose, as if someone had run a chilly finger across his skin. There! A pale, unmoving figure in a dusty window to his left. Jamie stared at it for several seconds before realizing it was only a wooden tailor's dummy left to get cobwebby in a disused draper's shop. He walked quickly away, his heart rattling his ribs.

Then something touched him.

Jamie almost leapt in the air. He looked down. A black cat was sitting in the road, regarding him with huge orange eyes. Jamie was not overly fond of cats. They always seemed to be looking at you as if you had just done something very stupid, or were just about to. The cat miaowed, and rubbed itself against his ankles again.

"Go away," said Jamie crossly; and as if it were being obedient (in a way cats never were) it trotted away from him down May Street.

When he didn't immediately follow, it stopped and looked back over its shoulder, for all the world as if it were saying, "Come on, Jamie Wave, hurry up."

Annoyed, Jamie followed it for another hundred metres, when it suddenly stopped and sat down in a doorway, where it cleaned its paws and face and waited for him to catch up.

It had stopped in the doorway of number twenty-seven. A sign in faded gold script above the door read:

The Maskmaker

In the window, unsurprisingly, were masks. Hundreds

of them, their hollow eyes all trained upon him expectantly.

The cat stood up and stretched. It too looked at Jamie expectantly, as if waiting for him to open the door.

Summoning his courage, Jamie Wave placed his hand upon the door handle. It turned smoothly beneath his grasp and the door opened with a creak of old hinges. The cat wove itself neatly between his legs and disappeared into the gloom inside. Nervously, Jamie followed.

7 THE MASKMAKER

Jamie had expected Miss Lambent to be in the shop waiting for him, but to his surprise it was deserted. Except for the masks. Rows and rows of them stared down at him from the shelves with their empty black eyeholes. It was like being in the catacombs, where the skulls of the dead are stored. It was like being in a dream. Or a nightmare.

Even the cat had vanished.

Everywhere he looked there was something to beguile the eye. Some of the masks were elegant white Venetian half-masks, ready to be worn to a midnight ball, your identity hidden as you went to join in the revels; some were hideous creations designed to scare small children – or adults – at Halloween. Some were full rubber head-masks bearing the likenesses of prime ministers or presidents of the United States, which you might wear to a fancy dress party, or to rob a bank. A mask of Elvis

Presley seemed to be deep in conversation with Mickey Mouse. Harry Potter and Osama Bin Laden occupied one corner with Tom and Jerry and Cristiano Ronaldo, whilst in another Dracula and Madonna leaned companionably against one another. Jamie could see masks for Superman and Batman, Spider-Man and Wolverine; Bart Simpson, Muhammed Ali and David Beckham – or was it Brad Pitt? They were all ranged in neat rows on the shelves that lined the walls of the shop; and here and there were gaps in the display as if the odd mask had been sold, or rented out, and not returned. There were masks from ancient civilizations, Indian, African, Maori and Aztec; the head of an Ancient Egyptian pharaoh and a Native American chieftain complete with feather headdress. There was a mask of a Viking, complete with horns on its helmet. The head of Ganesh the elephant god held court with Frankenstein, William Shakespeare and Darth Vader. There were masks you might wear to a fancy-dress party – firemen and cowboys, gorillas and dinosaurs; a wizard's mask with a tall pointed hat and long grey beard. A lot of the masks Jamie did not recognize at all; some looked as handmade as his tiger, while others seemed as old as the hills. There was an ancient Greek warrior with a horsehair crest on his helmet, a pair of garish great animal heads, a horrible-looking ghoul with worms crawling out of its mouth and, presiding over them all, his face and beard formed from twined leaves and birds, a Celtic Green Man.

They all peered down at Jamie, waiting.

The air in the shop felt still and close, as if a thunderstorm were brewing. Suddenly all Jamie wanted to do was to leave the maskmaker's shop and get out into the fresh air. He wanted to run all the way up May Street to the high road and jump on the first bus that came along and go home and curl up on the sofa with his mother in front of a comforting game show or talent competition. He turned on his heel and walked quickly back to the door. But when he reached out his hand to it, he couldn't find a door handle; and when he pushed it, nothing happened.

Something moved in the gloom at the back of the shop. He turned, and there was Miss Lambent.

"Please, miss, I did what you said and came here, but I want to leave now," he said, fighting down the panic that rose to engulf him.

"Now that you're here, I'm afraid there's only one way out," said Miss Lambent softly. "You must choose a mask, Jamie."

Jamie didn't want to choose a mask. There were too many to choose from, and they were all staring at him. He remembered what had happened with the tiger mask. He began to feel dizzy. Perhaps he should just take one and she would let him leave. . .

He scanned the shelves, his head swimming.

Pick me, pick me. . .

No, me. . .

Be a wizard for a day. . .

Come riding across the plains. . .

The rhythm of the dance will capture you. . .

Can you feel the flames?

Find out what it's like to be really famous. . .

Try a taste of human flesh. . .

In times of stress Jamie told himself jokes to take his mind off the bad things that were happening. When his dad had left he had told his mother and sister joke after joke after joke. His mum hadn't laughed at many of them and Cadence had usually groaned and rolled her eyes but at least they had listened to them. But now, try as he might, he couldn't remember a single joke. Or rather, he could remember hundreds of little bits of jokes, but they were all jumbled together, with the wrong punchlines.

What's Mary short for? Two sausages are in a frying pan. My dog's got no nose. How do you kill a circus? One of them says to the other, Jeez it's hot in here, and the other says. . . Wait at the buzz stop. Knock, knock. . . How does it smell? She's got no legs. Nothing: he just gave out a little whine. Go for the juggler. . . Terrible. . . Argh! A talking sausage. What did the grape say when the elephant stepped on him. . .

"No!" cried Jamie Wave. He was beginning to sweat.

Miss Lambent turned to the masks, apparently addressing each wall in turn. "Now then, don't frighten him. Be quiet and let him make his own choice." She was very pale, Jamie noticed, except for two spots of colour in her cheeks.

"Choose a mask, Jamie Wave," she repeated. "I'm depending on you." She paused and her voice dropped almost to a whisper. "Cawstocke is depending on you."

Jamie stared at her. He was beginning to feel really ill. Perhaps it would be best to get it over with as fast as possible: then he could go home and forget all about it. In a sudden access of fear and recklessness, he reached out and grabbed a mask at random and cradled it against his chest.

Miss Lambent beamed. "Well done," she congratulated him. "You really are as brave as a tiger. Do you know why I chose you for this task, Jamie?"

Jamie wondered with dread what "this task" might be.

"It was because of the mask you made. Like the tiger you have a great heart and great courage, though you might not realize it. Yet. You will need them: and other resources besides. Tell me, Jamie, are you feeling as brave as a tiger?"

Jamie shook his head. "Not really. Not unless tigers' knees knock too.'

Miss Lambent smiled. "Truth, and courage and a sense of humour and humility: the perfect makings of a proper hero. Though not that many legendary heroes I've come across had much of a sense of humour. I don't remember King Arthur ever cracking a joke; or Merlin, either. And Sir Francis Drake was just a bore."

Jamie's eyes widened. "You knew them?" He felt stupid even as he said it. Of course she couldn't have known any of them. They'd died centuries ago. Even before his gran.

"Before you put your mask on, Jamie," Miss Lambent said, leaning close as a conspirator, "I shall take mine off. It's only fair. But you have to promise me you won't tell anyone."

"C-cross my heart and hope to—"

Miss Lambent put her finger to his lips. "Ssh, or someone'll hear you and take you at your word."

Jamie's heart skipped a beat. But things were about to get stranger still. He watched, puzzled, as her fingers moved busily amongst the roots of her fair hair, as if seeking to get hold of something. Which she then did.

Jamie watched in terrified amazement as Miss Lambent pulled a corner of something pale pink and pliable away from her forehead. A sort of thin plastic, or latex. What on earth—?

A few seconds later he began to see why, and wished he hadn't.

For beneath the pale perfection of the latex mask, Miss Lambent was hideous.

8 THE MIRROR

"So you see. . ." Miss Lambent said, finally removing the long blonde wig to reveal coils of ratty silver-grey locks flattened against a head that was little more than a skull. The skin lay on it like fine white tissue paper that someone had screwed into a tight ball, then tried and failed to smooth out again. Only her extraordinary toffee-coloured eyes remained as clear and lucid as he remembered. "So you see," she repeated, "things are not always as they seem. But now you see me as I really am. No one else knows this truth about me; at least no other person in this world. I hope I can trust you with my secret."

Jamie felt as if he had had all the air knocked out of him. He nodded slowly. Even if he told someone, who would believe him?

"Why do you wear a mask?" he asked, shock making him forget his stutter. *Mind you,* he thought, *if I looked like that, I'd wear a mask too.* It wasn't just that the figure before him was obviously very, very old: it was as if there was hardly any life left in her, as if it had been sucked out of her with a straw by something very greedy.

"That's a very long story, and a very strange one," Miss Lambent said. "I'm not sure now is the best time to tell you. Perhaps when you come back I'll tell you more. But for now, let me just say that I am in hiding from someone. Someone . . . terrible. Someone who wants to see me dead."

Jamie Wave's mouth fell open. Who would want to kill Miss Lambent? In either of her guises – as school art teacher, or this old lady? This very, very old lady.

As if she could read his question in his eyes, Miss Lambent shook her head. "Not now," she said. "Things will become clearer as time passes. Time has a trick of making everything clearer. Now, though, I must introduce you to your guide."

She turned, and the black cat which had run into the shop before him appeared, as if by magic. With a single, fluid movement it leapt up on to the counter beside the book and gazed at Jamie with its orange eyes. Then it said, "Good day, Jamie Wave. My name is Jasper. I am delighted to make your acquaintance."

Jamie nearly fell down. "It talks!"

The cat bristled. "I might well say the same of you! And

how would you like to be referred to as 'it'? Very rude, I must say."

Miss Lambent laughed and ran a hand down the cat's head and shoulders, along its back and right up to the tip of its tail, and it shivered its coat and narrowed its eyes in appreciation. "Now, now, forgive him. You took him by surprise." She looked back at Jamie Wave, whose eyes were round. "Jasper will accompany you on your journey. He will help you to find what you are looking for."

Jamie gazed dubiously at the cat and it stared back at him unblinking, as if it had no eyelids, or didn't know how to use them. Jamie looked away, feeling more like a mouse than a tiger. "What will I be looking for?"

"All will come clear," she promised him. "Let's have a look at the mask you've chosen."

Jamie slowly turned over the object he held against his chest. At first he didn't really know what he was looking at. It seemed to be all made of fabric, of a dusky blue-black colour with an odd metallic sheen to it. He turned it this way and that, puzzled, until at last he realized it was a sort of turban which covered the whole of the top of the head and wound around the rest of the mask's face, leaving only a slit for the eyes.

Who would wear such a bizarre thing? Mind you, it was a very useful disguise. Wearing one of these, no one would know who you were. Though you might stick out a bit at school. . .

"Come with me," said Miss Lambent, holding out her hand. She led him through the beaded curtain at the back of the shop, and the cat followed them soundlessly. Behind the curtain lay a tiny room like a black-walled cabinet with a single floor-to-ceiling mirror. It was dark in there. Dark and enclosed. Jamie's heart started to beat faster. He really didn't like small, dark spaces.

"Put the mask on," said Miss Lambent, her voice low and urgent.

Jamie did as he was told. At once he was engulfed in dusty fabric that felt hot and foreign and uncomfortable. He couldn't see a thing.

Miss Lambent tugged at the mask, making a few adjustments; and suddenly, just like that, it fitted him so well it was as if it had melded itself to his skin. The eye-slit gave him a clear view out. It was like being hidden inside a cave. He felt claustrophobic. It was a very unpleasant sensation.

"There you are," she said at last, standing back and admiring him. "A proper Tuareg."

Inside the turban, Jamie frowned. What was a Twa-reg?

"You'll soon find out." She smiled. "In you go." And she pushed him gently towards the cabinet.

In where? Jamie looked around. There *was* nowhere to go. He turned to see if there was a door hidden in the black wall to his right. Nothing. He turned to his left. Not even a crack in the smooth black plaster. Which left. . .

A mirror. A mirror surrounded by an extraordinary frame of tarnished silver into which were etched curls and swirls and strange symbols.

But it *was* a mirror. Jamie could see his reflection in it, and very odd he looked, too. Then he realized he couldn't see Miss Lambent, except as a vague outline behind him. A sudden horrible thought occurred to him. If she had no reflection, was she a vampire? Now that he thought about it, she had seemed remarkably interested in the blood that had come out of his mouth when he was wearing the tiger mask. Had she lured him here to sink her fangs into him and drain his veins? His heart started to beat very fast as he prepared to push past her and make a break for the shop's door. Surely if he pushed it hard enough. . .

But now something else caught his attention. As he stared, the surface of the mirror started to shimmer and change colour, and suddenly he could see sand, and rocks, and blue, blue sky.

Without even realizing, he had taken a step forward and found himself walking into the scene. . .

*

For several seconds the light was so hot and so strong that it was as if his face had been scorched off and he couldn't see anything; and in the same instant he became aware that the world was moving, and in a very disconcerting way. It was lurching, in a bizarre, circular sort of fashion, so that he found himself tipping backwards, sideways, forward, sideways, then backwards again. It was like being on some mad fairground ride that had lost momentum and was going really, really slowly. In fact, if you just relaxed into it, it was quite soothing. Was he dreaming?

He forced his eyes open, and got a load of sand in them for his trouble. He couldn't have dreamed that: he could feel the grains, each one of them gritty and sharp against his eyeballs. It was the most uncomfortable thing he'd ever felt, worse even than getting soap in your eyes; worse than getting hit by Mouth. He blinked and blinked till tears ran down his cheeks and into the folds of the fabric that encased his head. Without really thinking about it, he pulled the material further up so that there was now an even narrower slit, but at last he had cried the sand out and was able to see, even if it was rather like peering through a letter box.

Sand. That was what he could mainly see. Tons and tons of sand. Not like the sand on the beaches they used to visit in the summer – flat and painted with ripples by the gentle sea – but piled up into massive great hills and arching dunes. The scene lurched again, and now he could just make out the faint, far-off silhouettes of a mountain range, outlined against blue sky; and then lurched again and he could see the sand down below, and the big, flat, split-hoofed feet of some large creature. He realized suddenly he was a long way up in the air.

Jamie had always had a thing about heights. He just didn't like them. Their flat was three storeys up in the block and that didn't seem too bad unless you leaned over the balcony and looked directly down into the street below; but when he was seven he'd been taken on an outing with his junior school to a local castle, and when they'd got up to the battlements and looked over the top he'd come over all odd and felt so dizzy he'd had to lie down and everyone had laughed at him.

Being where he was now wasn't as high up as that, though with the movement it felt worse. But where, precisely, was he? And who was the owner of those vast feet?

"You're on a camel," came a voice, very close by. "In the desert. To be very exact, in the Sahara Desert, deep in the south of Algeria."

Jamie had to tilt his head awkwardly to see who was speaking, and suddenly found himself nose to nose with the black cat from the maskmaker's shop.

"Jasper," the cat reminded him, enunciating precisely.

He recoiled so sharply he almost fell off whatever it was he was sitting on. A saddle: that's what it must be. A camel-saddle. It was not very comfortable, though it was covered in a brightly woven carpet, and ornamented with bands of colour and inlaid metal that sparkled in the sun. The beast he was mounted upon lurched violently and he grabbed at the horns of the saddle and held on for dear life.

"Why on earth I am in the desert riding on a camel?" he wailed, and even as the words came out of his mouth, they sounded odd, as if he were speaking a foreign language. Perhaps he was speaking Cat. The entire situation was weird enough for anything to be happening.

"Best not to worry too much about the strangeness of things," came the cat's voice again. "It'll only get stranger."

Try as he might, Jamie could not see its mouth move. Perhaps its fur was in the way. Perhaps – and this was not an entirely good thought – it was reading his mind. . .

"That's right," the cat said cheerfully. "When you're near the White Lady's masks you can hear me speak, and I can hear your thoughts. So better not go thinking anything too unpleasant! Now, to answer your question, you are here to find something. Something very special that she wants."

Questions whirled around Jamie's mind; but before he could ask any of them, something happened that made them vanish out of his head as if they had never been there.

9 THE DESERT

Three other camels had appeared alongside his own. They were enormous beasts, tall and majestic, of a slightly darker colour than the sand over which they swayed with their alien grace, and he remembered how he had once heard them described as "ships of the desert". On their backs were the most extraordinary-looking people he had ever seen.

The first image that occurred to him was of Christmas cards showing the three kings riding to Bethlehem bearing their gifts for the baby Jesus. These figures were equally magnificent, but they wore no crowns, only all-encompassing turbans of gleaming indigo cloth, which showed nothing of their faces but the glitter of their eyes; and their voluminous clothing was not multicoloured but all of black or blue. Silver amulets – great squares of silver marked with tiny patterns and suspended from leather cords – bounced against their chests. Across their backs were bound long, narrow objects which looked remarkably like swords. Swords! Jamie's heart skipped a beat as the three riders all turned their heads in his direction, but it was impossible to know whether they were regarding him with curiosity or menace, for he could see nothing of their expressions.

The leading rider came up beside Jamie's camel, and Jamie's grip tightened on the pommel of his saddle. The man bowed his head. "Greetings, Far-Rider!" he said. "We have been expecting you."

Or at least that was what Jamie heard in his head. The man's words sounded different, but somehow he understood them.

"Have you really?" He was so surprised he forgot to stutter.

"Now we know that our plan is surely blessed. My name is Ali ag Igbouchi, and these are my lieutenants, Anan ag Brahim and my brother Salim ag Ibouchi."

"Bow your head," the cat hissed suddenly, "and tell them your name."

Jamie bowed his head. "My name is Jamie Wave."

"Just Jamie Wave?" the chief queried. "That is a very strange name. Do you have no father; or are we unworthy to be gifted with the details of your lineage?"

"The name of your father," Jasper supplied urgently. "Tell them quickly or we'll be mincemeat."

Jamie felt himself colour underneath the folds of his turban. He had already managed to insult three fearsome nomad tribesmen and he'd only just met them. "My father's name is Tom . . . Thomas Wave," he said quickly. "But he's no longer with us."

At this, the men made complicated gestures with their hands, as if warding off wasps, or something else unpleasant.

"The loss of a father is a grave loss indeed. So now you are the head of your tribe, Jamie ag Tom-Thomas. You are now chieftain of the Wave People."

Jamie had never really thought about it in these terms before. Both his mum and Cadence were much older than he was, but somehow they seemed . . . helpless, in the grip of some sort of inertia. "Yes, I suppose I am," he said at last, then quickly changed the subject. "What did you mean about 'our plan'?"

Ali laughed. "Ah, it is a good one. You will like it. We are going to visit our neighbours."

His lieutenants laughed heartily.

Visit neighbours? That didn't sound like something you could call a plan. But at least it didn't sound too dangerous. Beneath his turban, Jamie smiled.

"Yes," said Salim. "It is a *rezzu*."

The word he said was definitely *rezzu* but Jamie heard it as "raid".

"A raid?" he echoed. He must have misunderstood.

"Yes. They stole some camels from us last week, and we intend to take them back. And something else besides."

"But what?" Anan asked. "What can we take that would shame them and add to our honour?"

"Yes, what indeed? A few goats are hardly worth riding so far for."

"Their women?" suggested Salim hopefully. "I hear the chieftain has a beautiful daughter."

"Tch," his brother scolded him. "Women are a nuisance. They will chatter and complain till you wish your ears would fall off. That is NOT a good idea."

Jasper whispered something to Jamie. Jamie stared at the cat. "But I don't want a sword," he told it sharply.

"A sword!" cried Anan, catching this last word. "A sword for the boy!"

"Perfect," declared Ali ag Ibouchi. His eyes gleamed through the slit in his turban. "And not just any sword, but Mohktar ag Badi's own. Yes, the Far-Rider must have the chieftain's own sword to reward his long journey to be our talisman on this raid!"

Jamie's mouth made a despairing round shape, but he said nothing. He didn't really want a sword. He had no idea how to use one, and trying to take away a chieftain's own sword seemed like an extremely dangerous thing for someone to attempt.

"Yes," agreed Salim. "And it will surely be fitting if the Far-Rider should take it for himself: for surely he must be a very courageous young man, wearing the *tagelmust* as he does at such a young age."

Tagelmust: the veiled turban. The word came effortlessly into Jamie's mind.

"A test! A test for the Far-Rider!"

This plan seemed to amuse the men greatly. They clicked their tongues at their camels and galloped on ahead, whooping, their mounts kicking up great clouds of sand as they went. But Jamie's stomach clenched in fear. For a moment he thought he might be sick. Which really wouldn't be a very good idea when wearing his *tagelmust*. All at once, he wanted to tear it from his head and show them he was only a boy, and a very ordinary boy at that, whatever Miss Lambent had said.

"Whatever you do, don't do that," Jasper told him severely. "If you lose the mask, you will never be able to get back to the shop."

Jamie looked down at the cat, and its orange eyes gazed steadily back at him. It looked, he thought, as if it was just about managing to suppress a smile. He was beginning to think he really didn't like cats at all.

"Oh, I'll grow on you," the cat promised him.

"Like warts?" Jamie suggested.

"No need to be rude. You just need to realize that you cannot get back to Cawstocke from here without the mask you wear."

"Anything is possible," Jamie said. Where was Algeria? He had a vague memory of seeing it on a map of Africa, but more than that he could not say. "I could get a plane!"

Now Jasper's mouth opened to show two rows of sharp little white teeth and a wide pink tongue. His eyes closed to slits of vast amusement and he began to shake. Was he ill? But after a moment, Jamie realized the dratted thing was laughing at him.

"I could!" he told it hotly. "Someone would help me get home."

The cat finished its little paroxysms of laughter. "You'd have a long walk out of the desert, and then you'd have to stow away on a ship, probably a pirate ship bound for Britain to steal more captives for the white slave trade; and if you survived that, you'd have to swim for it and then walk a long way again; and after all that find that the Cawstocke you know doesn't yet exist. That you don't yet exist."

Jamie stared at it. "Now you're talking rubbish," he said. "How can I not exist?"

The cat gave a minute shrug: a hard thing to do if you're holding on with your claws to someone's robe in order not to fall off a camel. "It's a conundrum," it admitted after a while. "But, you see, we're actually in the year 1663 here: so I don't think you'll be getting on a plane any time soon. In fact," it calculated, "I'd say you'd have somewhere in the region of three hundred years to wait for a commercial flight. Give or take a few years or so. But what's a few years between friends?"

"We're not friends," Jamie told it shortly.

"Not yet."

"Not ever."

"I wouldn't be too sure about that, if I were you."

Jamie thought about this for a long time as his camel swayed along in the wake of the three nomads. He was in another century, and his mask was the only key he had to returning to his own. It couldn't be true, could it? He pictured himself falling off the camel and opening his eyes to find he had just fallen out of his own bed, at home, relieved to discover it had all been a dream. There were, after all, a lot of dreams going around Cawstocke.

"About that," the cat said, gazing up at him. "The dreams, I mean."

Jamie stared at Jasper coldly. "I don't like you reading my mind."

"Well, stop thinking so loudly, then," it said pleasantly. "These dreams: there's a reason for them, you know."

"What, like eating cheese before you go to bed?"

The cat rolled its eyes. "That's an old wives' tale. Though I have to say some of those old wives knew a thing or two. I've worked with quite a lot of them in my life. Or should I say, my nine lives? Anyway: look, the dreams have a cause; and not just the dreams, but the disappearances, too."

"Disappearances? What, like my dad?"

Jasper looked shifty. "Maybe."

"You'd better tell me what you know, or—"

"Or what?"

Jamie was about to devise something that might persuade the infuriating animal to explain when there came a cry from ahead of them, and he saw the three nomads jump down from their camels.

All at once, as if it had a mind of its own (which it most certainly did: camels are very individual creatures with strong personalities, who only do what they feel like doing) Jamie's camel started to run towards the others. It was only with the utmost difficulty that he managed to hang on.

"Come, Far-Rider, see this!"

Salim was on his knees in the sand, with Anan and Ali looking over his shoulder.

Jamie's camel stopped suddenly and lurched violently forward, throwing Jamie hard against the saddle. Jasper, who would otherwise have been squashed flat, meanwhile made an acrobatic leap in the air and landed, as cats always do, on all four feet, looking infuriatingly nonchalant. Now, the camel folded its back legs under itself as well and sat back, and Jamie's world stopped moving. Cautiously, in case it lurched to its feet again, Jamie got down. At once, he nearly leapt back up on to the camel again, for the sand had burned his feet. "Ow!" He looked down. No wonder: he was barefoot! Where were his Nikes, his precious, precious Nikes? And where, for that matter, were his favourite jeans? He was wearing – well, a dress. He supposed the proper term for it must be a robe; but it looked pretty much like a dress to him. What on earth would Mouth say if he could see him? He'd never live it down.

His surprise must have been apparent, for Salim stopped examining whatever it was he was examining and looked up. "Yes, indeed, how? They have made good time. Come here: see, this?" He indicated what looked to Jamie like a scatter of dull, whitish pebbles and a lot of churned, wind-blown sand. "Eight men came past here three days ago, leading twelve camels." (This was beginning to sound like one of Mr Reynold's maths puzzles. The sort of puzzles Jamie couldn't do.)

Salim held up one of the pebbles. "Mina. This tells me it was our camels that came this way."

Jamie couldn't imagine how a stone could tell him that.

"Perhaps now is a good time to stop and take tea," Ali suggested.

Jamie frowned. How very odd: tea, in the desert. He picked up one of the pebbles, weighed it in his hand. It felt hot and dry, and lighter than he would have expected. He picked up another.

"He is a proper desert man," Anan said. "See how already he collects fuel for the fire. Thank you, Far-Rider; place them in this hollow I have made."

The three nomads went away to fetch tea-things from their saddle packs, leaving Jamie and the cat, which nobody had once mentioned. Jamie made a pile of the pebbles, as instructed. The last one he picked up, he sniffed. "This is a very funny sort of stone," he said. "How could he tell all the stuff he did just from looking at it? And how can they make fire from stones? It's all very weird."

The cat made a wheezing sound.

Jamie stared at it. "What?"

The wheezing went on and on. "It's not a stone," Jasper said at last.

"Well, what is it, then, wood?"

"Let's just say it's an organic waste product."

"You don't mean—" Jamie dropped the thing he held as if it had burned him. "Ugh . . . and they're going to heat their tea by setting fire to camel . . . poo?"

While the nomads brewed their tea, Jamie went away and sat by himself on top of one of the dunes, looking out across the desert, all shapes and shadows and endless sand. It was another world. In 1663. Would he ever get home again, and if he did, just when would it be? His mother would be worried sick.

After a few moments the cat had tracked silently up the dune in the footsteps he had made and sat down beside him, arranging its tail tidily around its paws: he could not be rid of it, it seemed, no matter what he did.

"If you're determined to follow me, you'd better tell me what's going on," Jamie said at last. "All this stuff about the dreams and my dad." He paused, frowning. "And who's trying to kill Miss Lambent. And why I have to steal some chieftain's sword."

"I don't think you're ready to hear all of it at once, for it's a most bizarre story; and if you find lighting camel poo strange, I'm not sure you're going to cope very well with something much larger and stranger. Let me just say for now that it's all connected. Something very terrible is happening to Cawstocke and its people."

Jamie scratched his head, taking this in. "And what about this sword?"

The cat glinted at him. "Ah, yes. Mohktar ag Badi's sword. Mohktar is the chieftain of the Kel-Ajjer tribe and a very fearsome man he is too, cruel and ruthless."

"You're not making me feel any better about this."

"The hilt of his sword is set with an enormous tiger's eye."

"Ugh." Jamie imagined this. Wouldn't it be all soft and squashy in your hand?

Jasper sighed. "It's a semi-precious gem, a topaz: a beautiful stone polished to an earthy golden-brown. The White Lady, or Miss Lambent as you call her, wants it."

"Why? It's just a stone."

"Ah, but that's where you're wrong. It may look like a stone, but there is a lot more to it than meets the eye. Appearances can be deceptive."

Which was exactly what Miss Lambent kept saying.

"It's very important, to the White Lady, and to the people of Cawstocke, that you get hold of this stone and bring it safely back to the maskmaker."

"And how I am supposed to do that?"

"You will find a way, Jamie Wave."

Which wasn't very helpful.

10 THE RAID

Just as the Tuareg men finished drinking their tea – which came in tiny decorated glasses rather than the chipped china mugs Jamie's mum used – a dozen or more camels appeared on the crest of the dunes behind them, each bearing a tall rider.

Jamie sucked in his breath.

"Fear not, Jamie ag Tom-Thomas, they are our brothers," Ali said. "They have come to join us on the raid."

"How many brothers do you have?"

Ali ag Ibouchi laughed so that the folds of his turban shook. "All the men of my tribe are of my family, or the family of my mother's brothers. It would be easier to count the grains of sand in this dune" – he flung his hand out in an extravagant gesture – "than to count the men of our tribe."

Jamie suspected this was possibly not the case, but wisely decided not to say anything. Instead, he approached his camel, who regarded him with its long-lashed eyes, then let out an ear-splitting bellow which made him leap backwards.

"My name is Taorka," it said. "I am very honoured to carry you on your mission."

Another creature that could talk. Jamie, surprised, bobbed his head. "Thank you," he said. "That's very nice of you, Taorka." He climbed aboard carefully, wishing he had something to give to her – a carrot or an apple, like you were supposed to with horses.

Jasper gave him a superior look. "She carries her own store of food."

"She does?" He looked around, but saw nothing by way of a bale of grass or a sack of grain.

"You're sitting on it."

Jamie shifted his seat gingerly. "I'm sorry, I didn't mean to."

Cat and camel wheezed and snorted. They were laughing at him, he knew it. He patted the saddle and the carpet that covered it, and an old joke slipped into his head:

Why was the camel in a bad mood?

Because it had the hump.

"It's in her hump, right?"

Jasper looked disappointed, as if Jamie had spoiled their fun. Then he leapt up beside the boy and fixed his claws tightly in his robe as the camel lurched to her feet and joined the others who were now milling about.

An hour later, they were all lined up along the ridge of a dune, gazing down at a collection of dark brown tents. To one side of these, many camels wandered, grazing beside a pool fringed with palm trees.

"I can see my camels Mina and Bazu," Anan said quietly. "Tonight they will rejoin their own tribe." His knuckles whitened as he gripped the hilt of his sword.

A little way from the tents groups of men sat cross-legged around several campfires, brewing tea or boiling pots of stew. They all wore turbans of deep indigo blue like Jamie's, only their eyes visible between the folds of cloth. But no matter how relaxed they seemed, their swords were at their sides, and curved daggers hung at their belts. Between the tents, women moved, herding goats and children, laughing and singing. Unlike the men, they wore no veils, and although the older women had covered their heads with bright head cloths, the younger women went bareheaded, their hair braided into many long plaits, or hanging loose in shining black waves. They all wore silver bracelets and necklaces, and long earrings that flashed in the sunlight.

Salim sighed. "We could take just one or two—"

Ali shook his head. "No women. The camels only; and Mohktar's sword. Are you ready, Far-Rider?"

Jamie gazed at him without the least idea of what to say. Ready for what? To run down the dune, single out the chieftain of the enemy tribe and run off with his sword? There was an easy answer to that.

"Just say yes," urged Jasper.

That wasn't the answer he'd had in mind. But his mouth was so dry, he could say nothing at all, and Ali laughed and clapped him on the shoulder as if his silence was assent.

Salim took half the raiding group and tracked off around the side of the long dune. Ali kept Jamie and the rest of the raiders with him.

"Salim will attack them from the north," Ali explained, "and when they run to defend themselves from that direction, we will come charging down on them from the west, against the sun, and they will think we are *djinns* come out of the desert air itself!"

Jamie smiled uncertainly. It sounded like a good plan. "What are *djinns*?" he asked the cat when the chieftain turned to brief his men.

"Evil spirits," Jasper explained. "The *djinns* can inhabit all four elements of the world – earth and air, water and fire – though they were born of fire. Everyone is afraid of them. They can cause all sorts of mischief and trouble."

Jamie laughed. "But that's just a fairy tale."

The cat turned its orange eyes upon him and regarded him solemnly. "Evil is not a fairy tale, Jamie Wave. Evil is all around us, ever-present and growing in strength. It is a mighty force, so mighty that maybe nothing can withstand it."

More than that could not be discussed, for down below there was a sudden hubbub as Salim and ten camel-riders came thundering out of the dunes to the north of the encampment, whooping and shouting and waving their swords in the air.

At once, the men around the campfires snatched up their weapons and leapt to their feet. They ran at the raiders, who circled their camels easily around them. Half of them galloped towards the stolen camels, the other half towards the tents, as if they were about to carry off the women. Jamie was surprised to see that the women and children did not scream and run, but hurled stones and sand and anything else they could lay their hands on at their attackers. He saw kettles and cooking pots flying through the air, and a great iron ladle which narrowly missed Salim's head.

Instead of racing into action, Ali ag Ibouchi roared with laughter. "What songs of shame my little brother will have to endure if Mohktar's daughter knocks him off his camel!" He seemed to be enjoying himself mightily.

One of the raiding party raced right through the herd of goats, scattering animals everywhere. Camels plunged and reared and tried to evade capture. It was chaos. The cries of the goats mingled with those of the attackers and of the women, with the outraged bellows of the camels and the shouts of Mohktar's men. There was so much sand in the air that after a while Jamie could not see what was going on.

It was at this point that Ali raised his sword and yelled, "Charge!"

"Hold tight!" cried Taorka. She lurched forward and Jamie found himself flying down the slope of the dune at a terrifying pitch and speed, heading straight for the middle of the encampment. He gripped the saddle horns so hard it felt as if his knuckles might burst, but still he was thrown this way and that with every thumping stride of his camel, and knew that if she stalled for even a second he would go sailing through the air, right over her ears, and land in a crumpled heap on the ground, where every other camel could trample on him.

Ali, in contrast, seemed to be having no trouble negotiating the breakneck downhill charge. He turned nonchalantly towards Jamie, apparently glued to his saddle with some invisible substance, for his sword gleamed in his right hand and a long shield of hide had appeared in his left. "This is the life, eh, Far-Rider? There is no finer way to pass an hour or two than to ride one's camel like the wind into the heart of your enemy's ground, scattering them like so much chaff and dust! Do you see Mohktar ag Badi?"

He pointed with his sword, and Jamie could just make out the figure of a tall man in a white robe and a dark turban climbing on to a big white camel.

"I shall challenge him!" Ali declared. "And while I do that, you may steal his sword."

And with that he was off, head down, his camel throwing out its feet like huge dinner plates in the sand so that great clouds of it came flying up into Jamie's face. Taorka followed without the least encouragement from her rider. Needles prickled Jamie's chest suddenly, and when he looked down he found that Jasper had dug his claws in so hard in the attempt to stay aboard that they had pierced not only his robe but his skin, too. There was no opportunity to complain about this, however, because a second later they almost cannoned into Mohktar's big white camel.

The enemy chieftain, however, was not looking at Jamie. All his attention was trained on the sudden arrival of Ali ag Ibouchi, who was advancing on him, his sword outstretched as if he might just try to kebab him. Mohktar's own sword remained scabbarded over his back. A great golden-brown stone glowed in its pommel, as if soaking up the last of the sun's rays before shining them out again, hot and changed.

"There it is!" hissed Jasper. "You could get it easily!"

But as he moved towards the sword, Mohktar's camel wheeled suddenly to bellow at his attacker.

Jamie could see Ali very close now, swinging his sword in a menacing fashion around his head and calling out insults about goats and dogs, but not striking the other man, who shouted back equally horrible insults and gestured at Ali with his dagger. Neither seemed interested in cutting the other, except with words.

"Your father walks on four legs and snuffs at the ground!"

"Yours slithers in the dirt and hides amongst the rocks if so much as a shadow falls upon him!"

It seemed that contests between the Tuareg were less about inflicting damage on your opponent than about making them appear foolish or less glorious than yourself. More symbolic than real. If only Mouth and his gang would follow the same rules, Jamie thought suddenly.

"Go on!" urged the cat. "Now's your chance."

Jamie reached out towards the chieftain's sword, but his arms were just not quite long enough.

"Again!" cried Jasper. "You nearly had it!"

Jamie swung a leg over to the right side of his camel,

holding tight to the saddle horn with his left hand and reaching desperately with his right. His fingers grazed the sword but couldn't get a grip. Just another inch—

And then he was falling. The world turned upside-down and suddenly there were feet everywhere: great, horny three-toed things, kicking out, thudding into the sand just in front of his face. Jamie rolled into a ball and pushed himself blindly away. No one kicked him, and for a moment he thought he had escaped the worst of the danger. He had got to his knees and was preparing to make a run for it when someone grabbed the back of his robe, just between his shoulder blades, and hauled. For a moment he found himself kicking out wildly and making no contact. Then he landed face down across something hard and spiky and all the air rushed out of his lungs.

"Ha!" a voice cried triumphantly. "Your son, I imagine, Ali? He has the Ibouchi stamp, crawling feebly in the sand like all his kin. It seems that I shall profit more from your raid than you!"

He had been taken prisoner by Mohktar ag Badi.

11 PRISONER

They rode, away from the oasis and the encampment, eventually making their way into the shadows of a rocky canyon, where other members of Mohktar's tribe had also gathered; and all the women and children too. From what Jamie could gather from the various conversations around him, Ali and his men had recaptured their camels, including Taorka, and then given up the chase. They might ransack the tents, but there was not much of value left behind: some fine rugs, drinking vessels, perhaps a little jewellery. The goats had scattered into the dunes, but they would easily be gathered up tomorrow.

Jamie sat astride the big white camel and looked around him. The landscape had changed again, the rock-forms towering above him like huge buildings, all pitted and scoured by the winds into strange shapes, casting cold black shadows upon the riders as they wound their way between them. In some places, Jamie saw pictures that had been painted or carved into the rocks – leaping gazelles and running camels, dancing women and hunting men; even something that looked like a giraffe, then another that resembled an elephant! In the desert! He remembered other ancient pictures he had seen, of bison and lions, hidden in caves and other secret sites in places where those animals no longer existed. They no longer ran and jumped and breathed in a world that had changed around them till it became unrecognizable.

Jamie knew that things changed and not usually for the better. But seeing these joyful creatures leaping above barren desert sands made him think of his family – how happy they had once been, how they were now. He thought about life in Cawstocke, which was becoming another sort of desert. Then he wondered how he would get back to Cawstocke at all, for of Jasper the cat there was no sign. Somehow during the fall from Taorka, they had been separated. He didn't much like the cat, but he hoped it was OK, that it hadn't been trampled underfoot by the camels.

He had lost his guide.

If he lost his mask as well, he would never be able to go home.

Now, the nomads halted their camels, which folded their knees up beneath them like enormous deckchairs so that their riders could dismount.

Mohktar ag Badi lifted Jamie down to the ground and held him at arm's length. He was an older man than Ali, there was grey in his eyebrows, but his eyes were as sharp and bright as an eagle's. "So, who do we have here? What is your name and lineage?"

Jamie stared right back at Mohktar. "I am called Jamie ag Thomas, also known as the Far-Rider."

Mohktar's eyebrows shot up. "The Far-Rider, eh? And why would they call you that?"

"Because I, er, come from a long way away?" Jamie suggested.

"From where?"

"A place called Cawstocke." Normally under such stressful circumstances he would surely stutter; but here he didn't. That was interesting. He would have liked to ponder this oddity further, but he realized that the chieftain was glaring at him as if Jamie were trying to make a fool of him.

"Cawstocke," he repeated. "In the south of England."

Now the tribesmen began to murmur. They had heard of England, a far-flung, exotic land. They all stared at him. Jamie was an object of much curiosity. Feeling very uncomfortable, he adjusted his *tagelmust* to hide even more of his face.

"What are the people of Cawstocke renowned for, Far-Rider?" Mohktar demanded.

That was a good question. Jamie couldn't think of a single thing. Their football team, much as he loved it, was pretty useless, the silver mine was closed, nothing was made in the town any more, they had no celebrities that he knew of, and no well-known landmarks, either. The countryside around about was quite pretty, and there were the Delving Caves, which were scarily impressive but not very visible. It didn't seem much to boast about.

"What are your finest skills, then, Far-Rider?" Mohktar pressed into the silence. "Why does Ali ag Ibouchi keep you beside him?"

There seemed little point in explaining that he was here by some sort of strange magic and didn't really know Ali at all. Jamie scratched his head. What could he say? That he wasn't bad at drawing, or making masks?

"I know quite a lot of jokes," he said at last, and immediately felt like clamping his hand over his stupid mouth.

"Jokes?"

"Funny things, riddles. . ."

"Ah!" Mohktar's expression became hooded and cunning. "I see we must put you to the test," he declared.

As the chieftain walked away, Jamie felt his knees go to water. What sort of test? Perhaps he had been wrong about the Tuareg favouring symbolic violence after all. Perhaps these Tuaregs were going to torture him. . .

Just as he thought this, a voice sounded beside him. "Don't panic, Jamie Wave. It will only be a contest. It is a Tuareg tradition."

It was a voice no one else appeared to have heard. He felt himself start to grin. "How did you get here?"

"Oh, it was easy." The cat appeared in the shadows of the rocks, its eyes glinting in the gloom. "I just jumped from Taorka to Amud, the white camel, and hung on to Mohktar's cloak." It flicked its claws out and examined them carelessly. "I knew you'd need me."

Jamie had been really pleased to see the cat. Now it was being its usual annoying self. "You haven't been much of a guide so far," he grumbled.

"Be like that," said Jasper. "If you think you can manage on your own I shall leave you to it." And he lay down in the lee of a huge boulder, wrapped his tail around him, buried his nose in it and went to sleep.

"Come with me." Mohktar had returned. He led Jamie to where the nomads had made a fire (out of bits of brushwood rather than anything worse, it appeared) and were gathering in a wide circle around it as if in anticipation of a spectacle. A knot of dread began to twist in Jamie's stomach. What were they going to do to him?

"We shall have a battle of wits," Mohktar declared. "My riddles against your own. I am known as the wisest man in all the desert, and no one has ever defeated me. If you answer my riddles and make me laugh, you shall choose your prize. If I win, you shall stay here as my slave."

Jamie stared at him. What chance did he stand against the wisest man in the desert?

12 A BATTLE OF WITS

He was led to a space before the fire where two huge colourful cushions had been set opposite one another. Mohktar held out his closed fists to Jamie. "In one of my hands is a pebble," he said. "If you choose that hand, you can go first. We shall each have three riddles to ask the other. If you cannot answer one, you lose."

Jamie reached out and chose a hand. Slowly, the chieftain uncurled his fingers. It was empty.

Mohktar's delight showed in his eyes. "Excellent. Then I shall begin!" He settled himself on one of the cushions and gestured for Jamie to sit on the second. Then he took a deep breath. "An easy one to start with, perhaps, to test your mettle, Jamie ag Thomas.

"No legs have I to dance,
No lungs have I to breathe,
No life have I to live or die
And yet I do all three.

What am I?"

Someone in the crowd burst out laughing, and after a moment others joined in. It was obviously a riddle they knew well. That, or they were a lot smarter than Jamie.

What on earth could dance without any legs? It made no sense. Did fish have lungs? he wondered suddenly. You could say they danced in the water – well, sort of. . . But they were alive, so that couldn't be right.

He looked around at the assembled throng – veiled men and women in colourful headscarves and silver jewellery, children clutching dolls made out of bones and rags. They all gazed back at him expectantly with their dark eyes reflecting the flames of the campfire. No help there, then.

What on earth could dance, and live and die?

Without legs, or lungs, or being alive?

He closed his eyes to concentrate, and on the inside of his lids the after-image of the flames . . . danced.

His eyes shot open. "Fire!" he shouted triumphantly. "The answer is 'fire'!"

Mohktar looked disappointed. "Very good. Your turn." And he glared at Jamie as if by sheer force of will he could force him into silent stupidity.

Jamie trawled through his mental storeroom of jokes. Most of the ones that came immediately to mind were useless because they required some knowledge of the modern world in order for someone to find them funny. If he asked Mohktar – *what's grey and goes round and round? an elephant in a washing machine* – he would have to explain the concept of a washing machine, and most likely an elephant as well. The chieftain would probably stare at him as if he were mad, or disqualify him, or something. He didn't want to be a slave. . .

His mind went blank. Completely blank. As if someone had put *it* in a washing machine and washed it white and clean. Then, out of nowhere, he said, "When can three big camels fit under one little tree and not get wet?"

The chieftain's eyes narrowed. People started to whisper to one another in the crowd. "Sssh!" Mohktar hissed at them, and they fell abruptly silent.

The Tuareg's feet began to tap, and his hands to knot themselves together as if he was thinking furiously. Then a great laugh suddenly burst from him.

"Simple! When it's not raining!"

There was a great burst of applause at this. The women trilled their tongues and clapped their hands; the children laughed and cheered.

"Ha! When it's not raining!" Mohktar was delighted by his own brilliance. "Very good, young man. It will take a lot more than that to catch out the great Mohktar ag Badi! Now

I have one for you. Tell me, then, what's as big as the biggest camel, but weighs nothing at all?"

Now it was Jamie's turn to knot his brows and rack his brains. Everything he could think of – sand dunes, elephants, trees, tents, a very fat person – all weighed loads and loads. He remembered an old riddle he had once heard about feathers. What weighs more, a pound of iron or a pound of feathers? The answer being that of course they weigh the same – one pound. It must be something like that, something tricky. . .

He looked at his feet, which were tapping nervously on the ground, just like Mohktar's had, the light from the fire sending their shadows leaping out across the sand.

His head came up and beneath the turban he grinned from ear to ear. "What's as big as the biggest camel but weighs nothing at all? Why, its shadow, of course!"

"Hurrah for the Far-Rider!" someone shouted, then subsided quickly as the chieftain glared at them.

"So you think you're clever, do you, Jamie ag Thomas of Cawstocke? Cleverer than Mohktar ag Badi, chief of the Kel-Ajjer, no doubt?"

Jamie shook his head quickly. He was useless at loads of subjects at school. "Er, no, sir. Of course not."

"I should think not. Come along then," Mohktar said briskly. "Your next test for me?"

All Jamie could think of was camels now. It was hopeless. He didn't know any more camel jokes or riddles, no matter how hard he tried. He thought about other animal jokes he knew; but what if the Tuareg were unfamiliar with cows, or frogs, or fish? Even if it was a good joke, the chieftain would say it didn't count and he would lose.

He thought of a frog joke, then realized that he could substitute the word "camel" for "frog", because it was the concept of the joke that worked rather than the actual animal. Secretly, beneath the *tagelmust*, he smiled to himself.

"What type of camel can jump higher than a tree?"

At once, the audience started to whisper to one another, discussing the merits of one another's camels, which one was fastest and which one had the strongest legs and all that sort of thing. You could make them jump a stream – but jump up in the air? That was a different thing. Perhaps it was a matter of training. . .

But Mohktar ag Badi wasn't listening to them. He had his eyes shut and was concentrating hard. He pulled at his turban, scratched his ear, rested his elbow on his knee and his head on his hand as if it was suddenly too heavy for him with all the thoughts tumbling through it.

Then he stood up and walked around, muttering, as if

debating with himself, testing out theories and answers.

Jamie bit his lip to stop himself laughing. It was such a stupid joke. Such an easy one, really. But they always were when you knew the answer. . .

Suddenly Mohktar whirled around and clapped his hands. "Ah ha ha ha ha! Ah ha ha ha!" He slapped his knee, and doubled up again in laughter. "It is very silly. A very silly riddle indeed."

Everyone stared at their chieftain warily, as if he had gone a bit mad.

"The answer," Mohktar declared solemnly, "is any type of camel." He gazed around at the gathered tribespeople, who were frowning and looking puzzled. "Because trees can't jump!"

Jamie nodded. He was, of course, right. Now he began to panic inside. What was going to happen to him if the chieftain's last riddle was too hard to answer? He really, really didn't want to stay here for ever to be the chieftain's slave. Cawstocke could be horrible, with its all its problems and sadnesses, but it was still home, and he wanted to go back there.

"My last riddle, then," Mohktar said grimly. "And it shall be my best riddle. The hardest one I can think of." He mused on this for a few moments; then a wicked smile lit his black eyes.

"I have it! Golden treasure am I, guarded by hundreds and thousands of armed guards. I am stored in a labyrinth where no man can walk, yet men come often to steal my gold. What am I?"

Jamie stared at him in disbelief. That was way too hard, and far too complicated! He had absolutely no idea. How could anyone steal gold from a maze they couldn't even walk in? Did they drop buckets down and scoop it up? Or use huge magnets, or something? But then he remembered an experiment they had done at school with magnets. Michael Rose had tried to clamp his magnet on to Angela Horne's gold hoop earring, and it hadn't worked. Only things with iron in seemed to be magnetic. So that was no good. His thoughts were going round and round in useless circles, and getting nowhere.

Mohktar fixed him with his eagle's eyes, as if he could see right through the mask and Jamie's skin as well, to the very interior of his thoughts. Like the cat. . .

The cat.

Yes?

Suddenly Jasper was there.

I need help, Jamie said humbly. He didn't say it aloud, but thought it very clearly.

Oh, I know, Jasper said into his head. *I could hear your thoughts falling over themselves, making such a racket I couldn't sleep any more.* He yawned. *And really, it's such a simple puzzle.*

Jamie grimaced. It didn't seem very simple to *him*. He felt himself starting to think something not very complimentary about the cat and stopped himself quickly.

"Hurry now!" Mohktar said. "I think by your silence, Far-Rider, that you do not know the answer." He rubbed his hands together in glee. "Ah, how good it will be to have a new slave. You can haul water from the wells for us and clean my camel. You can rub my feet for me after a long day's ride. . ."

Jamie's eyes turned helplessly to the chieftain's feet. They were huge and horrible, with cracked heels and yellow, horny nails like talons.

Shall I give you a bit more time to come up with the answer yourself? the cat asked sweetly.

"No!" roared Jamie, and everyone stared at him.

"No, you don't know the answer?" Mohktar prompted happily.

Tell me, Jamie thought at the cat. *Tell me what this golden treasure in a labyrinth is!*

You'll owe me a favour. Jasper smiled smugly.

Anything!

When we get back to Cawstocke, you will help me find my wife and kittens. That's the price for the answer of the riddle.

Why, where are they?

If I knew that, why would I ask you to help me find them?

But how could you lose them?

How could you lose your father?

A good point. Chastened, Jamie gave a mental shrug. *I don't understand how you could have lost your family, but yes, OK, I'll help you look for them.*

He felt the creature's satisfaction wash over him, and behind that, something else, something he couldn't quite catch, a glimpse of something wild and dark. Then it was gone.

You can't read my mind, the cat chided him. *So stop trying. The answer is easy. It's honey. The golden treasure. In honeycombs in a beehive: where no man can walk. And the armed guards are the bees, with their stings!*

It was simple, but it was also ingenious. Jamie laughed out loud. "Honey!" he declared with a grin.

Mohktar ag Badi stamped his great feet. "How did you know that?" he roared. "How could you?" Sand flew everywhere as he stamped and stamped. The audience looked away as if it was shameful to see their chieftain in such a rage.

At last Mohktar subsided on to his cushion. "Go on, then, Far-Rider," he said. "Give me your final riddle."

Jamie had already thought of one. It had popped into his

head as if by magic. He stared at the cat, but it gazed back at him unblinking. He could not tell whether it was his own idea or Jasper's. In the end, he decided, it didn't matter, as long as it worked.

"How many camels," he asked the Tuareg, "can you fit in an empty tent?"

Mohktar stared and the crowd fell silent, thinking. There were so many sorts of tent, and all of different sizes, depending on how rich you were, how many goatskins you could afford to use; whether it had been handed down by your mother and you had added to it; how big your camels were. You could probably fit quite a lot of baby camels into Mohktar's biggest tent. They considered their fingers and toes, calculating.

The chieftain paced up and down. He paced sideways. He drew something in the sand, as if doing a maths puzzle. Then he scrubbed it out with his foot and started again. Time ticked on.

"I'll have to hurry you," Jamie said cheekily.

Mohktar glared. "A moment more is all I need," he declared through gritted teeth. He stared at the tribe's gathered camels, trying to picture them squeezed into a tent. It would be a hard task: camels did not like to be enclosed. They would stampede without warning, probably tearing the tent from its anchors, flattening it, or ripping it apart. . .

"Your time is up!" Jamie said. "Do you have an answer for me?"

Mohktar growled like an angry dog. "It isn't a proper question!" he roared. "Ask me another."

There was a shift in the crowd, a murmur like a wave.

"It was a fair question," someone said quietly.

"Answer the boy," said someone else.

"Shame on you, Mohktar!" cried a woman's voice.

"I want to know how many camels you can fit in an empty tent!" cried a child.

Mohktar ground his teeth. "You had better tell me the answer, then, Far-Rider," he declared. "And it had better be good, or I shall beat you every day when you are my slave."

Jamie looked around at the crowd. He hoped they would support him. He hoped they would understand the joke.

Quietly he said, "You can only fit one camel in an empty tent. Because after that, it's not empty any more."

There were some seconds of silence; then someone cheered.

"A fine piece of logic!"

"Give the boy his prize!" cried one of the seated men.

"I wonder what he will choose," one of the girls said loudly, pushing her way to the front of the crowd and batting her long eyelashes at Jamie.

"Sit down, Zaina. You are noisier and more trouble than a camel with a fly upon its bottom!"

"What will you have then, Far-Rider?" Mohktar asked with a sigh. "Do you want silver, or a flying carpet? Perhaps a good camel?"

A flying carpet? Now that would be a prize indeed. But it was not what he was here for. Jamie thought of Miss Lambent and the task he had been set. He drew himself up. "I would like your sword, please, sir."

Mohktar's eyes bulged. "My *sword*?" he spluttered.

Someone laughed.

Mohktar stared into the crowd and the person who had laughed became very, very quiet. He turned back to Jamie. "You must mean this." And he handed to Jamie his small, curved dagger in its pretty, ornate scabbard.

Jamie shook his head. "No, your sword. The big one with the golden stone set in its handle."

Mohktar paled. Jamie could see that he had, even though all he could see through the eye-slit of the man's turban was the little bit of skin around his eyes and across the bridge of his nose.

"I will only give you the sword," Mohktar said craftily, "if you take off your *tagelmust*. I must know to whom I am handing the Tiger's Eye. It is an ancient sword, passed down to me by my father, and to him from his father, as has been the case for a hundred generations before them. I cannot simply give it away to a stranger whose face I have never seen."

You cannot take it off! Jasper hissed into his mind. *If you do, you will be lost for ever. Tell him you respect him too much to expose your face, that it will bring evil down upon him. All Tuareg men know that evil resides in the mouth. That is why they always cover their faces.*

Jamie glared at the chieftain. "You ask the impossible, Mohktar ag Badi. Were I to remove my *tagelmust*, evil would come upon you, and I respect the chief of the Kel-Ajjer too much to do such a thing."

Mohktar looked furious but said nothing. For a moment, Jamie thought he had won his argument; then the chieftain lunged forward, grabbed his turban and started to haul it off.

Jamie howled. Images of Cawstocke whirled through his mind: his bedroom, with its posters of Cawstocke FC and the Blue Flamingos, his school playground, the park, his mother trying to hold her lips steady and not cry while she applied her lipstick. He thought about Cadence and Jinny and Michael Rose and even Mouth; and the maskmaker's shop and Miss Lambent. All the people and places and things he would never see again if Mohktar took his turban away from him. And then he thought about his tiger mask . . .

His howl turned suddenly into a deep, throaty roar.

Around the edges of the fire, women screamed and children burst into tears. Men reached for their weapons.

"A *djinn*! It is a *djinn*!"

Mohktar ag Badi leapt backwards in surprise. His eyes never left Jamie's face. He watched warily, as if the boy might at any moment reveal himself as the evil shape-shifter he was, throw off the turban and robe to reveal the powerful, terrifying beast beneath.

With shaking hands, he held out his sword.

"Take it, Far-Rider, and be gone."

"Thank you," Jamie said in an entirely normal voice, and took it quickly, before the chieftain changed his mind. The sword weighed heavily in his hands and the tiger's eye which gave it its name glowed in the firelight.

Now bow and walk swiftly away amongst the tallest rocks you see to your left, Jasper instructed him.

Jamie did as he was told. He felt a hundred eyes boring into his back as he walked as fast as he could towards the towering boulders.

Once they were hidden from sight, Jasper ran swiftly in front of him. "This way," he said.

He wove between the awesome rock formations, sniffing at the base of each one, until at last he gave a sigh.

"Here."

Between the towers was a place where two great

boulders leaned together, leaving a narrow gap between them like a doorway. Through it, Jamie could see the last rays of the sun streaked red and apricot across the sky. Soon it would be dark. His stomach clenched with fear.

"Quickly," said the cat. "Follow me through the rocks, and hold on to the sword. Don't lose it, or your mask, whatever you do. We must leave before it gets dark. We must be back in the shop before night falls."

"Why?"

"Night is another's realm," the cat said, "and you will have no protection." Without bothering to explain any further, he leapt into the gap between the rocks. One moment he was there, with his black fur gleaming and his orange eyes shining like lamps; the next he was gone. Disappeared. Really disappeared: as if he had winked out of existence. And perhaps he had.

Taking a deep breath and holding the Tiger's Eye cradled tightly to his chest, Jamie stepped into the void.

13 THE FIRST STONE

The world spun sickeningly. Then Jamie crash-landed on his knees. Disoriented, he tried to look around, but he couldn't see a thing. Feeling around with his hands outstretched, he found thin carpet on the ground, nothing in front of him, and a cold, smooth surface behind him. The mirror in the maskmaker's cabinet. Or at least, that's what he hoped it was. Gingerly, he pushed himself upright, took a step forward, tripped over something and sat down again hard.

"Ow! Maaaroww! That was my paw!"

Someone laughed, and a light came on. Silhouetted in the doorway was Miss Lambent, mercifully wearing her mask once more. Beside her sat Jasper, licking a paw and looking most disgruntled. Miss Lambent's gaze flicked over the boy on the floor and fixed itself on the object he carried and in that moment she looked nothing like his pleasant art teacher. Her eyes burned with greed and intent.

"Ha! Well done, boy, you have brought me back my Tiger's Eye! Give it to me – give it to me at once!"

Jamie levered himself to his feet, using Mohktar ag Badi's sword as a crutch. His knees hurt from the shock of hitting the floor and he felt sick and dizzy from the strange, swift transition he had made between a seventeenth-century desert on the other side of the world and the maskmaker's shop. But, he realized as he looked down, at least he had his precious Nikes on; and his jeans.

He had meant to hand over the treasure for which he had risked his life with a flourish, but he was too slow. Miss Lambent's hands shot out and seized hold of the sword. They were gnarled and threaded with lumpy blue veins, an old lady's hands, mottled with age spots, the joints all swollen and contorted. But even as he watched her fingers close around the hilt, they began to change. A light came into them – it was the only way he could describe it to himself – a golden light, exactly the same colour as the polished gem she called the Tiger's Eye. This light seemed to infuse Miss Lambent's hands, as if she cupped a candle-flame. At the same time Jamie felt the light enter his own skin. It felt hot and dangerous, as if it carried inside it all the heat that had ever been trapped in the desert he had just left behind. Alarmed, he let go of the sword and took [illegible] away.

The hot light coursed up Miss Lambent's arms, making them glow as if they had been set on fire. Jamie expected her to cry out in pain, but instead she threw her head back in what seemed like triumph, or joy. The light burned more brightly still, gaining fierce orange sparks like some sort of bizarre internal firework; then abruptly it dulled to a deep dark red, and went out, as if someone had thrown water on the flames. For a moment there was silence and all Jamie could see was the after-image of the fiery light etched against his eyelids; then, gradually, his vision returned to normal.

Miss Lambent stood exactly where she had been standing before, but of the sword there was no sign, except for a small pile of smouldering ash at her feet. She was staring at the thing she held in her hands, something walnut-small and dark. All Jamie could stare at were her arms. They glowed with health and vigour. Gone were the knotted veins, the swollen knuckles, the age spots and thin, old-lady talons. The skin was rosy-golden, smoothly muscled, perfect.

At her feet, Jasper's fur bristled from ears to tail. He looked as if he might dash away at any moment in fear for his life, and Jamie knew exactly how he felt.

Miss Lambent smiled. There was a new, golden light in her eye.

"Don't be frightened," she said softly. "This is all quite

natural. Just a little injection of the energy I've been in need of for a long time. A very long time indeed." And she threw the object she had been holding to Jamie.

He caught it with a reflex action that would have made his sports teacher proud. Whatever it was, he had been expecting it to be hot, like a spent coal still yielding some of the heat from its fire; but the object was quite cool, and smooth, and dead. He had feared a resurgence of the golden light, but when he saw what he held in his palm he found with a flicker of disappointment that it was just a stone, black and dull. It was as if everything that had made the Tiger's Eye beautiful and precious had been sucked out of it. Sucked into Miss Lambent.

Which he suspected, with some new-found insight, was precisely what had just happened, and this knowledge scared him, since it tallied with nothing he understood about the way the world worked.

But then, neither did travelling through time and space merely by wearing a mask.

And in his world, cats and camels did not talk.

Magic.

The word shivered through him, thrilling and terrifying in equal measure.

"That's right," said Miss Lambent. "We are in the presence of magic. It is the most rare and precious resource in the world, and to see it work is a great and secret privilege." She leaned closer to him. "But it must remain our secret, Jamie Wave. Do you understand me?"

He nodded quickly.

"Good. Because the consequences – not just for you or me, but particularly for whoever you might tell – would be terrible beyond imagination or description."

Jamie didn't know what she meant by this. He didn't want to know. "I won't t-tell anyone," he said. The stutter was back, and it was by this small detail that he knew without doubt that he was neither dreaming nor in another world. "I-I'd like to go home now."

Miss Lambent beamed. "Of course, my dear. I shall see you at school on Monday, as usual." She flexed her arms, sighed. "I had forgotten what it was like to live without aches and pains. I feel . . . wonderful. As if I could fly."

She watched Jamie's mouth fall open.

"But of course I can't. More's the pity. Not yet, anyway."

Jamie closed his eyes. All he wanted now was to be back in the flat with his mum and his sister, having beans on toast, with the television on in the background and everything back to normal.

You have to help me find my family. The cat's voice scratched at him.

I've got to go home now.

Then when?

Jamie knew he had made a promise, but he felt exhausted. *I can't: not now. Another day,* he told it, and watched its eyes narrow angrily.

Miss Lambent lifted an eyebrow as if she had caught the tail-end of this exchange. She walked back into the shop, and Jamie followed her, his heart hammering. The masks were all in their rows looking down at him, but this time none of them said a word. He felt no emotion from them as he passed, nothing except a prickle of curiosity, as if he was being scrutinized. Past Miss Lambent's shoulder he could see the outside world: it was getting dark.

At the door she turned to him. "Remember, Jamie Wave, this is our secret: you cannot mention it to anyone – not to Cadence, not even to your poor mother, all right?"

He knew that Miss Lambent had met his mother at Parents' Day; but he also knew for certain that she had never met Cadence. Cadence went to the local comprehensive, had never set foot in Cawstocke High. He had no idea Miss Lambent knew he had a sister; let alone that she knew her name.

"See you at school on Monday," Miss Lambent said brightly, as if nothing out of the ordinary had happened at all.

14 NIGHTMARES

But on Monday at school there was no sign of Miss Lambent.

More than that, half of the rest of the teachers were away. And so were a lot of Jamie's classmates.

Something was happening in Cawstocke: something strange and disturbing.

When Jamie arrived home he found his mother lying on the sofa, propped on one elbow, the wan light of the television illuminating her pinched features. On the screen a woman in brightly coloured dungarees and a hairstyle ten years too young for her age had been singing a song about ducks and monkeys and dancing in a stupid way. His mum didn't look up. Instead, her eyes listlessly followed the dungaree-woman's every movement, as if the flickering cathode image was the centre of the universe and the rest of the world was a shadowy illusion.

There was no sign of his sister either. She hadn't got up

at all the previous day, and when at last he'd stuck his head around her bedroom door, he'd found her curled up in bed; and when he'd called her name and asked if she was all right, all she had done was to huddle further into her duvet and refuse to say another word.

So now Jamie just stood there, listening at her door. He couldn't bear to go in and see her like that again, so he turned and went away into the kitchen. After his adventure at the maskmaker's shop, he'd felt a bit scared and confused. He'd wanted to feel safe with what was left of his family, but instead it was as if his mum and sister were living in some shadowy other world, as if only their bodies were present in this one. Suddenly he missed his dad badly. Despite Miss Lambent's warning, he felt pretty sure his dad would have been a good person to tell about his experiences. He'd have taken what Jamie said seriously before telling him not to worry, that everything would work itself out. Jamie tried not to think too much about his father these days. When his dad had first left them, Jamie had missed him all the time, had started talking to him before realizing in mid-sentence that he wasn't there. Had left a space on the sofa for him and laid a place at the table for him. On the bus, he'd searched the faces of the people on the streets of Cawstocke for a glimpse of him, even though he knew he could hardly still be in the area without their knowing. Even so, when the football team had played on TV, he'd scanned the crowd, in vain. His father had simply . . . vanished.

To be honest, he didn't really understand what had happened to make his father leave home. Everything had been fine: and then it hadn't.

After his dad had left, nothing had ever been the same again, and now it was worse than ever. Something was very wrong with his mother and his sister and he had no idea what he could do about it.

Sighing, he opened the fridge . . . and found it empty. He realized he was pretty hungry.

"Mum, it's gone lunch time and there's nothing to eat. If you give me some money I'll go to the shop."

She didn't say anything, so he opened her handbag and put her purse in her hand. His mother tore her eyes unwillingly from the TV, where a man with a manic grin had arrived to join in the dungaree-woman's dance. The man looked disconcertingly like his dad, his skin the same shade of dark chestnut brown, his hair braided in a similarly intricate way.

Mrs Wave sighed as she shook out the contents of the purse. "I'll make a list. Mr Patel will put the rest on tick for us."

But Mr Patel wasn't in the shop when Jamie got there.

Instead, a young woman stood behind the counter, hefting a small child on one hip. She was shouting at a pair of boys to get out of the shop unless they were going to buy something, sounding angry and afraid at once.

"Bloody Paki!" one of them shouted. He sent the magazine rack crashing and magazines spilled all over the floor. The baby began to wail.

Jamie watched the boys run down the road. He knew them: two of Mouth's gang. Then he knelt down and gathered up the scattered magazines and stuffed them back into the rack.

"Thanks," said the girl with the baby, giving him a weary smile. "I'm sure life's not supposed to be like this. What's your name?"

"Jamie Wave." He hesitated, shopping list in hand. "Um, where's Mr P-Patel?"

"Dad's not well," said the girl, sighing. "That's why I'm helping out. What can I get you?"

"My mum's not very well, either," he said after a pause. "She's not been able to get to the bank, so all I've got is £5. If it's more, she said to ask Mr Patel if she could pay him next week."

"What's the matter with your mother?"

What *was* the matter with his mother? Jamie didn't really know. It wasn't as if she had flu or a broken leg. That would be easy to explain. "She's . . . um . . . just tired all the time."

"Sounds like my dad. He's not sleeping properly. Last night he had the worst nightmare ever. Me too." She shivered. "Must be something going around."

She went around the shop with him, putting the things on the list into a wire basket; then she totted up the price, fished Mr Patel's little notebook out from under the counter and wrote "Wave: £4.10" and the date. When she handed the carrier bag over to Jamie he saw there was a Crunchie bar lying on top of the groceries. "Just to say thanks. For helping with the magazines."

The Crunchie was delicious: the high point of his Sunday. While he was eating it, the honeycomb bursting like golden sparkles on his tongue, things had almost felt normal again. But when he got home, he found a black cat sitting by the entrance to the flats, its stance alert. He recognized it at once, with its sleek coat and orange eyes. It was Jasper.

"What are you doing here?" Jamie asked.

But the cat just stared at him with its secretive, unblinking gaze, a tangible reminder of his strange adventures. He had the odd feeling that it had come to spy on him. But he hadn't wanted to dwell on something so unsettling, and instead a joke had popped into his head.

"What does a cat like to eat on a hot day?"

No answer. He had forgotten that Jasper couldn't speak to him if he wasn't near a mask. Then the cat stood up, stretched first its back legs, then its front legs, and finally curled its long tail into a question mark.

"Mice cream."

He could have sworn it grinned. Then it gave a long miaow, and walked away. He watched it go, and only then remembered that he had promised he would help it. A sudden hot wash of guilt swept over him. It had helped him in the desert. Without it he would still be in the Sahara, rubbing the Tuareg chieftain's horrible feet for the rest of his life. He would have to make it up to Jasper, and soon.

He lay awake for hours, watching the flame on his tealight candle throwing weird shapes on the wall. When he finally fell asleep he felt as if something was trying to invade his dreams. Something with long, chill fingers. Something that wanted to give him nightmares. . .

"Jamie?"

Someone in the playground had just said his name. He turned around and saw Jinny Briggs gazing at him curiously, as if his nose had suddenly turned into a hamster or something.

"Sorry, what did you say?"

"I said, how did *you* sleep last night?"

"Why do you ask?"

"My mum said she dreamt of the King of Shadows. He whirled her away to his kingdom under the hill and she danced and danced all night, and then she dreamt she escaped and when she got home, a hundred years had passed in a single night and everyone she knew was dead and buried." Her lower lip trembled. "Including me."

"The King of Shadows doesn't exist!" Michael Rose and Mouth had appeared behind her. It was Michael Rose who had spoken: his chipolata lips were twisted into a sneer.

"You shouldn't say his name out loud," said Andy Grant. "If you do, he'll come and get you when you sleep."

Michael rolled his eyes. "You're all such wimps. The King of Shadows is just a fairy tale used to scare babies. Babies like you!" He'd avoided Jamie ever since the tiger incident, and seemed a whole lot braver when he was with Mouth.

"Shut up, Rosy," Mouth hissed suddenly. "What do you know about it? I say he's as real as you or me."

"What about you, Jinny, have you been having nightmares?" Jamie asked, to defuse the dangerous atmosphere.

She nodded. Her dreams for the past two nights had

been confusing and bizarre. But one image had haunted her ever since. The bell for class rang. As they were walking in she said quietly, "Jamie . . . you aren't in any danger, are you?"

"What makes you say that?"

"I saw . . . I saw you . . . with a weapon at your throat."

Jamie felt his knees go weak. His mind raced. Had she somehow eavesdropped on his journey into the Sahara? But that was impossible. Wasn't it? He had to know. "Where was this, Jinny? Was it in the d-desert? Were there camels and men in turbans?"

Her eyes opened wide, as if in shock. She had dreamed of the desert. But that had been almost a week ago. The image she retained of Jamie from the previous night's dream had as its backdrop another landscape entirely, a landscape filled with towers of ice and swathes of snow.

And fearsome-looking men brandishing weapons. . .

And there had been a monster, too. . .

"Take care, Jamie," she said earnestly. "Even in your dreams."

"Oooh, take care, Jamie." Mouth pushed himself in between them, his face all twisted up, mimicking Jinny's concern. "Jinny fancies Jamie Wave!" he shouted out to anyone in earshot, which, given the tremendous volume of Mouth's mouth, was pretty much everyone.

Jinny looked as if she might burst into tears. "I do not!" she wailed, and fled.

Jamie glared at Mouth. "You shouldn't have done that," he said grimly.

Mouth pushed him. "Oh yeah, and what are you going to do about it?"

Jamie drew himself up. He didn't know what he would do, but he had survived amongst the desert nomads and come away with Mohktar ag Badi's treasured sword, and his life, and in comparison with that test, surely fighting with Mouth was nothing special.

He balled his fists, and at that moment Mr Wilkinson appeared.

Mouth pushed him again, surreptitiously. "See ya later, Jamie Wave," he promised.

Mr Wilkinson was sitting in for the absent Miss Lambent. He gave out drawing paper and pencils, yawning all the while.

"Draw—" He gave another huge yawn, then rubbed his eyes as if forcing himself awake. "Draw . . . draw whatever you like." And he went to sleep right there in front of them, seated at the desk with his head on his arms. When he started to snore they sniggered, and when Michael Rose poked him and he didn't wake up, they laughed. But when he started to mumble and cry out they all fell silent.

Normally if there was no teacher around they would all have been shouting and throwing things at each other until an adult came to make them stop, but there was something very wrong about a teacher falling asleep there and then in the classroom when he was supposed to be keeping order. They felt in charge instead, as if they had to keep an eye on Mr Wilkinson, make sure nothing bad happened to him while he slept. It was like turning the world on its head. Jamie felt that if he were to look out of the windows he would find that night had fallen, or that there were two suns in the sky.

All of which was no stranger than walking through a mirror into another time and place. He pushed that thought away. But as soon as he stopped thinking about that, he thought about Mouth instead and his threat to see him later. What had he been thinking about, getting into a fight with the school's worst bully? Then he remembered how he, or rather the tiger-Jamie, had attacked Michael Rose. Perhaps he was changing. And perhaps not for the better. . .

Mouth wasn't waiting for him after school, which was a relief. And he wasn't around the next day, either. When Jamie entered the school gates on Thursday, he saw Miss Lambent instead. His heart began to thump. A shiver ran up his spine.

She crossed the playground with a new spring in her step and as she reached the door she turned and winked at him: or was he imagining that?

In his maths class Mr Reynolds got all confused and seemed to forget how quadrilateral equations worked. He stopped writing a set of them up on the whiteboard, his hand poised with the marker in the middle of a number two like a robot that someone had just switched off. Then he rubbed his forehead and sat down behind his desk and didn't say another word for the rest of the lesson, even when Michael Rose threw a paper aeroplane at him. In their drama class they were rehearsing for the Christmas show; but everyone forgot their lines and Mrs Willis got angry and shouted at them. She even gave Helen Russell detention and Helen immediately burst into tears: she was usually the star of the class and teacher's pet and had never been given detention for anything before.

Everyone was talking about how weird things were, how the teachers were all so bad-tempered and forgetful. They made jokes about it, but beneath the joking lay a sort of suppressed anxiety. Teachers were supposed to be in a position of authority. They were supposed to keep order, to punish you only when you deserved it and not to fall asleep in lessons. They were supposed to know more than you, and they weren't supposed to drift around the school like ghosts of themselves. It was as if no one knew what to expect any more, as if the rules of the world were being rewritten in a language no one could read.

Jamie had no art class on Tuesdays, but even so, Miss Lambent sought him out just as he finished his lunch in the school canteen.

"How are you, Jamie?"

He wasn't sure what to say. The truthful answer would be "nervous" or "shaken". He shrugged. "Don't know, really. Everything seems really strange."

"Quite so. It's got worse since Saturday, hasn't it?"

It was true: everything had got suddenly worse. Since his visit to the maskmaker's shop. But surely there couldn't be any connection? He was only twelve, but he had already learned that it was wrong to see yourself as the centre of the universe, to blame yourself for the things that went wrong around you. *But*, a little voice nagged at the back of his mind, *it was your fault that Dad left: Cadence said so*. . . And since he had been to the desert – if he really had been there – people's nightmares *had* got worse.

"Since you fetched the Tiger's Eye for me?"

It was as if she was reading his mind again.

"Y-yes."

"I think so too. And I know why. But I also know how

we can make things better. Do you want things to get better, Jamie?"

What did she mean by "we"? Surely there was nothing he could do about all the adults behaving so oddly? That was a problem beyond anyone's power to put right, let alone a schoolboy and his teacher. But he knew very well that Miss Lambent was not at all what she appeared. He tried not to think about her mask, about the coursing of golden light up her arms, about the way the sword had gone to ash in her hands.

He shook his head.

Miss Lambent put her head on one side and regarded him steadily with her bright eyes. He felt her gaze boring into him and had to look away.

"Yes, I do. I do want things to get better. But I don't know how I can help to do that. It's all so . . . big."

"You can help me. And if you help me, I can do great things. We can do great things together, Jamie. Come to the shop again on Saturday and take another journey for me. There is another object I need you to bring back for me."

"Another stone?"

"Another stone."

"I don't really understand how that will help."

Miss Lambent smiled. Her smile was radiant, so

gleaming, he was transfixed by it. Had she always smiled like that?

"Oh, it will help: believe me. Will you come?"

He found himself agreeing before he knew what he was saying. After that, it was all he could think about for the rest of the week.

15 THE BLACK CAT

The following Saturday morning Jamie sneaked out of the flat. Well, sneaking out wasn't quite accurate since both his mother and sister were still in their rooms, neither of them having got up for breakfast, or even lunch.

He pressed the button to call the lift, but nothing happened. He waited for a while, but it didn't arrive and the motor made no sound at all. He realized it must have been broken. He ran down the stairs instead, passing balconies leading to dozens of other flats in the block. Normally on a Saturday morning there would be people everywhere: Mrs Wright hanging out her washing, Mr Bridge watering his tomato plants, the Terry twins kicking a ball up and down the corridors, and generally making a racket. Today it was oddly quiet. He passed the fat old lady from the flat on the second floor who usually ruffled his hair and asked him for a joke, which she would then laugh at uproariously. She didn't even smile at him but looked away when he said hello and went into her flat, banging the door behind her.

Feeling rather unnerved, Jamie reached the ground floor of the block. There was no "Out of Order" sign by the lift, and no workmen either. The block's caretaker, a cheerful man called Mr Richards, was nowhere to be seen, but by the door of his office sat Jasper, the black cat. As soon as Jamie came around the corner, the cat got up and walked to the door which led to the outside world as if it had been expecting him. Jamie wondered how it had got in. You had to punch a number code into a keypad outside the security doors to open them – or go in with someone who lived in the block. Maybe that was what Jasper had done. He felt guilty that he hadn't kept his promise to the cat, but seeing it waiting for him was creepy all the same.

"Did Miss Lambent send you to fetch me?" he asked crossly.

The cat just blinked at him.

Jamie shook his head. "I must be going mad, talking to a cat."

Jasper grinned.

Jamie pushed the heavy door open and the cat followed him outside. It followed him out of the estate and on to the main road. It followed him to the bus stop. It was only when they got there that Jamie had a nasty thought. He patted his pockets. Then he dug inside them and brought out the stub of a pencil, the card Miss Lambent had given him, and the tangled earphones for his CD player. He dug deeper and found two sticks of chewing gum that he'd had for goodness knows how long, an acorn, a magnet, a whole lot of fluff and a 50-pence coin. But the fare into town from here was a pound. Perhaps he'd go halfway and walk. . .

"*Meearow-wow!*" said Jasper suddenly, and left the bus stop at a trot.

Jamie felt a sudden sense of relief. Perhaps he wouldn't have to go to the maskmaker's shop today after all. Perhaps he could go and have a kick-around with the other lads down at the park. (Though to be honest he hadn't done that for a while, and neither, it seemed, had anyone else.) Perhaps he should just walk down to the shopping centre and mooch around like most of the other people in his class did on Saturdays. He might bump into Jinny.

He was just thinking this when a car drew up to the kerb.

"Hi, Jamie!"

It was Jinny Briggs, waving at him from the back seat of her mother's car. What a weird coincidence.

Mrs Briggs leaned out. "Hello, Jamie. I don't think the buses are running today – I haven't seen any, anyway. Perhaps they're on strike. Would you like a lift into town?"

"Yes, please."

Jinny opened the back door and shuffled along to make room for him, smiling. Then she looked past him, over his shoulder. "Is that your cat, Jamie?"

Jasper had leapt up on to the bus-stop seat, staring directly into the car, miaowing loudly. You could almost see sparks of fury coming off him.

"No," said Jamie Wave, very firmly. "It's not."

He could feel Jasper's unsettling amber gaze boring into the back of his head as the car drove away down the road.

"Where are you going?" Jinny asked.

"Oh, um, nowhere." He wished he could tell her, but he was too scared of Miss Lambent. Instead, as they passed a pub called The Good Man's Arms, he remembered a joke. "A man walks into a bar with a roll of tarmac under one arm and says to the barman, 'A pint for me, please. And one for the road.'"

Jinny's mum snorted with laughter. But Jinny's little brother, Josh, turned around and regarded Jamie critically. "Wouldn't a road be really heavy? And how would you roll it up? And why would it want a drink?"

Jinny rolled her eyes. "Take no notice. He's very . . . literal."

Jamie grinned at Josh. "Those are very good questions. But you know, things are not always what they seem."

Josh frowned, digesting this. Then he turned around and stared out of the window as if trying to catch the world doing something it shouldn't.

Jinny grinned at him. And just like that, a joke popped into her head. Which was weird, because she was a serious girl who didn't often tell jokes. But it was as if Jamie had given her a gift with his joke, and now she wanted to give a gift to him, too. She took a deep breath and said in a rush, "A dyslexic man . . . walks into a bra."

Josh stuffed his hands over his mouth and giggled. "That's rude!"

Jamie felt a huge smile blossom on his face. "I've not heard that one before."

"I made it up." Jinny was blushing furiously, wishing she hadn't bothered.

"So what are you going into town for?" Jamie asked, seeing how flustered she was.

"I've got a ballet class at the leisure centre."

"Oh." Why did he feel a sudden, sharp disappointment?

"But if you'd like to meet up with us later, Jamie," Mrs Briggs said into the silence that followed, "you could share a pizza with us. I'll call your mum to make sure it's OK with her, shall I?"

"No," said Jamie, too quickly. "There's no need. I'd love to."

Mrs Briggs raised her eyebrows. But she didn't say

anything. They drove in silence for a while; then suddenly she jammed on the brakes. Jamie and Jinny shot forward in their seats and were brought up painfully short by their seat belts. The engine juddered and stalled. Someone honked a horn loudly and impatiently. Josh burst into loud tears. Mrs Briggs sat there shaking.

"I'm sorry, I'm sorry," she kept saying over and over. "I was yawning. I must have squeezed my eyes shut for a moment and then, when I looked up, there was a cat in the road."

"A cat?" Jamie asked cautiously. "What sort of cat?"

"A black cat," said Mrs Briggs.

"It was! It was!" Josh shrieked. "It had really big orange eyes, and it looked right at me. And when it did I saw bad things in my head!"

Mrs Briggs gave a nervous laugh. "I think that's just the shock, dear."

Jamie felt his stomach lurch towards his toes. Jasper. It had to be. But if it had been Jasper, why had he done such a thing? He could have killed them all. Didn't he want Jamie to help Miss Lambent? Was he really so angry that Jamie hadn't kept his promise? He wondered how the cat had followed them all this way, and got ahead of them. It was surely impossible. They'd been travelling at twenty-five or thirty miles an hour most of the way. Surely no cat could run that fast for any length of time? He found that his heart was beating very fast, as if it was trying to get out of the cage of his ribs.

They had stopped near the junction with the high street.

"I can walk from here, thanks," Jamie said, unbuckling his seat belt. "It's not far." Suddenly it seemed really important that he keep Jinny and her family safe; and for some reason that meant away from him.

"Nonsense," said Mrs Briggs. "Tell me where you're going, dear, and we'll make sure you get there. Your mum wouldn't thank me for dropping you in the middle of nowhere, not with so many odd things going on nowadays."

"I . . . er," Jamie stopped. He could hardly tell Mrs Briggs about the maskmaker's shop. "Just the shopping centre," he lied.

"Excellent," she said briskly. "We'll use the shopping centre car park and walk across to the leisure centre from there. I can get some things while Jinny's in her class."

There was no avoiding it. They parked and took the lift down to the ground floor.

"I feel a bit sick," Jinny confided as they stepped out into the shopping centre. "The seat belt squashed my stomach. I hope I don't throw up in ballet." She did look a bit pale.

"I've got some chewing gum somewhere," Jamie said.

"That usually helps." He dug in his pocket and pulled out the two sticks of chewing gum, all twisted up in his earphones. The rest of the contents of his pocket cascaded out as he disentangled the chewing gum. Jinny took the chewing gum gratefully and helped him gather up the fallen stuff. She handed him the magnet, his 50p, and the acorn.

"We'll meet you in the Pizza Shack at 5.30 – is that OK, Jamie?" Jinny's mother asked.

Jamie nodded. "Thanks for the lift."

Jinny's little brother crossed his eyes and stuck his tongue out at him: Jamie made a face back and everyone laughed.

Then the Briggs family turned towards the exit that led to the leisure centre. Jamie watched them walk away, getting smaller and smaller until eventually they disappeared into the crowd. Suddenly he felt more alone than he'd ever felt before. He wanted to run after them, tag along with Mrs Briggs and Josh while Jinny had her ballet lesson. Anything rather than do what he knew he had to.

With a sigh, he trudged towards the opposite exit, the one that led towards May Street.

The cat appeared at the top of the street as he had known it would. It had been perched on top of a heap of rubble beside one of the rusting cars. Now it jumped neatly down to stand in front of him, regarding him solemnly with its orange eyes, its tail curled into a question mark.

"Yes," said Jamie wearily. "Yes, I'm coming."

He followed it to the door of the shop and hesitated with his hand on the door handle, knowing that as soon as he went in, there would be no going back till he had taken whatever journey the masks required of him. Would he ever get back to the Pizza Shack at all, let alone at 5.30? How long would this take? He had no idea, and that was scary in itself. But he pushed the thought aside, remembering instead what Miss Lambent had said about making life in Cawstocke better than it was now. The sooner he went in and met the challenge head on, the better.

He turned the handle, and entered the maskmaker's shop for the second time.

"Good afternoon, Jamie."

Miss Lambent was standing in the shadows behind the counter with Jasper the cat in her arms. As usual, he hadn't seen it come in. He gave them a tight smile.

"I came."

"I brought him," corrected the cat.

"I can see that. I'm very glad to see you."

The cat stretched in her arms and started to clean one of its paws in a nonchalant fashion. Miss Lambent set it down carefully, beside the big old book that was open on the counter.

"Go ahead and choose a mask, Jamie."

He regarded the shelves of masks resolutely and they looked back at him. Did he imagine it, or were they less insistent than they had been the first time? He had felt then that they were all trying to insinuate themselves into his mind with their wheedling promises and attempts to persuade him to choose them. Now, they were quiet, just waiting. It was as if he had passed some sort of exam the first time. They had tested his mettle and decided that he might be up to the task, whatever that task might be, and had concluded that he was capable of making his own decision.

So what would it be?

His gaze skimmed past the ghouls and monsters and Chinese lions. A cowboy? No, he'd had enough of riding last time. A bank robber? That might be fun. Though he didn't want to shoot anyone, and he certainly didn't want to be shot. Superman? The idea of soaring around the city, saving people, was tempting, but what if his flying powers failed? He didn't want to be a famous actor or a footballer – he didn't have the skills to do what they did. Darth Vader? He loved the Star Wars films; but he didn't really want to be the villain. He hesitated when he came to the wizard's mask, with its tall pointed hat and long grey beard. Perhaps he'd learn to do actual magic. That would be really interesting. He reached towards it, but as he did so, another mask fell off the shelf and he caught it automatically.

He turned it over in his hands. It was a Viking mask: or at least he thought it was. It was composed of a close-fitting helmet with a patterned nose-guard and a pair of horns curving up on either side. He'd read about the Vikings. They seemed a rather bloodthirsty lot, raiding and pillaging all over Europe. But he'd also read some stories about their other achievements: how they wrote poetry and told stories, how they had sailed their longships across the oceans and discovered America and Greenland and Iceland. He remembered sitting on the sofa with his dad watching an old film on the TV in which Kirk Douglas ran along the oars of a Viking ship, something that had really impressed him at the time. The memory of this made him suddenly very sad, and he put the Viking mask back on the shelf.

But it refused to stay there. When he reached for the wizard's mask once more, the Viking mask tumbled off again. And again, by sheer instinctive reaction, he caught it by the horns.

"I think the mask has chosen you, Jamie," Miss Lambent said quietly.

It seemed that way to him, too.

"Now off you go, and bring me back the second stone."

He followed Miss Lambent and Jasper to the cubicle at the back of the shop, put the Viking helmet on and stepped into the mirror.

16 AN ARCTIC ADVENTURE

As soon as he touched it, the surface of the mirror shimmered and rippled. But this time when he walked through it, it felt as if the mirror was swallowing him whole, and instead of stepping on to solid ground, he fell, and fell, and kept on falling. Air rushed past him. He clutched at the helmet in case it fell off, remembering what Jasper had said about not being able to make it back to his world without the mask.

What have I let myself in for? He really had no idea where – or when – he was going. He knew the Vikings had existed much earlier than the Tuaregs he had visited in the seventeenth-century desert, but he was a bit vague as to the actual dates. Now he wished he had paid better attention in history. Were they around before or after the Norman Conquest? All he could remember was that the Battle of Hastings had taken place in 1066. That was over a *thousand* years ago. Would he ever make it back from there to his own time, let alone in time to meet Jinny in the Pizza Shack?

All these thoughts tumbled through his head as he tumbled through time, as if they were just as displaced and out of control as his body, until – bang! – he landed on something very hard and very slippery.

His feet went out from under him and he fell on his bottom.

Ow!

When he opened his eyes he thought for a horrible moment that he had gone blind, for everything was black. He blinked and blinked and stared around and at last made out faint silver sparkles above him: stars! A lot of stars, some brighter than others, and a full, fat moon, a great silver disc hanging as big as a shield in the night sky.

As big as a *shield*?

That was hardly a normal comparison for a boy from twenty-first-century Cawstocke. Was he being possessed by the mask? Beneath the helmet, Jamie frowned. What would he usually say? As big as . . . a dinnerplate, or as shiny as . . . a CD. Well, that was a relief – he was pretty sure the Vikings didn't have CDs, so he was still Jamie. This all managed to distract him for several seconds from the fact that it was night and he was out in the dark, all alone, and had no idea where he was.

He reached out with his hand and felt that the ground was cold and smooth. When he snatched his hand away again the palm was wet. Ice. He had landed on ice. He started to get up, and found as he did so that something weighed heavy around his neck, as if his shoulders were being pressed down by an invisible hand. Determined, he straightened and shoved himself to his feet, and suddenly the weight was gone, replaced by a lot of hissing and spitting and snarling which eventually resolved itself into words.

"Aaaagh! Cold! Horrible! Freezing! Miaowwww!"

"Jasper, is that you?"

Something sharp dug into his thigh and then his arm and the weight settled itself around his shoulders once more.

"Of course it's me, you idiot! Gah! Don't move!"

"Don't be such a weed, it's only ice."

"If you had to stand on it in your bare feet, you'd soon complain too."

Jamie realized his feet weren't cold. In fact, he felt pretty warm. He could feel the chill of the air on his hands and face, but the rest of him was really quite toasty. As his eyes adjusted to the pale light of the moon, he looked down at himself and found that the lower half of his body appeared to have changed, becoming sturdier than usual, and . . . furry.

How weird. It was as if he had changed into a bear. Or half of him had. He patted himself and was relieved to discover that although whatever it was once might have belonged to a bear, it was something he *wore* rather than *was*. Like bear trousers. And on his feet, lifting them up to inspect them, despite Jasper's yowls, were big soft boots which insulated him very effectively from the ice.

It could be worse. And at least he knew he'd get his Nikes back when he returned. But returned from where? Where on earth was he?

"Greenland," said Jasper. "At least, that's where we're supposed to be."

"How do you know?"

The cat sniffed awkwardly. "I just do."

"Well, what are we supposed to do now?"

"I don't know."

"You're not much use as a guide, are you?"

"You're not much use as a friend, or a keeper of promises."

Jamie felt a pang of guilt. "I'm sorry about that. I will help you find your family, but you need to tell me why, and what I can do."

Jasper sighed. "I will. When we complete this task and get out of this godforsaken place."

"So, let's get on with it."

"I think that might be a bit . . . difficult."

Was it mocking him now? With cats it was hard to tell; they acted so superior all the time. "Why?"

"Trying using your eyes," the cat said rudely into his mind.

Jamie tried. It was hard to make out very much – he wasn't a cat, after all, and couldn't see in the dark – just acres and acres of light and dark shapes. Then he realized what was wrong.

They were moving!

No! That was impossible. How could land move? He squinted hard. Overhead, the stars seemed constant, but something about his relation to them had changed. He turned and stared behind him, focusing all his senses, until he could hear the soft *slap, slap, slap* of water . . .

He was afloat. On a raft of ice – an ice floe – which was drifting quietly along in the black ocean with a whole load of other floes: for now he could see them, patches of white against the dark background like a giant jigsaw puzzle that had been broken apart and thrown into a massive bathtub.

"Yep," said Jasper. "You got it. We're stranded."

"Perhaps we could swim to the shore," Jamie said.

The cat hissed. "Just put your hand in the water and then tell me we're going to swim!"

Jamie walked a few paces to the edge of the little ice-island, hearing the squeak-crunch of the snow beneath his feet. Careful not to dislodge Jasper – for although he didn't much like the creature, it did seem to know more about their situation than he did – he dipped his fingers into the liquid blackness.

"Whoa!" He snapped upright as if burned. In fact, his hand felt as if it *had* been burned. It was so cold it hurt.

"Don't fancy a dip, then?" said Jasper, curling his lip.

"Definitely not." Jamie loved to swim, in the warm waters of the leisure centre. If he tried to swim here, there would soon be a new type of ice lolly in Jamie Wave flavour. "What do we do now?"

"We wait."

"For what?"

"For whatever happens next."

"Like what?"

"I don't know."

"You don't know much, do you?"

Jamie felt the cat's fur bristle against his neck. Then it rasped, "Look, I didn't choose to do this, you know. I was designated to this task. I'm here to help you, though I don't seem to be getting much thanks for it."

"Help me how, exactly?"

"You'll know when it happens, believe me."

Jamie's fingers were throbbing now, throbbing with hot-aches. He remembered the last time his hands had felt like this, years and years ago, when he'd been seven and Cadence eleven. He'd been up on Churnock Downs with his dad and sister, in the first proper snowfall he had ever seen. He remembered how it had covered everything in a great soft duvet of white, disguising the landscape, softening the contours of the hills, and how the sunset had striped it with incredible colour. Overhead, crows had tumbled and banked, playing in the air currents, cawing raucously, while they built their snowman and then hurled snowballs at one another. The snow had melted through his woollen mittens, soaking his hands in freezing water, but he hadn't cared while he was running around, shrieking, trying to dodge the showers of white missiles with which Cadence and his dad were pelting him. It was only as they walked home that his hands had started to ache. Just like now.

"Would you like to find your father?" Jasper said softly, into the silence.

Jamie started. "You're reading my mind again," he accused.

"It's what I do."

Silence fell between them again. Then Jamie said, "Do you know where my father is?"

The cat gave him a flat-eyed look. "I do."

"Well, where is he then?"

"I suppose I could tell you . . . or I could hold back that information until you help me find my wife and kittens. . ."

Jamie glared back. "You can be really mean."

"Do you blame me?"

There was nothing Jamie could say to that. He gazed at the black cat helplessly. "I really miss him, you know."

"Not half as much as I miss my family."

This argument could have continued for a very long time but just then something erupted from the water beside their ice floe.

Moonlight illuminated the long wedge of a head, pale against the dark sea; a wide black snout, small, coal-black eyes, and a lot of sharp white pointed teeth.

It was a polar bear, the great white bear of the Arctic! Jamie had always wanted to see one. But maybe not quite so close, or under such intimate circumstances.

Now, it placed its huge yellow-white shovel-like front paws on the edge of the floe and heaved itself up out of the water, digging its long claws in and pulling, just like a climber using ice-axes to drag himself inch by inch up a frozen waterfall. Jamie backed away. What if the ice floe tipped up from this sudden exertion of force, from the weight of this monster? What if he and Jasper were capsized into the ocean? He didn't know which was worse: to be eaten by a bear or frozen to death in the icy sea.

He began to wish he still had the sword of the Tuareg chieftain.

"Gerrrrrowowowow!" the bear roared, and then: "What have you done with my cousin?"

So shocked to hear it speak, Jamie stopped in his tracks and stared at it. "I don't know your cousin."

"How can you not know the one you are standing in?"

That was most confusing. "I'm sorry," Jamie said nervously, his mind skittering all over the place. "I don't know what you mean. Is it a joke? I know some good jokes. What does a polar bear eat for breakfast?" He took a breath and rushed out: "Ice Krispies!"

No one laughed.

The bear regarded him suspiciously. "Seal. Usually. I eat seal. Sometimes white hares, or the odd Arctic fox; but mainly I eat seal. For breakfast, lunch and dinner. But" – it narrowed its little black eyes at him – "I am also partial to *innuq*." And it licked its enormous black mouth for emphasis. "Especially an *innuq* who is wearing my cousin Siku."

Jamie looked down at his furry legs, and realization struck him like a hammer. "Ah. Look, I didn't do anything to your . . . cousin – I just arrived here from . . . um . . .

somewhere else, and when I got here I was just . . . wearing these . . . er . . . trousers." As excuses go, he had to admit it sounded pretty feeble.

The white bear finished levering itself on to the ice and took two lumbering steps towards Jamie Wave. Jamie's knees began to quiver, but he stood his ground, remembering something his father had said. *Never show your fear to an angry dog. If you show him you are afraid, he will bite you.* He wondered if the same could be said for polar bears.

His gamble paid off. The bear stared unblinking at him with its bright black eyes. "You certainly don't look formidable enough to be able to kill my cousin. And no hunter worth his salt would ever end up stuck on an ice floe floating at the mercy of the ocean's currents." It peered closer. "And what is that thing you have around your neck? Surely I have never seen anything like it. Is it a malnourished dog-child or a fox which has fallen into a fire?"

Jasper started to bristle all over, as much out of fear, Jamie suspected, as in fury.

"That," he said, "is a cat. Where I come from there are a lot of them. Have you never seen one before?"

The polar bear squinted. Then it curled its lip. "It is a thing of no consequence, hardly even a snack unless I were starving. And a great hunter like Nanuq the Destroyer is never *that* hungry! But I am hungry enough to eat *you*!"

"Oh, I'd taste horrible," Jamie said quickly. "If you ate me I'd give you terrible indigestion."

The bear considered this. "Perhaps if I ate you whole, you might." It looked cunning. "Well, then, little *innuq*, I will make a bargain with you. Tell me who it was who gave you Siku's pelt to wear and I will only eat *half* of you."

That didn't sound like a very good deal to Jamie Wave. He was quite attached to his head *and* his legs. The cat shifted on his shoulder, and he felt its warm breath against his ear as it whispered its advice.

He nodded, then took a step towards the bear. "I'm afraid I can't tell you who killed your cousin Siku. But if you help me to reach the mainland, I will lead you to those who know."

"You are very brave for such a little man, to think to make such a bargain with me." The bear swung its head back and forth as if loosening a kink in its great neck. Then it seemed to come to a decision, for it turned its back on Jamie and lowered its haunches. "All right then, I shall do as you suggest. Climb aboard!" it roared.

And so it was that Jamie Wave, with a black cat wrapped around his neck like a furry scarf, came to be sitting astride a giant white bear which swam with slow steady strokes towards the shore, as the sun rose over the eastern horizon and painted the icebergs, the floes, and the ice cliffs they passed with a brilliant fiery light.

17 THE HORNED BOY

It was a lone hunter from the Tasiilaq hunting band who first spotted them. The only one to have stirred from the warmth of his furs in the igloo that dawn, he had just made a hole in the ice and begun to set up his fishing pole. He blinked sleepily in the rosy light as he realized that something was moving in the fjord. Perhaps it was a whale! Perhaps he should wake everyone, tell them to bring their harpoons. But he'd better make sure; they wouldn't thank him for waking them unnecessarily. He rubbed his eyes, and stared out into the narrow inlet. Out in the shining waters was one of the great white bears, carrying what appeared to be a small dark creature upon its back. His shout of surprise caused a dozen ice gulls and eider ducks to burst upwards into the cold morning air, crying out their harsh alarm calls. That started the dogs barking and yelping, and the brief serenity of the morning was well and truly shattered.

*

"We have been seen," the bear said, swivelling his head to eye Jamie Wave. "Little *Innuq*, is he one of those who took my cousin Siku?"

"I cannot tell yet: we are not close enough," Jamie replied carefully. He was actually rather relieved to see someone, especially someone standing on what appeared to be solid ground.

"I shall know soon. No one has such a fine nose as Nanuq. I can almost smell the scent of Siku's death upon him from here," said the bear, striking out even more strongly.

More hunters had appeared on the icy headland now, men with spears and harpoons. Jamie watched as three came running, then four, six, nine. . .

The polar bear kept up its steady paddling towards the shore as if it did not care how many of them came.

Jamie didn't want to see anyone get hurt. "If you keep going they will throw their spears at you." *And at me*, he thought.

The bear said nothing, just kept on swimming straight towards them.

"What's the point of letting them kill you?"

"I must avenge my cousin's death. It is a matter of honour."

"And if you kill them, what then?"

"I will have avenged Siku. If more of them come, I have achieved my goal and will die honourably."

"So they kill Siku and you kill them and they send more hunters to kill you." Jamie shook his head. "It seems wrong to me, a waste of life."

"The code of life is harsh."

"It sounds to me more like the code of death."

"In the Arctic, life and death are ever close."

There was nothing Jamie could say to this, so he said nothing, but trained his gaze on the hunters who were watching them from the ice. They were short, solid-looking men, dressed from head to foot in thick animal skins and furs, with hoods framing their faces. Their breath rose into the freezing air in soft white clouds.

We are still out of range, Jamie thought, *but they will surely throw their spears at us as soon as we approach the shore*.

But they did nothing of the sort. Soon, the bear had swum in close enough to the land that Jamie was able to make out the features on their faces, which were wide and flat and impassively handsome, their eyes as dark as Nanuq's. They stood unmoving, holding their spears tightly, like an honour guard at a royal event.

The polar bear stopped swimming and trod water instead. "I do not understand. What are they doing? Why are they not casting their weapons? I do not like this. It is unnatural. What is natural is that the *innuq* and the *nanuq* should fight one another. How else will the circle of life and death continue?"

"Can't everyone live together in peace?"

"Ridiculous! We eat them and take their dogs to feed our cubs, and they kill us and wear our pelts and eat our flesh, and thus it always was."

"It doesn't have to be like that," Jamie said, thinking of his wildlife videos and the conservation groups who fought to save creatures like polar bears from being killed. "If we all kill each other, there'll be no one left."

The bear snorted. "You are spoiling my appetite. I was looking forward to eating the *innuq* who slaughtered Siku, but now the hunger has left me and I no longer feel like fighting them. I shall likely be killed for nothing at all." He sighed. "Ah well, perhaps it is my time to join the Old Ones." And he started swimming once more, slowly and steadily, towards the shore.

"I won't let them kill you," Jamie said fiercely, though he had no idea how he would stop them. "I promise."

Nanuq blew water through his nose. "And where would be the honour in allowing a small person like you to protect a great bear like me?"

"It is my honour that is at stake this time," Jamie assured him.

The bear considered this, but it said nothing.

Soon the water was shallow enough for Nanuq to wade through it, and before long they were standing on a pebbly strand. The hunters watched them wordlessly; then one of them turned to the rest of the group, and the one who seemed to be their leader called out loudly, "Welcome, Horned One!" and they all dropped their weapons and bowed their heads.

"This is most strange," Nanuq said, stopping in his tracks.

Horned One?

They mean you, idiot, Jasper said silently. *It's the mask.*

The man who had greeted them came forward now. "Our shaman told us of this, but we did not believe what was said. A horned boy, borne by a white bear. We thought Qilak was mad. Our shaman is very old, and sometimes the thoughts of the old ones wander."

"It is you who is wandering now, Samo!" hissed another of the hunters. "Make him a gift, or he will strike us all down!"

Samo dug in the leather bag he carried across his chest and brought out something small and round. He held it out to Jamie, keeping his eyes averted as if he were afraid.

The bear's nose twitched curiously. Jamie slid down

from its back and took two steps towards the man. Why was he giving him a ball?

Euugh! Jasper smelled it before Jamie could; and when he did he thought he might throw up. It smelled powerful and rancid and very horrible indeed. Worse than the dead rabbit he had found rotting by the roadside on his way to school.

The man was extending the thing to him. "Please take this, Horned One, as a token of our esteem. A little something to nourish you after your long journey. We will roast a seal for you tonight if you will come with us to our village, but this is the very finest *kivioq* in all the White Earth."

Jamie took the *kivioq* and stared at it. It was dark and knobbly and a bit shiny, and it felt soft in his hand. Whiffs of its awful smell assaulted his nostrils. Whatever was he supposed to do with it? *Nourish you*, the hunter had said. Surely he couldn't mean. . .

"Eat it, you fool!" the bear growled.

No way, Jamie thought. "Whatever is it?"

"My lord, *kivioq* is made by stuffing a seal's intestine with the bodies of six small birds; then the end is sewn up and we smother it with seal fat to keep off the flies and then store it under a cairn of stones for the space of two moons until it is ready to eat. Amongst our people it is considered a great delicacy: it is extremely delicious, and we share it only with our most honoured guests."

You'd better eat some of it, Jasper said, *or they'll think* you *rude! And if you were to offend them . . . well, it's probably better not to.*

Jamie closed his eyes. He couldn't imagine anything more disgusting. A seal's intestine – that was bad enough – but the idea of the six little birds left to rot for two months under a pile of stones made him feel sick, and he knew if he ate it he would throw up. Perhaps if he pretended to take the tiniest little bite – not much more than a lick.

Suddenly his hand felt oddly . . . light.

He opened his eyes, and found that the *kivioq* had disappeared. Just like that. Nanuq was sitting in front of him, his jaw working nineteen to the dozen and his eyes all soft and dreamy.

"You ate the whole thing!" Jamie said reverently.

The hunters looked appalled. "That is very bad luck," said Samo.

"Nonsense," said Jamie, grinning widely. "It is very *good* luck. Now take me to your village."

By the time the dogs had been harnessed into their traces and the hunters' spoils and gear had been strapped on to their sledges, the sun was in the north and the breeze was sharp. They set off at some speed, the huskies howling with excitement, their breath frosting the air, and Nanuq, Jamie and Jasper following behind. The sledges swung along the gleaming ice and the bear thundered after them.

Jamie remembered swaying along on the back of Taorka the camel in the Sahara Desert, but that had been stately progress in comparison with this. It felt as if he were flying, and soon he was grinning from ear to ear. All around, the great snowy landscape sped past, glittering in the sun, which threw different shadows and colours in their path – silver and turquoise, jade green and powder blue, lilac and indigo and purple. Glaciers reared up on one side of them, lit from below by a shining dark lagoon. Above them the sun hung pale and gold, offering light but no heat.

Fragments of ice thrown up by the sledges and the polar bear's paws stung his face like a thousand tiny pinpricks. But all the time the Viking mask stayed safely on his head, and his polar bear trousers, boots and furry black neck-scarf (otherwise known as Jasper) kept him toasty and warm. So he was almost sorry when, nearly two hours later, they arrived in sight of a village.

A little group of low huts were scattered here and there, made from rocks that had been piled upon each other, cemented with earth and roofed with turf. Hundreds of fish hung drying from frames like socks on a washing line. Dogs mooched around, nosing for scraps, children played in little groups, and men and women went about their tasks, pounding skins and preparing food. Above them all curved a great white cliff of ice as graceful as a swan's wing.

The barking of the sledge-dogs brought everyone away from their tasks; and if they had been surprised at the early return of their hunting party, they were astonished at the sight of a giant white bear carrying its strange rider.

As soon as they saw Nanuq, the people looked terrified. Many of them turned and ran away. Children started to cry. Those who stayed took up whatever weapons they could lay their hands on – ladles and cooking knives, fire-sticks and cudgels.

"They think we're chasing the hunters!" Jasper chortled. "They think the bear is trying to kill them!"

Jamie laughed; then sobered. If the bear sniffed out the hunters of his cousin Siku, they wouldn't be too far from the truth.

"Stop, Nanuq," he said to the polar bear. "They are frightened of you."

The bear laughed. "And for good reason. Do they really think they can stop Nanuq the Destroyer with their little sticks?" But he halted in his progress and stood waiting, his hot breath making little clouds in the chill air.

They watched the hunters draw into the village and shout greetings to their friends and kinfolk. They all looked towards Nanuq, Jamie and Jasper, then started talking and gesticulating wildly. Through the midst of this group came a small figure, bent almost double over the staff it used as a walking stick. Ignoring the returned hunters, this small person carried on, past the sledges and the yapping dogs and the lines of fish, straight towards Nanuq and his rider.

A few paces away from them it stopped.

Nanuq began to growl, quietly at first, then with a deep, throaty roar. Jamie could *feel* the sound as a vibration which rumbled up through his limbs where he sat on the bear, and settled in his bones. Then the polar bear shuddered and started to back away, his ears flat to his skull, his tail low against the snow. Jamie felt the bear's great muscles tense as if he was suddenly going to turn and break into a run.

"Wait, stop!" Jamie cried. "Where are you going?" Who knew where he might end up if the bear fled?

"I think you had better get down, Little *Innuq*," it growled to Jamie.

The small person took another step towards them.

"Get down!" roared Nanuq, backing away faster.

Jamie scrambled down from the bear's back, hitting the ground with a thud that shook every bone in his body.

"Ow!"

By the time he had picked himself up, all he could see of the polar bear was a flurry of snow cast up by its huge, fleeing paws. And he hadn't even had time to say thank you, or goodbye, let alone to fulfil his promise to find those who had killed the bear's cousin. Disappointed and confused, he turned back to look at the person who had caused such panic in Nanuq the Destroyer.

It was, he realized with sudden shock, an old lady. An old lady swathed in the strangest garb. A toothless little old lady smiling up at him out of a face as wrinkled as the leather of a battered old boxing glove.

"Come with me, Horned Boy," she said, extending a hand. "I have long been expecting you."

But all Jamie could look at was the staff on which she leaned. It was curved and whitish and covered all over in intricate carvings. And on top of it was fixed a skull, which grinned at him, showing long, sharp white teeth.

She may call you Horned Boy, said the skull. *But I will call you Jamie Wave.*

18 THE SHAMAN

Jamie had heard of the phrase *out of the frying pan into the fire,* but no one had ever said anything about the dangers of slipping out of the clutches of a polar bear and into the hands of a scary old lady who carried a talking skull on a stick.

Half of him felt like running after Nanuq and begging him to take him away from here; but the other half was rooted to the ground by the sight of the skull and the sound of its voice in his head. Set in the centre of it was a shining stone of emerald green.

Jamie knew – just *knew,* though he couldn't explain how – that it must be the stone he had come here to retrieve for Miss Lambent. He also knew, without any understanding of how he had come by the knowledge, that the skull belonged to a polar bear. He stared at it, terrified.

"Do not be afraid," the old lady said, her slanted eyes shining. "It is only magic. I am the one they call Qilak, which is our word for sky. They call me that because my spirit flies in the air and communes with other spirits, seeking out knowledge, and bringing it back to my people. I am what they call a shaman, and I have seen you coming for many months past. I did not see your friend, however." And she leaned in close to examine the black cat.

If Jasper had bristled at the attentions of the polar bear, now his hackles were really raised. Little jags of fur stood up along his back, all the way from the crest of his head to the tip of his tail.

I have a bad feeling about this, he said into Jamie's mind. *We should leave – now!*

"I thought I knew all the creatures of the White Earth," the shaman said, reaching a hand out towards the cat, who hissed and spat at her.

"In the sea, the seal and the whale, the fish and the walrus and narwhal – all the children of the goddess Nerrivik."

As she said this, she touched a necklace of bones that she wore about her neck, fingering each bone with every name she uttered.

"On the land the caribou, the fox, the wolf, the hare; the rat, the mouse and the dog." And as she spoke the name of each of these she moved her hand across the furs and skins she wore – the skins of her leggings, her cap of silver-grey fur, her jerkin of white fur, her sleek grey gloves, down to the furred-topped kamiks she wore on her feet.

"And of course, the polar bear." She tapped her staff on the ground. "While, from the skies, the birds. The gull, the eider duck, the swan; the sea eagle, puffin and guillemot." She swirled her cloak about her, and Jamie saw for the first time that it was made up from thousands of tiny wings and feathers all sewn together with a million tiny stitches.

"But I have never come across a creature quite like this." She cocked her head on one side and blinked her shiny little black eyes at him, for all the world like one of the birds whose bodies had been dismembered to create her cloak. "Tell me, Horned Boy, what manner of beast is it?"

Jamie found, quite unexpectedly, that he was feeling protective towards Jasper. He placed a hand on the black cat's head. "It's called a cat," he said quietly. "Where I come from, there are a lot of them."

"And where is that, exactly, Horned One?"

"Cawstocke."

The shaman tilted her head to the other side and regarded him speculatively. "Caw . . . stock. I have never heard tell of such a place. You shall tell me all about it. And then perhaps we will work out a trade."

"A trade?"

"I know that you have come for my jewel." And she tapped her horrid staff upon the ground.

Jamie felt something cold drop into the middle of his stomach. How did she know? His face must have betrayed him, for the old woman patted him on the arm.

"Don't be afraid. I have seen you coming for . . . a very long time."

"How?"

The old woman laughed, throwing her head back so that he could see the dark cave of her mouth.

"Let us say I have my ways. Special ways." She reached out and ran her fingers over Jasper's coat. "My, my, softer than the gossamer of a spider's web. Excellent. Now follow me." And she turned and trotted off back towards the village.

Jasper dug his claws hard into Jamie's shoulder. *No! We mustn't go with her. Something bad will happen if we do. She smells of death.*

Jamie shuddered, and not from the cold. *Let's just get the stone and get out of here.*

You do not know what she will ask for it yet.

That's true. But we're not going to find out by standing here.

I am here to advise and guide you. And my advice is that we leave. Right away.

But suddenly the hunters were standing before them, their eyes hard and their weapons in their hands.

"Come with us."

I don't think we have any choice in this, Jamie told the cat.

The old shaman led them through a village in which people peered at them from beneath doorways and furred hoods with suspicious, wary eyes. Jamie had never been looked at like this before, and he didn't much like it. Even the normally arrogant Jasper was burrowing into his tunic in an attempt to become invisible.

Through the village and out the other side they walked, flanked by the hunters, who seemed to have turned from the cheerful companions who had accompanied them across the ice into a stern armed guard. But as they approached the shaman's domain, Jamie noticed that the hunters hung back. He didn't blame them: for the path to Qilak's house, which was set into the ice cliff, was lined with bones and skulls. And as he passed them, they spoke to him.

Greetings, stranger. My name was Tarroq.

Hail, voyager, I was a mighty walrus once.

I am Uttoq, I was a grey seal.

I am Aua: I was a right whale.

I was a pack-leader, said a dog's skull. *I led the sledge-*

teams, and my sons followed in my footsteps. Soon they will join me here, too.

Don't enter the shaman's cave, said the tiny skull of an Arctic hare. *If you do, you'll never come out again, except like us.*

It was like being back in the maskmaker's shop with all the masks vying for his attention. If this was magic, he hated it.

He also hated caves: they scared him half to death. It was something about their chilliness, and the black, black dark of them. . .

"Tch, tch," said Qilak. "Don't think I can't hear you all chattering away. Stop bothering our visitors with your nonsense, or it will be the worse for you."

How could it be worse? Jamie thought. *They're already reduced to skulls and bones.*

You don't want to find out, Jasper warned him silently.

Inside, the shaman's cavern seemed to be a great deal larger than it appeared to be on the outside. They had had to duck their heads to get through the little door, but inside a great hall opened up, with tall carved pillars stretching up into the cold dark rock like petrified tree trunks, whilst long silver icicles hung down. When Qilak spoke, her voice echoed off the walls, and it seemed that she, too, had grown in stature.

"Welcome to my home."

Jamie was suddenly terrified. He could feel the weight of the world pressing down on the cave. For a moment he thought he couldn't breathe, but it was just panic making him hold his breath. He tried to relax, and transferred his attention to his surroundings, but everywhere his gaze fell he found something that made him even more anxious and made his breath go panting in and out like a dog's. An array of bizarre weapons lined the walls: knives and axes, spears and harpoons, and other things for which he had no name. There were swords and clubs and little short bows, slingshots and spiked sticks. All of them were the same creamy off-white colour, and all were carved with intricate patterns. Fish skeletons plastered the walls; some of them tiny, some of them vast, all of them swimming, fleshless, through an invisible sea. Here and there in the gloom were skulls of every size and type hanging from long brown strings, twisting and turning slowly in the heavy air of the cavern. And over there, a wide iron pot hung above a fire which burned brightly.

With green flames. . .

She may well call herself a shaman, Jasper said into Jamie's mind, *but she's not a true shaman. Where I come from she'd be called a witch. Believe me: I've had experience of witches.*

It was exactly what Jamie had been thinking, but agreeing with the cat didn't make him feel any better. "Um, what about this trade, then?" he asked quickly.

Qilak pushed back her hood. Under it, she had long, stringy grey hair in a hundred thin braids, and in each braid were a hundred thin bones. Her eyes glittered at Jamie.

"Trade? Ah yes. Our trade. First of all, tell me why it is that you want the Soulstone."

"The Soulstone?"

"My beautiful aquamarine." She ran a hand over the gleaming green-blue stone set in the skull that topped her staff, and the skull opened its jaws and let out a low, rumbling growl.

Jasper dug his claws into Jamie's shoulder so hard that he cried out.

"What's the matter, Horned One? Surely such a hero cannot be frightened of a dead bear?" She shook the skull in his face and the bear grinned and grinned.

"I'm no hero," Jamie said, backing away. Indeed, he had never felt less like one. "I have only come to take the . . . Soulstone back to the person it belongs to." It seemed the right thing to say, though he wasn't entirely convinced the stone was actually Miss Lambent's.

Neither, it seemed, did the shaman. "It belongs to me. I

can't possibly let you have it. There is a lot of magic in this stone. It would be extremely dangerous in the wrong hands. That is why I have set my friend here to guard it for me."

"But I thought you said—"

"Oh, the trade?"

Jamie nodded.

"That was for something else entirely. Your life for that of your companion."

"*What?*" Jamie could not believe his ears.

"I have forgotten the name you gave it. Its silky fur will make me a fine collar; but most importantly, its soul will give me dominion over another order of creature, one that I have never encountered before, and that will further increase my power. If you give me the . . . creature I will let you live. For a time, at least."

"I . . . I. . ." Jamie was so shocked he didn't know what to say. Did she really think he would simply hand over the cat in order to save his own skin? He didn't much like the animal, and certainly didn't trust it, but even so he didn't want to see it turned into trimming.

A lot of things happened at once. As the shaman reached out to grab hold of Jasper, Jamie took a step backwards, stumbled over something and lost his footing. Jasper launched himself away from the falling boy with a powerful kick from his back legs, and the shaman fell, flailing, on top of Jamie. As she fell she let go of the staff, which spun away into the darkness and went clattering on to the floor of the cavern.

"My staff!"

Qilak pushed herself to her knees, then painfully to her feet. She muttered something in a language he could not understand and waved her hands about in a complicated way and after a few seconds a small blue flame began to glow in her palms.

As she searched for the staff, Jasper hissed, *Now's our chance to escape! Run for the door!*

Jamie hesitated for a fatal moment. In that moment, Jasper reached the door to the cavern and, finding the smallest gap beneath it, wormed under it as if he were an eel. Jamie followed him a heartbeat later, but no matter how he tried, he could not open it, even though it appeared to be a flimsy thing made only from animal skins stretched upon a frame of driftwood.

"I can't get out!" he wailed.

There was no answer from the other side. The cat had gone. Jamie stared at the door in disbelief. So much for it being his guide and his friend – it had abandoned him! It had left him alone with an evil, soul-stealing witch!

Trembling, he turned back to face his fate.

19 THE SOULSTONE

As if by magic, the shaman appeared.

"Oh no you don't!"

She held up the staff, and the stone glowed with a bright green light, illuminating the wrinkles and creases of her ancient face like a Halloween mask.

"Your friend may have escaped me, but you most certainly shall not! Look into the Soulstone and tell me your true name, Horned One, and you shall join the spirits who aid me in my magic."

"No way!" Jamie retreated from her until he bumped up against the door, which now felt like iron against his back.

Jamie Wave, Jamie Wave, Jamie Wave! sang the skull.

Qilak cocked her head as if listening intently. "What a pity it is that the voices of the dead speak so indistinctly."

The voice sounded quite clear to Jamie: could she not hear it? It seemed as if she had heard the skulls chattering to him as he walked up to her cave. Perhaps she couldn't make out exactly what they said. That was interesting.

Hello, he said suddenly in his mind. *Do you hear me?*

I hear everything. The dead hear all. Why do you call upon me?

I need your help. The shaman is trying to kill me.

She has taken many of us; why should I care about one more?

Jamie remembered something the great white bear had said to him. *It's a matter of honour, the code of life,* he said silently to the skull.

It pondered this, then asked, *Why should the code of life mean anything to the dead?*

There was no answer to that. *I don't know,* Jamie admitted. *It's just something someone said to me.*

Nanuq used to say things like that.

Jamie shivered. *Are you . . . Siku?*

There was a pause. Then: *Yes, I am Siku the White, cousin of Nanuq the Destroyer.* It laughed, a rumble in his head. *Though Nanuq the Clumsy Oaf might be a better name for him. I remember the day he fell in the seal-hole. . .*

He is my friend, Jamie interrupted before the spirit of the bear could launch into a long story. *He would want you to help me. Tell me what to do.*

Do not let her touch you with the Soulstone, for if she touches your forehead with it, it will take your soul.

How can I stop her? Can you bite her?

Again, the hollow laughter rang in his mind. *I do not dare. You must challenge her somehow. She cannot resist a challenge.*

Challenge her how?

He could have sworn he heard it sigh. *Ah, well that is up to you, Jamie Wave.*

The shaman was almost close enough to touch him now. What sort of challenge could he set to a mad old witch who wanted to take his soul? The only thing he was any good at was jokes, and he suspected she was not likely to appreciate the sort of jokes that were jostling around in his head at the moment. (*What do you call a witch on a beach? A sand-witch. . . What do you call a witch who stands by the side of the road with her thumb out? A witch-hiker. . .*) But perhaps if he challenged her in some other way. . .

Ah, a riddle, the skull sighed. *How people love a riddle. We hear them around their fires at night, making up their nonsense. She always knows the answers.*

That didn't sound too promising. Still, what did he have to lose?

Your soul?

He didn't want to think about that. Riddles had worked

with the Tuareg chief, so perhaps they would work with the shaman. Jamie took a deep breath. "Qilak, if you are a great shaman, you must know the answer to many of the mysteries of the universe."

The old woman regarded him curiously. "Of course. I commune with the spirits, who tell me many things. It is an art confined to only a few strong souls. It has imbued me with great knowledge."

"Perhaps you will know the answer to this small riddle, then: they do not have feathers, or flesh, or scales, or bone. Yet they have fingers and thumbs of their own. What are they?" he said suddenly.

Qilak pursed her lips. "Is this a trick? Are you trying to enspell me?"

He shook his head. "It is just a test of your cleverness," he said. "I cannot simply give up my soul to someone who isn't clever enough to solve a few easy puzzles."

Silently, she considered the conundrum. "Fingers and thumbs, eh? Well, that rules out the squid and the eel, though eels have bones. Thumbs! Even bears don't have thumbs. . ."

Jamie grinned to himself. It was a very easy riddle, as long as you knew the answer. It came from a rhyme his mother had told him when he was little, and she was dressing him to go to school in the cold.

The shaman was stomping furiously around the cave, and as she stomped the light in the Soulstone began to dim. "Can't be fishes of any sort – they have scales. Birds have that backwards-facing claw that might be conceived of as a thumb. But are there featherless birds?" She clicked her tongue. "No flesh? Now that's a problem. It could be one of my skeletons, but they are all bone. . ." She ticked off possibilities on her fingers. Then she turned around, a manic grin on her wizened face. "Ha ha! I have it! Gloves!" And she waggled her silver-furred fingers at him. "Ha! No flesh, no feathers, no scales, no bones. Excellent! Ask me another."

In a way it was disappointing that she had guessed it so quickly: but at least he seemed to have diverted her from her purpose, for the time being. But now he had to rack his brain for a harder riddle. He gazed around the cavern for some inspiration. None came to him. He needed more time.

"I can't think very well standing up," he lied. "I need to be comfortable. I'm very cold."

Qilak gave him a long, hard stare. "I know what you're doing." Then she shrugged. "But it won't make any difference to the end result, so I will indulge you." She led him to a chair by the strange green fire and draped a fur around his shoulders. "Come along, then. Ask me another riddle."

By now, Jamie had seen something that jogged a memory of a riddle he'd once come across.

"Gleaming and glittering

Down I thrust

A sparkling spear,

I never rust.

What am I?"

The shaman screwed her face up so that all her features seemed to disappear. She pulled her nose. She pulled at her lips. She thumped the staff up and down on the floor and ground her gums together. The light in the stone was barely a glow.

"Sparkling spear, sparkling spear. . ." She stared at her walls. "Ha! A narwhal's horn!"

Jamie frowned. "What's a narwhal?"

"Silly boy! It's a great big sea creature with a spear-like horn on its nose!" And she pointed to where on the dark wall of the cave there hung a long ivory horn which spiralled to a point, just like a unicorn's horn in a fairy tale. "That will never rust. And if I polish it, it gleams. And when a narwhal dives, it's thrusting down." She put her hand on her hip, triumphant. "So there's your answer."

Jamie shook his head. "That's not the answer. I didn't even know what a . . . what that creature is. Try again."

For a good ten minutes Qilak paced the floor,

muttering, while Jamie darted glances around the cavern for possible avenues of escape. Could he dash into the darkness at the back of the cave in the hope of finding a way out? It was as black as night back there, with not a chink of light to be seen. It seemed unlikely there, was a way of reaching the outside world that way. Plus, he couldn't imagine giving himself up to that dense darkness and whatever it might conceal.

At last the shaman stamped her foot. "I don't know. Tell me the answer."

"Will you let me go if I tell you?"

"No!"

"What will you do if I don't tell you?"

"I will take your soul before you can utter another word!"

"Oh." There didn't seem to be much choice. "It's an icicle," Jamie said, hanging his head.

Qilak huffed. "That's not a very interesting riddle. Tell me another one and make it better, or it'll be the last thing you'll ever do."

A great wave of black despair swept over Jamie then. He couldn't think of any other riddle, let alone an interesting one.

Jamie Wave. . .

The voice was so soft as to be almost a whisper. Jamie's

head shot up. He stared wildly around. Had the cat, Jasper, somehow sneaked back in?

Up here.

Was there a bird or a bat up there in the darkness? He stared above him. One of the skulls hanging from the ceiling seemed to be swinging more than the others, and as he looked at it, it spoke again, though its bony jaws never moved.

I once was a boy like you. . . said the swinging skull. *I was a Viking boy, from a village in Iceland. My father brought us here to settle, but the Skraelings attacked us and killed us all. But no Viking ever wore a helmet like the one you wear.*

There was a low laugh from higher up in the cavern's gloomy air. *Of course not, lad: horns like that would catch a sword and you'd soon lose your helmet. It would be hopeless in a fight! We've all been laughing at you ever since you arrived!*

Erik Loosetooth had a helmet with horns on it.

Erik Loosetooth was a fool.

I was not!

You were.

Anyway, it was a joke. Look, are we going to help the boy in his plight?

Why should we? I'd welcome some new company up here. Be nice to have a new head amongst all you old bores.

Don't listen to him. Boy, I have an excellent old riddle for you.

"Each morning I appear
To lie at your feet,
All day I follow you
No matter how fast you run,
Yet I nearly die
In the midday sun
What am I?"

Jamie thought about this for long moments. Then he admitted, *I have no idea!*

Ah, but we know the answer. Just ask the old woman. It'll keep her busy for a while.

So Jamie repeated the riddle the Viking's head had offered him and watched as Qilak buried her head in her hands and gnashed her gums, and at last the light in the Soulstone dimmed to nothing.

Is there any way out of here? he asked the heads while the shaman pondered the riddle.

Hollow laughter filled the air.

If there were an escape, do you think we would still be here?

That wasn't very helpful.

Now the skull on the staff spoke again. *How is it that you know my cousin Nanuq, Jamie Wave?*

So Jamie told Siku of arriving on the ice floe and finding that they were stranded in the freezing ocean: of how he had come to make a bargain with the polar bear to save his skin and that of Jasper the cat. And he apologized about the trousers, but that indignity didn't seem to bother the bear.

What was the bargain you made? Siku asked him.

I promised I'd lead him to the men who killed you.

The air stirred as the jaws of the skull moved in silent laughter. *I think, then, Jamie Wave, that your promise will be an impossible one to fulfil.*

Why?

Why? Because it was no man who killed me, but a woman.

How could a woman kill a great creature like a polar bear? Jamie had imagined it must have been a dozen fierce hunters who had trapped Siku and speared him to death. Realization dawned slowly. *You mean, it was Qilak who killed you?*

She took my soul with that cursed stone. She had it set on top of a staff made from a whale's jawbone. I broke the staff in my death struggle, so she punished me by using my poor skull on her new stick.

It was a horrible thought that the Soulstone could be so powerful. Jamie wondered why Miss Lambent wanted it. What would she do with it? Would she use it, and if so, on whom? That was an even more uncomfortable thing to think about. When Qilak burst out cackling, he was almost relieved.

"Ah ha ha ha ha ha! I know the answer to your riddle, Horned Boy!"

He'd forgotten all about the riddle.

"It's your shadow!" she exclaimed. "Under your feet all the time, following you no matter how fast you go, long when the sun is high and vanishing almost to nothing when the summer sun is overhead."

That was clever: Jamie knew it was the answer as soon as she said it.

Qilak danced a little jig of triumph, tapping the staff as she went, and all the tiny braids on her head jinked and jumped with each step like writhing snakes. And with each step she took, the light in the Soulstone began to glow more brightly. At last, breathless, she stopped. "Ah, I am the wisest woman in all the world, not that I ever doubted it. Thank you for such entertaining diversions, Horned Boy. But I am bored with riddles now, so the time has come for me to take your soul instead." And she started to chant strange-sounding words into the air of the cavern. All at once, the carved bones on the walls started to glow with the eerie green light as the Soulstone burned with its terrible inner fire.

She advanced upon him until he felt the cold light upon his face.

Jamie knew he had failed in the task he had been set, and now he was going to die. His skull would end up swinging from a string in the shaman's hall like the other skulls, chattering dully to one another for eternity. He would never see his mum, or Cadence, or Jinny, or Cawstocke ever again. At that moment he missed them all sharply. It felt like a physical pain. He missed his dad. His dad would have found a way of dealing with Qilak, he was sure. He even missed Miss Lambent, the maskmaker's shop and the wretched cat that had left him to face the shaman's magic alone. For the first time in his life he gave up hope. He closed his eyes and waited for the stone to take his soul.

20 NANUQ THE DESTROYER

At the very moment that Jamie Wave gave up all hope there came a great hullabaloo outside.

Qilak grabbed hold of Jamie and shoved him hard away from the door. "Get back there while I deal with this rude interruption!"

Jamie fell headlong into the darkness. He got to his knees in time to see the most bizarre sight. The shaman flung open the door, to find half a dozen polar bears ranged outside, led by the gigantic form of Nanuq. Even more strangely, a small black shape appeared to be clinging to the thick white fur of his neck.

It was Jasper.

"We've come to save you, Jamie Wave!" he cried. "I ran and ran until I found the great white bear. . . Are you there, Jamie? Are you still alive? Are we in time?"

"Yes!" shouted Jamie. "I am here, and alive!"

"You are in time to join your friend!" the shaman smiled.

"But if you want him, you will have to step into my hall and allow the stone to greet you, one by one!" And she waved the horrible staff at them. "Just a little kiss on the forehead is all it takes. . ."

Nanuq reared up on his hind legs and Jasper promptly tumbled to the ground with a yowl of protest. "Step aside, old woman, or I shall bite your head from your shoulders!" the bear roared.

Qilak laughed. "I see you are braver now with your friends around you. Do they know that the last I saw of you was of your big furry rear disappearing in a great flurry of snow as you fled from me and my little stick?" And she chanted the words which made the Soulstone burn brightly.

Nanuq bristled. His forefeet thudded down so hard that ice fell in a shower of needles off the cliff above the shaman's home. "It is not you I fear, old woman, but your unnatural magic! But know that if you kill me, then Aput will step forward, and if you harm him, Imaq will come, and if Imaq falls, then Mala and Arn will take her place. You cannot kill us all!"

Bravely said, cousin!

Nanuq stared around nervously. "I heard a voice, the faintest whisper of a voice, but it sounded to me like the voice of my cousin Siku."

I am here, reduced to nought but bone. And the skull atop the shaman's staff rattled its jawbone together in a horrible clacking noise.

Nanuq's ears flattened, and all along the ridge of his spine, his hackles rose like an angry dog's. "Something is scratching at the inside of my head, but I cannot make out the words!"

"All that remains of Siku is the skull on the staff!" called Jamie Wave. "He is speaking to you, but it seems that no one but me can hear him. I said I would lead you to the men who killed your cousin, but it was no man who took his soul. It was the old woman, Qilak, with the evil stone that shines in the middle of Siku's head. It is called the Soulstone and it has stolen the soul not only from your cousin, but from all those whose bones adorn her house and grounds!"

All the bears began to growl as they heard this, for they had seen the many skulls and skeletons along the path to the shaman's dwelling, and the eerie green light the stone now emitted shone upon the skulls that swung from the strings in the cavern, and studded the cavern's walls. But the doorway was too narrow to admit them all at once, and the shaman was too astute to come outside.

But Nanuq stepped forward. "You may consider your promise fulfilled, Little *Innuq*, for now I shall avenge my poor cousin!" And the great white bear launched himself through the door at the shaman.

Qilak, moving with remarkable swiftness for such an old woman, wielded the staff as fast as a striking snake, trying to touch the bear's head with the green stone, but at the last moment, Siku's skull opened its jaws wide, tilting the Soulstone away from Nanuq.

"Ha! Now I know it is you, my cousin!" Nanuq roared. "What a team we made when we hunted the caribou and the fine fat seals!"

Again the shaman lunged, and again the skull prevented her attack.

Qilak took a step backwards. She reached up, grabbed hold of one of the skulls swinging from the roof, broke the leather thong from which it suspended as easily as if it were the stalk of a daisy, and hurled the skull at Nanuq. The skull wailed in protest as it flew before bouncing harmlessly from the bear's flank and flying off to shatter against the rock-hard ground. In the blink of an eye, Qilak had wound the string tightly around the jaw of the skull, binding it shut. "Now you shall neither thwart me nor mutter my secrets," she scolded it, even as she advanced upon Nanuq.

The Soulstone blazed as bright as a star.

Jasper!

Jamie Wave sent a desperate silent cry into the air.

Yes? The cat's response was quiet and hesitant.

On the count of three, you run between the shaman's legs and I will push her over. We cannot let her harm Nanuq! Are you ready? One, two, three. . .

Go!

Go on, Jamie Wave!

May the gods speed you!

It was as if the wishes of all the stolen souls propelled Jamie Wave, for he fairly flew across the cavern and, just as a small black shape rushed between the old woman's legs, pushed with all his might. Down Qilak went in a tangle of limbs and cat, and the staff went flying. Over and over it twisted in the air, foot-first, then head first, until it seemed to hover and then come down as fast and straight as a spear. With the Soulstone pointing right at Nanuq's upturned face. . .

Jamie had never been much of a sportsman at school. When they played football, they always put him in goal, since he got in everyone's way if he was out in the open field. He never managed to save a shot. Basketballs slipped through his hands as if someone had slathered them with butter. He had dropped every catch in cricket. But the life of his friend Nanuq was at stake. Jamie leapt into the air, higher than he had ever jumped before, and made a grab for the staff. But as he leapt, the Viking helmet fell from his head. He felt a moment of terror – would he be stuck in this freezing, terrible place for ever? The staff was above him and falling away. If the green stone touched Nanuq, the bear would die horribly. He stretched his body till every muscle felt it would burst and his desperately reaching fingers might shoot right off his hands.

His fingertips brushed the bone of the staff, but he couldn't quite catch it.

But he *did* knock it out of its trajectory. As he started to fall he saw the staff tumble end over end and plummet towards the floor, landing just to the left of the great white bear. Where the shaman, Qilak, lay sprawled. Quite what occurred next it was hard to say, for the Soulstone sent brilliant green flashes shooting across the cavern, blinding everyone. There was an ear-splitting shriek and then the whole place was plunged into deepest darkness and silence.

For a while Jamie could see nothing but the jagged silver-green after-image of the light stabbing across the inside of his eyelids.

After a time something warm and furry brushed against his hand.

"Aaargh!"

It's only me, said Jasper the cat, sounding huffy.

"Sorry. What happened?"

I don't think the old witch will be casting any more spells.

Even when his sight returned, it was hard to make out the interior of the cavern. The strange green fire had gone out, and the polar bears pressed against the doorway, blocking out the natural light. But as his eyes slowly adjusted, Jamie could make out the still form of the shaman, prostrate on her back, with the staff lying across her body, the skull of Siku the bear pressed against her own.

Suddenly a great rumble filled the cavern, and for a moment Jamie thought an earthquake had come. Then he realized the polar bears were all laughing. Why were they laughing? It seemed strange, and rather horrible, in the circumstances. He stared and stared into the gloom. Was Qilak dead? She wasn't moving, and her eyes looked weird. He focused harder, and suddenly realized why. The pupils had rolled back into her head, leaving only the whites visible. It looked as if someone had replaced her eyes with hard-boiled eggs. For a moment, Jamie felt sick. Seeing his first dead body didn't seem funny to him. He felt deeply shocked.

At last the chamber fell quiet again and Nanuq turned to Jamie. "Forgive our levity, Jamie Wave. We have seen justice here today, long-awaited justice, and a great deal of tension has been released. As my kin have reminded me, I have spent all these years vowing to avenge my cousin, but it seems he preferred the help of a Viking lad to that of his renowned cousin, Nanuq the Destroyer!"

"The boy saved your life!"

"He's a hero!"

"I'm not a Viking," Jamie said quietly. "Nor a hero." And he certainly didn't feel like one. "I'm just a boy from Cawstocke. And I'd really like to get back there. I don't want to have adventures like this any more."

But you are a hero, Jamie Wave, the cat told him. *Listen.*

Jamie listened but he couldn't hear anything. *I don't understand. What am I listening for?*

Can you hear the voices of the dead?

He couldn't.

You have freed them. Now that the shaman who took their souls is dead, they are finally at peace. You have broken the spell of the Soulstone. And now we can safely take it back with us to Cawstocke.

Jamie felt his heart lift. *We can? But how can I return without the mask?*

Jasper batted something with his paws till it came to rest at Jamie's feet. *It's a bit battered, but I reckon it'll get you back home. Now, take the stone from the skull, and we'll away.*

And there was the Viking helmet, between the black cat's paws, covered in dust and cobwebs, but in one piece.

Jamie picked it up and jammed it on his head. He had never been so relieved in his life. Then, with trembling hands, he touched the skull of Siku the bear. The bone lay inert beneath his touch, the jaws inactive, as if not even a whisper of his essence remained. And the Soulstone, too, lay quiet and dull, as if all the magic had gone out of it in the same instant.

Is it safe to touch it? He was still afraid it would take his soul.

Jasper came up beside him and bravely reached a paw to the deadly stone. Nothing happened as he patted it.

It will not harm you, the cat promised.

Gritting his teeth, Jamie took hold of the Soulstone. The blood pulsed in his ears, but the stone remained dead to his touch, and his soul remained his own. His fingers closed around it and he gently prised it away from the skull of Nanuq's dead cousin. It sat in the palm of his hand as heavy as a lump of lead. He tried not to think of all the souls it had taken, and perhaps still contained.

Can we leave now? he asked Jasper.

Yes, let's go home.

Nanuq carried the pair of them through the village, with the other polar bears following in a solemn procession, and where they passed the people gazed at them in fear and awe and no one dared to raise a hand to them. Even the huskies fell silent at their approach. They kept their haunches low to the ground in submission, and their strange pale eyes were filled with uncertainty. They had been on hunting raids to take cubs or a single wounded bear, but they had never seen seven of the great white bears together in a line, walking like kings through the middle of their own territory. This was not a tale to pass down to the pups: it was a matter of great shame.

When they reached the fjord where the cold black water lapped the strand, the bears made their farewells, each in turn bowing to the boy and the cat, then went their separate ways. Only Nanuq, Jamie and Jasper were left on the pebbly shore. Jasper scanned the bergs and floes floating on that black sea. He looked to the sun, hovering redly above the horizon, then back to the water as if making some sort of calculation.

"Over there," he said at last, pointing to a berg that looked like a shining white castle.

Nanuq swam to the berg and set them down on its icy flank. "Will I see you again, Jamie Wave?"

Jamie shook his head, and the Viking helmet slid around till the eye-slits were halfway to his ear. It felt as if something had been broken in its fall. He adjusted it so that he could see out again, and hoped that when they stepped back through the portal it would still work. "I don't think so, Nanuq."

"Then you must go and do what you were born to do: save your home."

Jamie gazed at him, a bit nonplussed. Whatever had Jasper said to the polar bear? He didn't know what to say. "Um, thank you . . . I think."

"It is you I must thank, on behalf on my clan," Nanuq said solemnly, bowing his head. "And my poor cousin Siku." He stared meaningfully at Jamie's lower half.

Jamie followed his gaze. "Oh, ah . . . yes. Er . . . sorry. Hang on a minute."

He struggled out of the furry white trousers, and was horrified to discover he had on nothing underneath except a wrap of soft leather. Feeling like an idiot – and pretty chilly, too – he held out the polar bear fur to Nanuq, who took gently it in his jaws, muttering something indistinct about a seal-hole which had been Siku's favourite place. Then the bear bowed his head to the boy and the cat and slithered back into the icy waters.

Jamie felt a lump rise in his throat. In the short time in which he had known Nanuq, he had become very fond of him. But his dad had always told him that boys don't cry, and while he knew that to be untrue, he always felt he had in some way failed his father if a tear escaped, and that his dad would never return if he was ashamed of him. So he swallowed the lump down and watched Nanuq swim slowly away until he was no more than a white speck against the black ocean.

Jasper shivered. "Let's get out of here before we freeze to death."

He led Jamie around the berg until they came to a spot that shimmered like a mirage in the chill air. "Ready?"

Nerves were making Jamie tremble almost as much as the cold; but just as they were about to step through the portal, a joke suddenly floated into his head.

"What do you call a cat that lives in an igloo?"

Jasper twitched his whiskers. "Don't know."

"An Eski-mew."

They were still laughing as they stepped into the void.

21 JINNY

The world spun so violently that it was hard to keep hold of the Viking helmet. But Jamie knew that if he let go it would spin away into infinity, and so would he. He clamped his hands around the mask and held it tightly in place, even though it vibrated against his skull until he thought he was going to be sick.

Crushed against his chest all the way was the black cat, Jasper. He could feel the little beast's sharp claws digging through his clothes, holding on for dear life, and for once he didn't mind. Over the course of this last adventure something had changed how he felt about the cat. He thought it had abandoned him when it had wormed its way under the shaman's door and run off into the icy wastes. But he realized now that it had followed the giant polar bear and somehow persuaded Nanuq to return with the other bears to save him from Qilak's terrible magic. That had been brave. A great white bear like Nanuq could surely swallow a small cat like Jasper in a single mouthful. But there was still the creepy way it turned up when you least expected it, and the way it had appeared in front of Mrs Briggs's car. Though perhaps that had to do with reminding him about his promise. Ah, yes, his promise. . .

Just as he was thinking about this he tumbled through the portal and came to an abrupt and painful stop. Was he back in the maskmaker's shop? There seemed to be no way of telling, for wherever it was he had arrived was as dark as night. Which made him shiver deep inside. Monsters came out in the dark. Monsters, and other scary creatures. *Don't think about that,* he told himself fiercely. *Just find out where you are and get yourself home.*

Don't forget your promise. . .

Jamie stood up, carefully detached Jasper from his clothing and set him down on the floor.

I haven't forgotten.

Ask her: ask her where my family is. Ask her before you hand over the stone.

Jamie took off the Viking mask and felt around for a way out. He touched something hard and smooth and cold – the mirror? And then a door. He opened this, but still no light came.

Feeling with his hands as he walked, Jamie made his way out of the little room and down a corridor. He came out into a larger space, but still everything was pitch-black. Where was he? And, indeed, *when* was he?

As he got used to the darkness, he became aware that hundreds of eyes were looking down at him, glinting in the moonlight. Hundreds of . . . faces. His heart sped up, battering against his ribs. He was so scared that it took him several seconds to realize that he was back in the maskmaker's shop, and he was just about to breathe a huge sigh of relief when one of them moved. . .

Jamie could not help himself from crying out. As he did so, a cold hand clamped itself over his mouth, stifling his shout.

"Sssh— Don't make a sound."

"Miss Lambent!"

"Keep your voice down. Wherever have you been? I've been waiting for you for hours!" Quick as a flash she grabbed up the black cat and shook it hard. "What did I tell you? Never in the dark!"

"There was no choice," Jasper rasped back, his legs dangling helplessly. "It was either by dark or not at all!"

The maskmaker set the cat down on the counter and gave it a hard stare. "I'll deal with you later. Move at your peril!" Then she turned back to Jamie. "Give me the stone."

Remember your promise!

Jamie felt his stomach knot. He fished in his jeans pocket

and, from amongst the earphones and the rest of his stuff, brought out the Soulstone. It sat as dull and uninteresting in his hand as a lump of spent coal, as if all the magic had gone out of it.

He watched Miss Lambent's eyes become round and avid. Light seemed to flash from them at the very sight of the stone. "Aaahhh," she sighed. "There it is, at last. The Soulstone. Give it to me."

Jamie took a step backwards. "I . . . I . . . have a q-question f-first."

He watched her eyes narrow dangerously.

"It's about . . . about J-Jasper's. . ."

He didn't even manage to complete the sentence. The speed with which Miss Lambent moved was not natural for an old woman. It was superfast, and her grip was powerful as she grasped his wrist. "Give me the stone!"

And she wrested the Soulstone right out of his hand. As soon as her fingers closed around the stone, it started to glow. He could see the green light oozing out of it, through the cracks between her fingers. Its illumination was so fierce he could even see the bones of her fingers like ghostly shadows beneath the skin. The look on her face was one of undisguised triumph; but worst of all, he could see the skull beneath the mask she wore, and the creases and wrinkles of her ancient skin. All at once he was terribly afraid, though he could not say what he was afraid of, exactly. Did he fear that she would use the stone on him? Or that if he stayed for another moment it would reveal the true Miss Lambent in all her terrible glory, and not just the old lady she had once revealed to him? Trembling with terror, he forgot all about Jasper, dropped the broken Viking mask on the floor and backed towards the door.

"I'll go now," he whispered, but she didn't seem to hear him.

The door swung open at his touch as if trying to get rid of him, and quite abruptly he found himself out on the cold, deserted streets of night-time Cawstocke.

Jamie had never been out in the night on his own before. He had once spent a night out in a tent with his dad on the Downs, and they had built a fire and his dad had pointed out to him all the constellations in the starry sky, and he hadn't even been scared when a great barn owl had slipped silently overhead, its face and belly feathers as white as a ghost. But May Street, without a single street lamp, was completely dark, and clouds covered the moon. It was horribly eerie. He was sure he felt eyes on his back, as if unseen creatures were watching him from the roofs of the abandoned shops, from beneath their eaves and behind their chimneys, from the gutters beneath the rusting cars. He moved up the road slowly at first, looking from side to side and turning around at intervals in case someone – or something – was following him. At last, unable to bear the sense of being some kind of prey, he broke into a run, his footsteps echoing noisily off the damp brickwork. That would surely alert anything out there to his presence, but at least he was a moving target, he thought, pounding around the corner and out on to the high street. Here, the sodium lamps threw their Lucozade light across everything, so he slowed to a walk. He passed the closed-down bingo hall, the pound-for-everything store, the shoe repairer, and all the nondescript little shops that lay outside the shopping centre. It was only when he came to the Pizza Shack that he remembered Jinny, and how he was supposed to have met her and her family there at 5.30. He wondered how long they'd waited for him and what they must think of him for not turning up, and he felt his cheeks burn hot.

He was still trying to come up with a reasonable excuse he could give to Jinny when he saw her at school on Monday when a car pulled up at the kerb and the driver stuck her head out of the window.

"Jamie! Jamie, is that you?"

It was Mrs Briggs.

The car screeched to a halt. The door was flung open

and Jinny's mother tumbled out of it in a tangle of hair and limbs. She looked frightful – literally full of fright and fear.

"Have you seen Jinny?"

"No. No, I haven't." Jamie stared at her. "Isn't she with you?" He knew it was a stupid question.

Mrs Briggs's eyes were shiny with orange light. "She went to look for you when you didn't come to join us for a pizza."

This was terrible, really terrible. "I haven't seen her anywhere," he muttered. How could Jinny have known where to look for him? He hadn't told anyone where he was going.

"I've been to the police, but they didn't seem to be at all interested, told me that people ran away and went missing all the time and that she'd either show up or she wouldn't. But I know my daughter. She's such a good girl. I know she'd never do anything so irresponsible as running away." The tears welled up and began to spill down her cheeks.

Jamie's heart was beating very fast. This shouldn't be happening, not on top of all the other weirdness he'd dealt with today. Adults weren't supposed to cry. Children cried and adults comforted them and made things better again, and if adults couldn't do that, then the world was truly broken. And Jinny was really missing.

"I'm really sorry, Mrs Briggs. I meant to join you for a pizza, but . . . er . . . something cropped up. . ."

She wasn't listening. Instead, she thrust a tattered piece of paper at him. "She left this behind when she went to look for you."

It was the card Miss Lambent had given him, the card for the maskmaker's shop. Jamie remembered with sudden vivid clarity how he'd excavated his pockets to try to find a piece of chewing gum when Jinny was feeling sick, and how everything had fallen out on to the ground. Including, he realized now, Miss Lambent's card.

"I went to the address on the card," Mrs Briggs was saying, "but as soon as I got there I realized there must be a mistake. There was nothing down May Street except all these boarded-up shops and abandoned cars. I didn't see a soul. And when I got to this place, it was in darkness and didn't look as if it had been open for a hundred years, what with all the dust and the cobwebs in the window. I knocked on the door and waited and waited, but no one came. And then I felt ridiculous, because why would my daughter be in a closed-up shop anyway? And I came back and looked for her in the shopping centre. I even got them to make an announcement, but she didn't appear; and eventually I went home, in case we'd missed each other and she'd made her own way back. But she wasn't there either. . ." The tears were falling faster now. She flopped down on to the car seat and buried her head in her hands. "What's happening to Cawstocke? There's something badly wrong here. People don't just disappear!"

Jamie felt terribly guilty, on three fronts. He had let down the cat once again. Moreover, it was late and he knew his mother would be fretting over where he was. But worst of all, it was his fault that Jinny was missing, and it was up to him to do something about it. He didn't know what to say to Mrs Briggs, so he didn't say anything. He just turned and ran, as fast as he could, back the way he had come. He ran up the high street with his trainers slapping against the wet pavement, past the everything-for-a-pound store, the shoe repair shop, the key-cutters and the old Grand Cinema. He ran till his muscles ached and his lungs burned. He ran till he reached the top of May Street. And then he stopped. It was terribly dark down there. Dark and forbidding. He really didn't want to go back to the shop, and he really didn't want to see Miss Lambent, shining with the light of the Soulstone, but he had to, for Jinny's sake. He just knew she'd been there, looking for him. What if Miss Lambent had hauled her inside and still held her prisoner there? Or maybe she'd been forced to choose a mask and had been sent off on some awful adventure and was now lost for ever in a different time and place? She wouldn't know that Miss Lambent was really a scary old woman: she'd just do whatever she was told to do, because when teachers told you to do things you did them, and Jinny was always a very well-behaved pupil.

Gritting his teeth and pushing his fear of the dark behind him, Jamie strode down May Street until he reached the door of the maskmaker's shop. He tried the handle, but it wouldn't budge. So he rattled it hard, and when that didn't work, he battered on the door with his fists. No one came.

Then something brushed his leg. He almost yelped till he realized what it must be, and sure enough when he looked down, there was the black cat.

"Jasper, Jasper, I'm so sorry."

The cat made an unintelligible miaowing noise and with a sinking heart Jamie remembered that he could only understand what it said when he was near the magic masks.

"Look, my friend Jinny is missing now, too. Have you seen her? Is she inside? Does Miss Lambent have her?"

Jasper looked hard into the window of the maskmaker's shop, then back at Jamie again.

"What? What are you trying to tell me? Is she in there?"

Jasper made an odd howling noise and ran up to the door of the shop.

"She's there, isn't she?" Jamie wrenched at the door

again, but it didn't give an inch. He peered in through the dusty glass but he couldn't see a thing. Inside, nothing stirred. Where was Miss Lambent?

There was nothing else for it. He ran across the road, picked up a brick from the pile of rubble between the rusting old cars, ran back and smashed it through the square of glass above the door handle. Jamie had never done such a thing in his life, not on purpose. He'd once broken a window with a football, by mistake, but he'd never vandalized anything like the gangs of boys on the estate who roamed around smashing up bus shelters and phone boxes and generally seemed to take a delight in destroying things. Jamie didn't like breaking things, he preferred mending them. The breaking glass made an appallingly loud noise. Even though the shop was tucked away down May Street, he half expected to hear police sirens at any moment. Still, no one came and nothing stirred within the shop. Nervously, Jamie knocked the remaining shards out of the hole he had made and thrust his hand through to try to find the lock. Then, and only then, he remembered that the door had neither lock nor handle on the inside. He was just cursing himself for his stupidity when the door swung slowly open, as if by magic.

22 CREATURES OF THE NIGHT

Inside the maskmaker's shop there was no sign of Miss Lambent.

Jamie shouted Jinny's name, but his cries met no response. He ran past the masks to the mirrored chamber at the back, but there was no one there. He ran his hand along the corridor and found nothing but dust and spiders – there seemed to be no other rooms in the place. At last, he came back out into the shop and stood there with all the masks staring silently down at him. Where could she be?

"She's not here. Your friend."

The black cat gazed at him, unblinking.

"Your friend was here. I can smell her. A girl: young. But she had been gone some time before we arrived back from Greenland."

"How do you know?"

"I smelled her touch on the outside of the door, but not on the inside."

"I don't understand."

"She did not leave by the door—"

"You mean, she went through the mirror?"

"It appears that way."

Which meant she must have worn one of the masks. But which one? Jamie stared at the ranks of gathered heads on the shelves in front of him. There were hundreds of them: how would he ever know which one she had used?

The mask of Elvis Presley was still in conversation with Mickey Mouse, and next to them Harry Potter, Osama Bin Laden, Tom and Jerry, and Cristiano Ronaldo; Dracula and Madonna, Superman and Batman, Spider-Man and Wolverine; Bart Simpson, Muhammed Ali and David Beckham (or it might have been Brad Pitt). There were the Indian, African, Maori and Aztec masks, the pharaoh and the chieftain. There was his Viking mask, where Miss Lambent had replaced it in the display. There was a gap next to the head of the elephant god where he had taken the Tuareg mask, then William Shakespeare and Darth Vader. Next there were firemen and cowboys, gorillas and dinosaurs; the wizard's mask with the tall pointed hat, the Ancient Greek warrior, then another gap next to some stupid colourful carnival mask, a horrible-looking ghoul and the Green Man.

It was all just as he remembered. Though even if he could work out which mask Jinny had taken, what could he do about it? Jinny's mask would have carried her to some far-flung corner of the world, at any time in thousands of years, and without the exact same mask, he would not be able to follow her and bring her back. Poor Jinny. She was on her own.

"I've lost her," he said miserably. "She's gone and I have no idea where, and it's all my fault. If she hadn't followed me this wouldn't have happened. But why? Why would Miss Lambent do such a thing?" It made no sense. Unless there were more stones to be retrieved, and she didn't trust Jamie to fetch them all.

"'Miss Lambent' is not what you think she is," the cat said cryptically.

"What do you mean?"

"She is very old."

Jamie knew that much: he'd seen all the creases and wrinkles that lay beneath the smooth latex mask that turned a gnarled old crone into beautiful Miss Lambent.

"How old, exactly? Seventy? Eighty?"

"To my certain knowledge at least four hundred, and before me she had other servants, so who knows?"

"Four hundred?" Jamie couldn't believe his ears. "How can anyone be four hundred years old? No one lives that long."

"No one normal. Miss Lambent is not normal."

"What is she, then?"

"She is a sorceress."

Jamie felt his skin prickle all over. *Magic. We are in the presence of magic . . . the most rare and precious thing in the world*. That was what she had said to him, and now he could sense it all around. He felt like a fly caught in a spider's web, struggling but unable to get free. "And you were her. . ." He searched his brain for the word.

"Her familiar, yes."

"But cats can't live for four hundred years!"

"You forget. Cats have nine lives. We come and we go, always the same, carrying our knowledge with us from life to life. I have been with my wife for three lifetimes. But our two kittens are the first who have survived. The human world can be a very hostile place. Especially with people like the White Lady in it."

All this was too much for Jamie Wave. He had once been a boy who hoarded jokes and riddles, because having a sense of humour seemed the best way to keep the bad things in the world at bay. They could make bullies laugh, and stop him thinking about things that might lurk in the dark. They could cheer up his mum and his sister when they were feeling blue, and when other people laughed, it made *him* feel better too. In fact, his mother had said it was

Jamie's way of bringing light into the world, "redressing the balance". That had been when she was less odd than she was now, before things had got bad, then weird. But in the face of the supernatural, it seemed that jokes were of no use at all.

"What are we going to do, Jasper?"

"Tomorrow we will come back and make Miss Lambent tell you where she has sent Jinny, and where she has hidden my wife and kits."

"Why can't we find her now?"

"You will not be able to find the White Lady at night: she is afraid of the dark."

Jamie knew what that felt like: but he didn't expect adults to feel the same way, and especially not a witch.

"Why?"

"She has good reason to be afraid. She has an enemy who rules the night."

"But she's a sorceress. Doesn't she have magic powers?"

"Her powers do not work so well after dark, while his grow night by night."

"Who is 'he'? And where does he live?"

The cat's coat bristled. "I should not even have mentioned him, not to you, and especially not during the darkness hours. It is simply too dangerous." It ran to the door of the shop. "You must go. It is not safe for you to be out. We must get you home. If he knows you are out in the darkness he will want to gather you to him."

This sounded ominous, but Jamie put it from his mind. "And what about you? Where will you go?" He remembered how cruelly Miss Lambent had shaken the black cat, how she had threatened it.

Jasper looked taken aback by the question. "I don't know."

"Come back with me," Jamie said impetuously. His mother wasn't keen on cats, he knew, but he was sure she'd be so happy to see him she wouldn't complain. And Cadence? Cadence loved animals of all sorts. It might even cheer her up.

The door opened as soon as he touched it, and as soon as he and the cat were outside, it closed again and would not budge. As he was staring at it, the space where he had broken the glass above the handle began to smoke and blur. He blinked, sure that his eyes must be deceiving him. As the smoke cleared, he realized that the pane was whole again, the new glass glinting in the moonlight, as if the shop had somehow healed itself; sealed itself off from the rest of the world, as if it was a magical space, not part of Cawstocke at all.

Jasper miaowed.

Even though he couldn't understand exactly what it was

saying, Jamie knew very clearly what it meant. *Let's get out of here.*

It was a long way between the centre of Cawstocke and the council estate where Jamie lived, but there was nothing for it but to walk. All he had was 50p, and the bus fare was a pound. Anyway there didn't seem to be any night buses on the roads. In fact, nothing stirred in the town – nothing human, at least. Twice they encountered other cats, which hissed and spat as they passed. Jasper took no notice of them, just stuck his nose in the air and trotted past at Jamie's heels with his tail held as high as a flag. Jamie felt their eyes on his back all the way down the road.

As they passed the recreation ground, though, a pack of dogs melted out of the shadows beneath the trees and came towards them, snarling. Moonlight lit their eyes and gleamed on their fangs.

Creatures of the night, at home in the domain of darkness.

Jamie tried to remember what his father had said: *if you show an angry dog you are afraid he will bite you.* But he *was* afraid. So was Jasper, for he had disappeared, leaving Jamie on his own.

The dogs advanced slowly, one pace at a time. There were a good dozen of them, and a couple were big – an Alsatian and a Rottweiler – though the rest were terriers and collies and cross-bred mutts. Even one of them could do him significant damage; a pack of them would tear him to bloody little bits. It would be a truly horrible way to die. Jamie looked around quickly. There was nothing he could see to throw at them, nothing with which to defend himself. He felt far more frightened than when he had been surrounded by Mouth and his gang. They were unlikely ever to kill him, and at least with Mouth he could try jokes to get himself out of the situation. There wasn't much chance of that with a pack of feral dogs.

Across the road was a row of parked cars. If he could climb on to the roof of one he might be able to get out of the way of their snapping jaws. He took a step to the right, then another.

Some silent communication took place between the dogs. He watched as they changed formation, one flank swinging around to cut him off from the cars, as if they knew what he was thinking. If they kept moving around like this they would soon have him encircled. Then he would be at their mercy. *Mustn't run,* he told himself fiercely. *If you run they will chase you down and attack you.* He could hear his blood beating in his ears now, as if it was surging around his body in a panic to get out. Then he felt a tang of it in his mouth, as if he had somehow bitten his tongue.

The sharp iron-taste of it brought something else back to him, some lost or hidden part of himself.

Jamie felt something building inside his ribs, thrumming through his bones. He felt it in his throat and vibrating against his teeth; a great pressure which he could not ignore or hold back. He opened his mouth and a roar split the night. Low and rumbling, it reverberated off the trees and houses, doubling and redoubling, as if a pack of tigers had suddenly entered the scene.

The dogs stopped in their tracks. They looked around fearfully. One of the smallest, a terrier, began to yelp. Its tail drooped. A collie started to bark furiously, a mad yapping sound. The Rottweiler's haunches quivered, and then it broke into a run, bolting away for the cover of the trees. One by one, the other dogs followed it until only the Alsatian was left, gazing at Jamie uncertainly, its ears flat against its skull.

Jamie tried to summon the tiger's roar again, but when he opened his mouth this time, nothing came out.

The Alsatian cocked its head, curious. Its ears pricked up again as its confidence returned. It was top dog here, not this strange little boy creature. It would soon show him who was master.

Its soft black lips drew back to reveal glistening fangs. A growl rumbled in its throat.

Jamie was about to sprint for the cars when something pale and ghostly glided overhead. It was a barn owl, its face as blank and unknowable as a mask. It skimmed the trees, then circled back, flying low over the dog and the boy.

It opened its beak and gave out a series of low hoots, before gliding noiselessly away again into the night.

At once, the Alsatian stopped its growling. It gave Jamie a long, steady look, then turned and walked back towards the recreation ground, where its pack-mates awaited it.

Jamie's heart resumed its normal pace, or something close to it. Then something appeared on the roof of one of the cars and yowled at him. It was Jasper. He looked very pleased with himself, his eyes a brilliant amber in the moonlight, his tail held high and curled over. He jumped down off the car and trotted over to Jamie, and then carried on up the road towards the estate where Jamie lived, as if nothing had happened.

Had it brought the owl? It was an odd thought; but no odder than the cat bringing the polar bears. It seemed as if the owl had said something to make the dog give way and go back to the park. And cats, dogs and owls were all creatures of the night. What if there was some sort of pact between them all? Something no human could ever really understand?

Jamie certainly did not understand what had just

happened here, but he was becoming more and more sure that the world was not the place he had thought it was even a few weeks ago. It was stranger by far, and full of things he did not understand. It was a world in which people disappeared for no good reason, a world in which an art teacher might be a four-hundred-year-old sorceress, a world in which magic operated, just out of sight. He shivered. Did anyone else know the things he knew? If they did, they did not speak of them.

He jogged after the black cat, and ten minutes later, he was home.

23 CADENCE

Despite the lateness of the hour, all the lights were blazing in the flat. Jamie, who had been ready to tiptoe in with the black cat in his arms so as not to disturb anyone, instead found his mother sitting on the sofa staring straight ahead, her eyes huge in her wan face. When he walked in, she flew at him and hugged him so hard she almost squeezed the life out of Jasper, who gave out a strangled yowl and promptly fled beneath a chair.

Mrs Wave looked astonished.

"Sorry, Mum. I know you don't like cats, but it sort of . . . saved my life, so I felt it ought to have somewhere . . . warm to spend the night. I didn't mean to be back so late – it was kind of . . . unavoidable." He started to fish around in his head for an excuse she might believe, but nothing presented itself. Lying to his mother was a skill he'd never mastered. He waited for her fury to blast into him, but she didn't speak.

"What is it, Mum? What's the matter?" But some small intuition was already whispering to him what she was going to say.

"It's Cadence. She's gone."

She handed him a crumpled sheet of paper.

In Cadence's clear, sloping writing it said:

Sorry, Mum, I have to go. I had the most amazing dream last night which told me where Dad was, so I'm going to find him. Say goodbye to the little squirt from me. (Sorry, Jamie. Love ya really.)

Cadence

xx

"She was gone when I woke up. And so were you."

Now Jamie felt dreadfully guilty. Where on earth could Cadence have gone? How could she know where anyone was just by dreaming? The day had already been strange, but now both his sister and his best friend were missing and it felt as if the whole world was unravelling around them.

From beneath the chair Jasper yowled suddenly. Jamie wished he had one of the masks with him – it sounded as if the cat was trying hard to communicate. Well, that would have to wait until tomorrow, back at the maskmaker's shop. Tomorrow, he was determined to get some answers.

He gave his mother a hug and felt her shoulders shake as she sobbed.

"Don't worry, Mum. We'll get her back. I promise. Go to bed."

Without another word, his mother got up and trudged to her bedroom like a sleepwalker. Her hand drifted to the door handle, and she turned it and disappeared inside. The light came on in a bright strip beneath the door. Half a minute later it went off again.

Jamie felt as if he had become the parent and his mother the child. Everything was upside-down. Everything was wrong. But sitting here worrying about it wasn't going to solve anything. Tomorrow he would confront Miss Lambent. She knew where Jinny was, and he bet she knew where Cadence was, too. She kept giving him hints about what was wrong in Cawstocke. Now it was time to ask her straight out and find out what he could do to put it right, since she kept telling him he had an important part to play. He was scared to know the answer, but he had to know, because he was beginning to believe he was the only person in Cawstocke to whom that answer might be given.

When he was sure his mother was asleep, Jamie realized he was starving. He went into the kitchen and made himself some toast, but couldn't find anything to put on it except Marmite, which he didn't much like. He scraped a bit of the bitter black spread across the toast and swallowed it down in large bites, trying not to taste it too much as it went down. Jasper stood up on his hind legs, rested his front paws on the kitchen table and nosed at Jamie's plate questioningly.

"Do you like Marmite?" Jamie asked him.

"*Miaoww-arow*."

Jamie took that for a yes. He broke a bit of toast off and pushed it towards the cat. A large pink tongue shot out, and in an instant the black topping on the toast was gone, and Jasper was rolling his orange eyes in ecstasy. The next moment, he wolfed down the damp toast and stared at Jamie expectantly.

"For a cat, you're a real pig," Jamie told him, pushing the rest across the table. Something about the way in which Jasper set about the toast cheered him up. It was as if the cat was saying, *Things may be bad now, but you still have to eat. Tomorrow things will be better*.

Having Jasper curled up on his bed intensified this comfort, and although dreams hovered around him all night, trying to get in, none of them were able to, for the cat, fortified with Marmite and determined to look after his friend, batted them all away. Jamie would need his sleep if he was to take on the challenges that awaited him.

The next morning, as soon as it was light, Jamie got dressed in his Cawstocke FC football shirt and his jeans and trainers, and he and the black cat left the flat. They walked and walked, and by the time they reached the town centre some desultory church bells were ringing and a few cars growled by on the road. High up a plane flew, leaving a white condensation trail against the pale blue of the sky, silent and serene as if there was nothing remotely wrong in the world it passed over.

"Come on," Jamie said reluctantly to Jasper, but even so he dragged his feet, knowing as he entered May Street that he was about to leave the world he understood – the ordinary world in which planes flew and cars roared along the bypass and church bells rang – far behind.

The door to the maskmaker's shop opened like a whisper. Inside, Miss Lambent stood with her arms folded, waiting, as if she had expected them at this very minute. Her green eyes sparked eagerly.

"Excellent!" she said. She sprang forward with an extraordinary whoosh of energy and shut the door behind them, effectively locking them inside.

She looked different, Jamie thought, as if she gleamed

from the inside out. As if the Soulstone was shining at the very heart of her. The very idea of that terrified him. What if she touched him?

"Quickly, then, choose your mask!"

Jamie stood his ground. "Before I do anything, I want you to tell me what's going on."

Miss Lambent looked faintly sad, as if he had somehow disappointed her. "I knew it would come to this sooner or later." Gazing at some infinite point behind Jamie's head, she said, "People don't trust the way they used to. They don't have the same faith they had in days gone by. They're not as afraid. Nowadays it's all questions and doubts, when they should be cowering in terror, falling over themselves to carry out my wishes." She brought her gaze to bear on Jamie now, and it was hard and piercing. "It doesn't do to cross me. As your little friend found out."

"What have you done with her?" Jamie demanded, furious that she wasn't even bothering to deny it. "Have you hurt her? If you have I'll—"

"Me?" She spread a hand against her chest. "Hurt little Jinny? Of course not, she's one of my pupils. I would never hurt a pupil. The teacher–pupil relationship is a sacred trust." But her eyes gleamed untrustworthily.

"Where is she, then?"

"Let's just say she's taken a little . . . trip."

"You've made her put on a mask! You've pushed her through the mirror!"

Miss Lambent smiled at him with slitted eyes.

Jamie pressed on hotly. "I'm not going to fetch whatever it is you want me to fetch unless you bring Jinny back safely: now!"

"Oh dear. I'm afraid I can't do that. She's gone rather a long way away."

The cat began to wreathe itself around his ankles in an attention-seeking sort of way. As if it was trying to communicate with him but didn't want to say anything in front of Miss Lambent.

"Oh, no you don't. I see what's going on here!" she hissed and launched herself at the cat, which fled from her, leaping up on to the counter and crouching there, ears pressed flat against its head. Jamie was sure that if he looked closely enough he'd see its heart beating against its furry little chest, and something about its vulnerability made him feel like the tiger he had once been. He turned on Miss Lambent furiously.

"What have you done with Jasper's family?" he cried.

Miss Lambent didn't reply. She just fixed the black cat with a look that made it quail. "You'd better not say another word, you little rat, or they'll be made sorry for it!" And she hissed what sounded like three magical words at the black cat, which reared back, its haunches quivering.

She turned back to Jamie. "Whatever he's told you, it isn't true. He's a liar and a sneak, always making things up, always has been."

"Always being . . . four hundred years?"

Miss Lambent narrowed her eyes at him. "I see he *has* been telling stories. What else has he told you?"

"That you're a sorceress!" Jamie blustered on, hoping by such a direct approach to shock her into telling him where Jinny was.

Miss Lambent just threw her head back and laughed. She laughed so long and so loudly that she ended up wiping her eyes. "Oh goodness me, is that all? I thought you knew that right from the start." Then she stopped smiling and took Jamie by the shoulder, and it was as if her fingers were made of stone. She bent in close. "Now listen to me, Jamie Wave, and listen well. You have a third task to perform, the final and greatest task of all, and only when you have performed that task can you save Jinny. Do you understand me?"

Jamie nodded, tight-lipped. "And what about my sister, Cadence? What have you done with her?"

Miss Lambent looked surprised. "I know nothing about

the whereabouts of your sister."

"I don't believe you! When I got home last night she'd gone. She left a note saying she'd had some sort of dream and gone to find my father."

"The affairs of your sister and father are nothing to me. And I don't deal in dreams. That little trick belongs to someone else."

Things were not going at all to plan: Jamie wasn't getting anywhere. He tried one more time. "You once told me that Cawstocke was depending on me and that I could help to make things better here, that together we could do great things. If I'm going to do this third task for you, I think the least you should do is to tell me why I'm doing it. I've fetched two magical stones for you – the chieftain's jewel and the shaman's Soulstone, and I've watched you drain the magic out of them – but for what? I want to know! I want to understand what all this is about! And I want to know where Jinny and Cadence and my dad are, too! You've got to tell me! Tell me, and then I'll go." It was the longest speech he had ever made in his life, and without a single stutter. By the end of it his voice had risen to a cry and his throat felt raw and hoarse, as if he'd been gargling with sand.

Miss Lambent's face darkened. "I haven't got time for this. And neither has your little friend. Take your last mask,

Jamie Wave, or you will never see Jinny again." And she took down a mask from the shelves and jammed it on his head.

"Don't forget your guide," she said silkily, and something small and black slipped swiftly past her and scampered into the shadows at the back of the shop.

Jamie stalked after it. "Come on, then, Jasper," he said through clenched teeth. "Let's get this over with."

Together they stepped into the mirror.

24 LORD OF THE HEAVENLY LAKE

Over and over Jamie tumbled, his arms and legs flung wide like a starfish. As he fell he clung on to the mask, which seemed determined to part company with him. To lose it before he even arrived where he was headed was the last thing he could afford to happen. Even as he thought this he realized with shock that he didn't even know which mask he was wearing. This time the choice had been made for him. Everything was out of his control.

I could be anyone, he thought suddenly. *Anyone, or anything. I could be going* anywhere. *Anywhere in the world, anywhere in history.*

It was a peculiarly uncomfortable idea, and as he spun over and over it was as if he had been cut adrift from everything he knew, no more than a formless atom tumbling through space and time, probably to be lost for ever. He wasn't sure how he felt about this, but while he was in the middle of deciding, the ground came up and hit him with a resounding thump which shook him to the bone. It brought the mask down over his eyes so that he couldn't see a thing. Wincing, he adjusted it, and suddenly light flooded in, as bright as a wish.

Of all places, this was nothing like he'd expected. After deserts and icy wastes he'd expected something far more extreme: something challenging; something scary. But this place was, quite simply, beautiful.

He found himself gazing out over a huge, placid lake, silvery-blue beneath a pale sky. Steep wooded hills and snow-topped mountain crests were reflected upside-down in its mirror-like surface and little white clouds drifted serenely through the centre.

"Are you just going to stand there?" came a voice from behind him. There was Jasper, high up in the branches of a willow tree. He had no idea how he knew it was a willow tree, or what distinguished a willow tree from any other sort of tree, but he just knew. "Or are you going to help me down?" the cat mewed.

Jamie put one foot up on the trunk, and realized he was still wearing his Nikes. And his jeans. And, it seemed, his Cawstocke FC shirt. That was odd. Every other time he'd made a magical journey his clothes had changed to suit his new environment. Perhaps it was because Miss Lambent had chosen the mask for him this time. Whatever the reason, it was strange. He got his left foot up on a branch, then moved up carefully until Jasper was almost within reach. Then the mask got in the way, and when he turned it got jammed between the branches and started to come off. Jamie's foot slipped, and now the mask was almost entirely off. A moment later something heavy landed on his head with a yowl, and together boy and cat fell out of the tree.

Jamie sat up carefully. Everything was black. Had he gone blind? But no, the mask had twisted around so that now the eyeholes and the mouth were at the back of his head. He twisted it until he could see out again, and found the cat sitting in front of him, smiling as if butter wouldn't melt in his mouth. "What did you do that for?"

"You should thank me."

"For what? Trying to kill me?"

"If that mask comes off, we'll never get back to Cawstocke."

There were times when Jamie didn't think that was such a bad thing. *Just imagine,* he thought, *a fresh start, no magic, no nightmares, no masks; no Miss Lambent, and no school. . .*

The cat regarded him with its head cocked to one side.

"You look ridiculous," it said.

"Thanks a lot. What am I, anyway?"

Jasper gave a sly little smile. "Ah, the age-old question. Can any of us truly answer it? Who am I, and why am I here?"

Jamie rolled his eyes. "I'm Jamie Wave, and I'm here to try to find Jinny Briggs."

"Bravo, Jamie," Jasper said softly. "You just remember that when things get strange or scary, right?"

"I can't imagine how they can get any more strange or scary than they already have."

"The world is full of surprises."

"I'm sorry I didn't get anywhere with finding out where your family is."

"Perhaps it'll be third time lucky," the cat said softly. But it didn't look very optimistic.

Jamie said briskly, "Are you going to tell me what this mask is, or not?"

"Why don't you go to the water's edge and see for yourself?"

Jamie was once more struck by the serenity of the scene. It was as quiet and blue and tranquil as the painted pattern on his mother's old china tea set. All it lacked was a pagoda with a curled-up roof and a little boat in the middle of the lake.

"Willow pattern," he said out loud. That's what his mother had called it. *China that comes from China,* she used to chuckle: the closest his mother ever got to a joke.

"That's right, we're in China," said the black cat.

Jamie gave it a hard stare. "Don't do that."

"Do what?" Jasper asked innocently, his eyes as round as saucers.

"You know what you were doing," Jamie returned severely. "And there's no need to make fun of me." For now the cat's eyes looked as large and round as dinner plates. He watched as Jasper's fur went all spiky and stood on end, as if someone had decided to style him as a punk cat and had added hair gel to the crest on his head and all the way down his back to the very tip of his tail. "Oh, stop it!"

From behind him there came a great whoosh of water.

Very slowly, Jamie turned around. And rather wished he hadn't.

For emerging from what had been the perfectly still surface of the silver lake was a monster – though what sort of monster it was he had no idea. He had never seen anything like it – in real life, or in books.

It was enormous, towering over him by a good six metres. It had what looked like the head of a camel, the ears of a cow, a pair of horns like the antlers of a deer, the fiery eyes of a demon, the thick, sinuous neck of a snake, and a pair of leathery wings like those of the world's biggest bat. It was a bright greeny-gold colour and when it reared up, the sun struck its skin so that it shimmered and shone. Floating a little way beneath its chin was a small, glowing ball which just seemed to hover in mid-air, changing colour second by second: now gold, now red, now a soft and pearly white.

"Who dares to disturb the Lord of the Heavenly Lake?" The monster did not roar this. It sounded more like music, the way it spoke, as if there were a dozen musicians just out of view who gave voice to its words with a variety of exotic instruments. Its gaze flickered over the black cat and came to rest on Jamie Wave.

Jamie gazed back, transfixed. He found that when he looked into the creature's eyes, it was impossible to look away. It had weird eyes: a shiny purple and black, and when it blinked, it blinked from side to side rather than up and down like normal people, and its pupils were not round but a long vertical black slit. He opened his mouth to answer and nothing came out.

"Well known it is that good things come in threes," the monster went on. "Three graceful cranes, three bales of lucky red silk, three wise counsellors bearing gifts. And so today it seems to be. Though methinks somewhat small and black and puny the third lion is."

Each of these words was familiar to Jamie, but something about the order of them caused the meaning to evade him. He blinked desperately, trying to focus, and found that when he wasn't looking into the creature's eyes he could think more clearly.

"I'm sorry . . . sir," he said, bowing low to avoid its gaze. "I don't know what you mean."

"Three lions have I seen today," the creature repeated.

Three lions? Jamie took a step forward and stared at his reflection in the now-calm water of the lake. Staring right back at him was the oddest sight. The mask he wore was a large, colourful head. It was yellow and green and red and black, and had big fringes over the enormous bulging eyes and all around the huge, smiling mouth, and a mirror right in the middle of its forehead. It didn't look anything like any lion he had ever seen – not the lions he had seen on wildlife documentaries, nor even like a cartoon lion. Instead it looked like some sort of giant carnival dog's head. How strange.

He risked a glance back at the towering Lord of the Heavenly Lake. "Am I a lion, sir? And if I am a lion, what sort of lion am I? And who are the other two?"

"Why, a philosopher it is. Capital, capital! What discussions we shall have in my watery kingdom. Long has this dragon waited for the one to entertain me thus," the creature crowed delightedly. It threw its head back and spread its little wings so that pale sunlight shone through the membranes like molten gold. The ball that floated beneath its chin spun and threw out silver light.

That's the third magical object, Jasper said into Jamie's mind. *That's what you have to take back to the witch. The Pearl of Wisdom and Everlasting Life. That's what she wants.*

Jamie found that it was much easier to stare at the Pearl than at the dragon, if dragon it was, though it wasn't much like any of the dragons he had seen in any of his books.

"Um, I'm not a philosopher, actually," he said. "I'm just a boy. Looking for a friend."

"Ah, a friend is it? A fine thing is a friend to seek. Better than gold, or silver, or" – and it lowered its huge camel-like head to his level – "or a *pearl*." The gleam of its gaze became sharp as knives, pinning Jamie to the ground, and the Pearl suddenly became very large, swelling beneath its chin like a great balloon. "Because many have come to the Heavenly Lake treasure seeking. A pearl, especially. My pearl in particular. It wouldn't be my pearl that you looking came for, would it?"

Inside the lion's head Jamie felt himself get very hot. He was hopeless at lying. If only Jasper hadn't said anything he'd still be none the wiser. He dragged his eyes away from the dragon and concentrated hard.

"My f-friend's name is J-Jinny Briggs," he said as firmly as he could manage. "And I wondered whether you'd seen her."

The dragon looked coy. "And what does a J-Jinny Briggs look like? Would it a long moustache have and a dish of mulberries carry? Or a knot of sleek black hair and a robe of celestial blue? Perhaps it with a sick child comes begging for my favour, burning incense and bringing me a bowl of cream as an offering?"

Jamie shook his head and the weight of the mask shifted awkwardly from side to side. "I don't think so. She's j-just a g-girl, about the same height as m-me. With r-red hair."

"Red hair, has she? Luck, the colour of. And luck you will need. Did you know I a brother have, whose colour is red? Fiery and strong he was, full of life." The dragon looked sorrowful.

"What to him happened?" Jamie asked, lapsing into the dragon's odd syntax. "I mean," he corrected himself, "what happened to him?"

"He swallowed the sun and to a cinder burned. Not very lucky at all. But then perhaps he was not a perfect red. There so many different shades are, and some luckier are than others. Perhaps if you told me the exact nature of the red of your friend's hair my memory it would jog. Was it, for example, the colour of sunset over the Yellow Sea, or the deep red of a ripe cherry, or perhaps the orange-red of the heart of a fire it is?"

This wasn't something Jamie had given much time to thinking about. He sighed. "Look, I'm afraid I really haven't got time for this. She's probably in danger and I need to find her as quickly as possible."

"Time, is it the little lion speaks of? Time? Ah, what is time? You poor little mortals so concerned are with it. How long are your lives?" It held its claw-hands and ticked off its talons one by one. "A mayfly – a single day. A grasshopper – fifty-one days. A dog – eight or ten years. A lion, maybe fifteen. A man? Sixty, seventy; maybe eighty. I once a man of a hundred-and-three met, but he withered was like old stick. To one such as I, such lifetimes are but the blink of an eye."

As if to emphasize the point, it fixed Jamie with its mesmerizing gaze.

"Do you have any idea how old I am?"

Jamie shook his head.

"Three thousand, two hundred and twenty-eight years, three moons and five days. Three millennia it has taken for me to evolve into the magnificent being before you

you see. An egg I was, a little egg like a jewel, and then for centuries barely more than a water snake. After half a millennium to a huge size I grew. Bigger than the biggest carp, scales and all. For another millennium in that form I inhabited this lake until my true head I grew and four little legs. Yet another five hundred years passed before had sprouted these fine horns on my head and I became *khoi lung*. Then the scales I had grew together to form the fine smooth skin I boast now, smoother than the smoothest lily flower.

"In that time I saw armies sweep across the plains and in a sea of blood die. I have seen their flesh by crows picked, and their very bones moulder to dust. Empires I have seen rise and fall and emperors come and go like summer butterflies. In that time have clouds rolled over me in waves, volcanoes have exploded and mountains have weathered to little hills, but the Heavenly Lake and its lord, the Heavenly Dragon, have endured.

"And now, a full millennium later, my wings I have, and I am *ying lung*. Three thousand years in which I powerful, wise and beautiful have grown, three thousand years in which I have grown my pearl.

"Poor little mortals, how my pearl they would love to take, more life to have. Already has one come today, and now another. Forewarned I am, and forewarned is forearmed."

And lunging suddenly it grabbed Jamie up in its clawed hands and squeezed tight.

Before Jamie could even gasp, the dragon had arched its great back and dived beneath the mirrored surface of the lake. Water streamed past him in a great flood. He couldn't see a thing but he could feel the speed at which he was travelling, down, down, down, the pressure of the water pressing the lion-mask tight against his face. Black stars swam before his eyes. Was he going to drown? He took a great gulp, realized that was a bad idea and shut his mouth again, expecting it to be full of water. But it wasn't. Inside the mask, Jamie frowned. Tentatively, he opened his mouth again and tasted . . . air. Or perhaps it was water. Whatever it was, he could breathe it. Had he turned into a fish? Or was he dreaming? Perhaps – and a cold hand of dread gripped his heart – he was . . . already dead.

But then the pressure around his waist lessened and he could feel his feet on the ground and he wasn't moving any more, at least not at the speed of sound.

It took a while to get his balance, for he seemed to be swaying (*like a weed underwater,* the joke part of his brain suggested), but when at last he stopped he peered out of the eyeholes of the mask. Whatever he had been expecting to see, it wasn't this. A great palace rose up before him, gleaming silver. Dozens of carved silver columns held up a shining silver roof with scrolled edges, and inside, a shining silver floor stretched as far as the eye could see, interrupted only by more carved pillars.

A pair of sturdy columns marked the entrance to the palace, on one of which stood a bronze lion with an oversized head and what looked as if it was supposed to be a cub beneath its right foot. It looked rather skinny for a lion cub, he thought. Very odd, the way the Chinese portrayed lions.

It was only when he had passed into the great pillared hall that he thought to wonder where the dragon was. Turning quickly, in case it was behind him, he stared around, but there was no sign of it at all. All he could see instead were a hundred or more odd-looking Chinese lions staring back at him. Terrified, he ran behind a pillar in case they all decided to spring out and eat him, but when he stuck his head out to see if they were coming, he found that they were all sticking their heads out from behind pillars, too. And that they all had huge garish lion-heads in red and green and black and yellow, with fringes over the eyes and around the mouth, and (even more weirdly) that they were all wearing sweatshirts bearing the Cawstocke FC logo, jeans and trainers. Stepping out from behind his pillar, he watched all the other lions stepping out as well and raised his hand to greet them and they all waved back. "Hello,

Jamie," he said quietly, feeling like an idiot, and the other lions all silently mouthed the words back at him – some from the walls, some from the floor, the rest from the ceiling. He was in a hall of mirrors.

Raising his voice, he called out again. "Hello?" The sound echoed off the pillars and bounced back at him, like a hundred lions. No one responded. He tried again. "Jinny?" The word doubled and redoubled emptily. And where was Jasper? He called out the black cat's name but nothing came back amidst the echoes.

It looked as if he would have to move deeper into the palace if he was going to find them. At the end of the hall of mirrors he found a pair of gigantic doors, their edges marked by a long, elegant sequence of twining dragons. Summoning his courage, he pushed them open.

Beyond lay darkness, relieved only by the flickering of a thousand tiny lights. He moved forward through the close air and the lights juddered and danced. They were candles. Tiny candles all over the floor.

"Hello?" he called again. He had expected the appalling hundredfold echo, but this time the darkness swallowed his voice whole, like a whale swallowing a minnow. Each candle illuminated only a tiny circle of light, but he could feel a vast space stretching overhead. It felt as if he was beneath the soaring, vaulted ceiling of the tallest, darkest cathedral. He took a step forward and as he did so the great door through which he had entered clanged shut behind him. It was as if by stepping forward he had triggered some kind of magical mechanism.

Jamie gulped. He felt for the door with his hands, but somehow even the edges of it, as well as the door handle, seemed to have disappeared. He was trapped. It was just like the door in the maskmaker's shop.

He was beginning to wonder if this was all some sort of elaborate trick by Miss Lambent, some obscure series of tests to see if he was the right sort of hero for her plans, when he heard breathing in the darkness. Vast, stertorous breathing like somebody pumping air into the room using the world's biggest pair of bellows.

25 THE CHAMBER OF TRUTH

Jamie's heart began to knock and he heard his own breath coming in short bursts, as if his lungs had shrunk to a third of their normal size. He was, he realized abruptly, very scared. Not much of a hero at all.

Now a strange greenish light began to glow in the darkness. Jamie watched it shimmer and pulse with his heart climbing into his throat. The light spun and brightened, gaining strength and focus, and suddenly he could see that it was the dragon's pearl. And as its light increased he began to make out, curled majestically above and behind it, in a vast silver throne, the Heavenly Dragon.

"Welcome to my mansion, little mortal," it intoned in a great rumbling voice that made Jamie think of earthquakes and thunderstorms and the beating of very large drums. "And in particular welcome to the Chamber of Truth, from which liars never leave. May I you invite above your head to look?" And it plucked at its pearl, which became small enough to fit the clawed hand, and sent it spinning upwards into the darkness.

Jamie followed the Pearl's trajectory. High up in the distant ceiling it stopped and grew and hovered for a second before slowly diminishing and descending again, and in the moment in which its light struck the ceiling it seemed to Jamie that he saw a thousand sharp, white, down-pointing teeth up there, glinting like knives.

"Those the teeth are of all the dragons who have served me in my long life. When they die their bodies melt away into the waters of my lake; only the teeth I keep. Everyone knows the magical quality of dragons' teeth. Sharper they are than the sharpest blade; harder than adamantine. A warrior who has the good fortune a dragon's tooth to find can never be defeated by another mortal's weapon." It paused, allowing this information to sink in. Then it said, "Do you know why liars never leave the Chamber of Truth?"

Jamie, unable to trust his voice, shook his head.

The dragon regarded him kindly. "Ignorance is the night of the mind, without the benefit of moon or stars. Allow me your moon and stars to be, enlightenment to bring." It gestured to the gruesome ceiling. "A lie will cause the dragons' teeth upon the liar to come crashing down, piercing him a thousand times. And if a dragon's tooth can shear through diamond, imagine how easily through flesh and bone it may cut!"

Jamie shuddered, dreading what was to come.

"Some questions I am going to ask you. Answer them well, and we shall see whether you are a lion or a liar. Do you understand me?"

Jamie nodded. *Perhaps*, a little voice in the back of his mind suggested, *this will just be another riddle contest*. If so, he might just survive. If he could manage without Jasper. Doubt gripped him, making his knees tremble.

"And when I my questions have asked, and if you still alive are," and here the Heavenly Dragon grinned horribly, "three questions you may ask of me. For I" – it spread out one taloned hand and polished its claws against its scaly chest until they sparkled – "the fount of all wisdom am. Which is why I bear the Pearl of Wisdom and Everlasting Life." The dragon leaned forward and fixed an intent gaze upon Jamie.

When he looked in its mesmerizing eyes, Jamie felt himself go all woozy.

"Who are you? Tell me your true name and lineage and clan-allegiances. Beware the dragons' teeth if falsely you answer."

So it wasn't going to be a riddle contest after all: more of an interrogation. His knees began to knock.

"My n-name is Jamie W-Wave. But I'm afraid I d-don't know what my lineage or clan-allegiances are."

The dragon rolled its eyes, which gave Jamie a brief respite. "Don't they teach you anything these days? Your lineage, lion-boy, is your ancestry, your parentage, your pedigree."

That made him sound like some sort of posh dog.

"I want to know about your family and your clan or tribe, and your region and whom you support, all that defines you so that in the hierarchy of all things I may place you."

Jamie didn't know what to make of this but he took a deep breath and started again. "My name is Jamie Wave. My mother is Jemima Wave and my father is Thomas Wave. My sister is Cadence Wave, and we all come from a town called Cawstocke in England. But I don't really belong to a clan or tribe or anything." A brainwave struck him. "I do support Cawstocke FC, I suppose, though they're a bit rubbish and have hardly won a match this season. They'll probably get relegated."

The dragon looked puzzled by this. "What is this Cawstocke FC?"

"It's our local football team," Jamie said helpfully. He indicated the club badge on his shirt.

But the dragon was none the wiser, and Jamie could see

that didn't please it at all. "What is this 'football'? I have never heard of it."

Jamie was a bit surprised by this. Then something occurred to him. "Ah, they call it 'soccer' in lots of parts of the world. America, for example."

"America?" The Heavenly Dragon scratched its scaly head with a gleaming claw. "What is this *America*?"

So much for being the fount of all wisdom, Jamie thought, and then quickly unthought it again, in case the dragon could read minds. "It's, er . . . a huge continent to the" – he had to think very carefully about his directions here, conjuring up a map of the world in his head – "to the east of China, if you pass Japan and cross the sea, or a long way west if you go all the way across Russia and Europe and then cross the ocean that way, and there's North America and South America, and both are huge, and they call North America the United States of America, because it's . . . ah . . . made up of lots of, well, states, and it's very big and rich and powerful." Which was about all he knew about America.

The dragon narrowed its eyes at him. "Bigger and richer and more powerful than China?"

Jamie felt as if he was getting into very hot water with this subject. Was America bigger than China? He wasn't sure. And as for being richer and more powerful, he really didn't know how such things were judged. And what was the right answer? Let alone the answer the Heavenly Dragon wanted to hear. He began to feel very hot and flustered inside the mask. Above him, he could sense the deadly dragons' teeth swaying in the dark air.

Whatever you do, he reminded himself, *you mustn't lie.* "I don't know," he said truthfully. "But I can explain about football," he went on quickly in case the dragon was angry with his ignorance. "It's a game played with eleven players. Well, twenty-two really, if you count both sides. And then there's a referee, and two linesmen and a fourth official, though at Cawstocke there are never enough staff. Sometimes half the team don't even turn up. And they, er, well . . . they kick a ball around a pitch and try to score goals." Even to his own ears this sounded a bit feeble, but the dragon leaned forward, looking interested.

"Goals?"

"There are these posts at either end of the pitch with nets stretched between them and a man with big gloves stands in the middle of the posts and tries to keep the ball out of the net." This was harder to explain than he'd thought.

"Just one man against twenty-one? The odds seem heavily weighted against him. He must quite a hero be, the Man With Big Gloves. I should like to meet him."

"Um, there are two of them actually, one for each team, so there's only ten players trying to score against each one. Though some are defensive players, so they don't generally attack. . ." He ground to a halt. This was hopeless.

"Even so," the Heavenly Dragon mused, "ten players outnumber one, by a factor of" – it thought about this for a moment, then declared with great pride – "ten to one! Even for the Man With Big Gloves that unfair seems."

"Ah," said Jamie, remembering something pretty crucial. "But that's where the offside rule comes in."

"The offside rule?"

Jamie's brain went completely blank. What were the rules regulating offside? Mr Jessop had tried to explain them to the class a couple of weeks ago, but Jamie found he had completely forgotten what he had said. At the time he really hadn't expected to have to store the information away for such an important purpose. Of all the things he could have imagined happening in his life, explaining the offside rule to a three-thousand-year-old Chinese dragon in an underwater palace with a thousand deadly blades poised over his head had not featured prominently.

"Er, it's rather complicated and I'm not too sure I really understand it myself. But football's a very popular sport. Millions of people all over the world watch when teams compete for the World Cup."

The Heavenly Dragon shook its head sadly. "Three thousand years have I passed in this world and still you mortals confound me. Millions of people, excited about a cup? Sometimes I think only I in the world sane am." It sighed. "Enough of this football. Tell me about your father."

That took him by surprise. "My f-father? Um . . . he's not with us any more. He left last year."

"And where is he now?"

"I d-don't know. Lost, somewhere."

"Lost. Somewhere," the dragon echoed sonorously. "I think that a contradiction is."

Jamie frowned. "I don't understand."

"If he lost is, he cannot somewhere be."

Though logical, this did not seem a very useful observation.

Jamie hung his head. "My father is, though," he persisted. "Lost, that is. And my sister, Cadence, too. She left home yesterday and no one knows where she went. And my friend Jinny is missing too, as I told you—"

"A father, a friend and a sister missing? That seems most careless." The dragon rested its little clawed hands on the pearl under its chin. Then it tilted its head as if listening to something Jamie could not catch. "Missing just means that something is not where you expect it to be," it said cryptically. "Nothing ever from the world is truly lost. A sly rabbit will have three exits from its burrow."

Jamie began to wonder whether three thousand years of being in the world might have sent the dragon a bit mad. But it was what the Heavenly Dragon said next that sent a cold current of fear jolting down into his stomach.

"Why have you come here, lion-boy? Answer carefully."

This was the question that Jamie had been dreading. It would take a lot of explaining, and he wasn't sure the teeth hanging above his head would understand long, complicated explanations. He closed his eyes. Above him, the teeth began to creak ominously. Jamie felt a drop of sweat run down his spine. What should he say?

Honesty is the best policy. It was what his mother always said. But if he told the truth, the dragon would surely kill him. And if he didn't tell the truth, then the teeth would. He took a deep breath and cleared his throat.

"It's a long story, so I hope you'll be patient with me."

The Heavenly Dragon nodded graciously. "Continue."

So he told the dragon about Cawstocke and what a strange place it had become of late. How the people had been plagued by nightmares that stopped them sleeping, making them tired and forgetful or bad-tempered all the time, and how some of them simply disappeared, including his own father. How those who were left seemed like shadows. How his own mother did nothing any more but stay in with the curtains drawn, fearful of the outside world, except as seen through her television screen.

Then he told the dragon about making masks at school and how his friend Jinny Briggs had helped him, and how when he put on his mask he had, just for a moment, *become* a tiger. After which, he told it about the maskmaker's shop, how during the week its owner was Miss Lambent, their art teacher at school, and how when you saw her then she looked, well, beautiful really. But she also wore a mask. He told the dragon how Miss Lambent had peeled off her face in front of him, revealing herself to be a very old lady indeed. Just how old he had not realized, not till the cat told him. Nor had he realized that she was a witch.

"Four hundred years?" enquired the dragon. "That's not so very old. I myself am—"

"Three thousand years," Jamie interrupted.

"Three thousand, two hundred and twenty-eight years, three moons and five days," the Heavenly Dragon corrected him patiently. "I am at least eighty times older than the mortal witch, and considerably more than eighty times more wise and powerful."

This was not a statement Jamie felt he should contest, so instead he went on with his story.

He told the dragon how Miss Lambent had invited him

to the maskmaker's shop and how there he had chosen the Tuareg mask and brought back the Tiger's Eye for her. How on his next visit he had picked out the Viking helmet and come back with the Soulstone. And he described the effect these two magical objects had had upon Miss Lambent, and the dragon looked very interested in that indeed.

"And you say she hid in the mask because afraid she is of someone?"

"She's afraid of the dark."

"What in the dark is there to be afraid of?"

"Well, there are packs of dogs around, creatures of the night, that sort of thing. But she said she was hiding from someone . . . terrible, someone who controls the night."

The dragon tapped its teeth with a thoughtful talon. "Interesting. Go on with how you came to be here, at Tianshan Lake."

So Jamie told it about Jinny going missing and how he had returned to the maskmaker's shop, sure that Miss Lambent had her prisoner.

"Except that she wasn't there. She'd made Jinny put on the other mask like this one and sent her here knowing I'd have to follow."

"But you said that the first two times the mask you chose. Of your own free will."

He thought he had, but perhaps it hadn't been such a

free choice after all. He remembered the odd way the Viking mask had fallen into his hands. Perhaps all this time Miss Lambent had been influencing him. After all, the cat had always seemed to know which object he was supposed to bring back. And the cat could read his mind. What if Miss Lambent and Jasper were working together and the cat was just pretending to be his friend? And the whole thing about Jasper's lost family was just a charade? He felt hot and then cold. But the cat had saved him from the dogs. It had come home with him and slept on his bed. It had told him all sorts of things. . .

But what if it was telling you the things she wanted you to know?

It was all too much to think about. . .

"So was it only for your friend that to Tianshan you came?" The dragon interrupted his thoughts.

Jamie quailed. Above him, he could sense the teeth, adamantine-hard, sharp enough to shear through diamonds. He gulped. But as he opened his mouth to answer he felt the world's worst stutter building up in his throat, blocking his tongue, tripping up the words. "And the p-p-p-p-p. . ."

"The Pearl?" the dragon supplied gently. "My pearl?" It sounded sad; but whether this was at the thought that someone would steal its pearl or that it was disappointed that that someone was Jamie Wave, Jamie couldn't tell.

"Y-yes." It came out as barely a whisper. He hung his head, feeling his cheeks flaming beneath the hateful mask. Now he was for it.

The dragon sat back in its throne. It caressed its pearl ruminatively, running its scaly claws first one way over it, then the other, so that its colours flowed and chased each other around its surface – violet and orange, crimson and umber and rose, all of them touched with a hint of nacre.

The weight of the teeth above him became an oppressive presence. He had told the truth, but he was sure that he would be punished for it even so. He had come to the conclusion that there was probably nothing supernatural about the teeth themselves, that they were unlikely to be imbued with the magical power to ascertain whether someone was telling the truth or not. He reckoned that the power resided somewhere between the dragon and the Pearl. And that there must be a mechanism the dragon could operate, an invisible cord which if released would bring the teeth crashing down, like the portcullis on a medieval castle's gate. He stared at the ground and waited and waited and waited, before realizing that since he'd told the truth, perhaps the teeth wouldn't fall after all.

He lifted his head a fraction. The dragon was still stroking the pearl so that it bobbled beneath its chin and its soft lights danced around the dark walls.

At last, he gathered the courage to speak. "I w-wondered . . . if you could p-possibly tell me where Jinny is. I could take her away, and we'd go back without the Pearl. I d-don't want to steal it from you. It's wrong to steal and I don't think Miss Lambent w-wants it for anything good, whatever she may say."

He'd have to deal with Miss Lambent's fury. But he'd cross that bridge when he came to it.

The dragon raised its head and regarded Jamie steadily. "I a decision have made."

What was it going to do?

"Come over here."

Was it going to bite his head off? Or wrap him in its coils like a gigantic boa constrictor? Perhaps the Pearl would do something to him. Perhaps it would wipe his brain clean and he wouldn't even know who he was any more, let alone why he had come. Perhaps it had already done that to Jinny. . .

Dragging his feet, he approached the throne, and was surprised when the dragon reached out and placed a clawed hand gently on his shoulder.

"Wise, the lion-boy is. Wise, and I believe honest. You this old dragon have intrigued with your strange story and for that I thank you. You now may ask three questions of me. Place on the Pearl your hands and ask your first question. And careful be. Only once I warn you."

Trembling, Jamie laid his hands on the object he had travelled all this way and time to steal, and at once the pearl swelled and its colours swirled and spun till he felt dizzy.

"Come along," said the dragon. "He who asks a question may feel a fool for five minutes, but he who never asks a fool for ever remains."

Jamie took a deep breath and thought hard. At last he said, "Where is Jinny Briggs?"

It was as if a mist inside the Pearl was burned away by the touch of a hot sun. Suddenly there was a clear picture of the Heavenly Dragon's palace with its gateposts in the foreground, surmounted by a single bronze lion. Jamie frowned, not sure why he was being shown this view. As he stared, the figure on the gatepost stirred. It began to lose its hard bronze colour and its squat, pugnacious demeanour, and became smaller and paler until at last there was only a girl in a garish carnival lion mask standing on the pillar. A girl with her foot pressing down on a small dark lion cub which had its pink mouth open in complaint.

"Jinny!" cried Jamie, delighted. "Jasper!" But of course they couldn't hear him. He gazed at the dragon in awe and was about to ask it whether they were OK and whether they would be able to go back with him when he realized that would constitute his final two questions, so he clamped his mouth shut.

"The girl came here yesterday. I knew she was sent by the one who sought my pearl, though she claimed she nothing of it knew. So I to bronze turned her. The best way to peace of mind. The other, a worthless scrap is. They return with you can, if so you wish," the Heavenly Dragon said, as if it had read his mind. Or perhaps the Pearl had. He stared at it in consternation but its colours just kept swirling like ink dropped in milk. "Now your second question ask."

Jamie marshalled his thoughts. Then, "Where is my sister, Cadence?" he asked the Pearl.

Again, the opalescence cleared to give him a better view of . . . something. But what was it? It wasn't anything he recognized, at first. It was dark and gloomy, hung about with shadows and cobwebs. This seemed very peculiar, since Cadence had a particular aversion to spiders and would never go anywhere so many of them lived. Of her own free will. But of Cadence herself there was no sign.

"Concentrate, you must," advised the Heavenly Dragon. "The Pearl your memory requires to locate your sister, for it has never knowledge had of her before."

And so Jamie thought hard about his sister. How she

was so proud of her yellow-gold hair and hated to tie it back. How she used to laugh at his jokes out of kindness. How she heartily disliked marmalade. And suddenly there she was with her long blonde hair gleaming in what looked like dancing firelight, and she was laughing with her head thrown back and her eyes shining, in a way he hadn't seen her laugh in ages. Not since their dad had disappeared. But where was she? As his eyes adjusted to the gloom of her background all he could see were long tall pillars that looked like half-melted candles, and lanterns that gave off little specks of light. Then he realized that the lights were moving, that they weren't actually lanterns at all but fireflies. The focus shifted and he began to see that there were a lot of other people there, too, and a bonfire, and above them, as if high on shelves overhead, he could make out an owl or two, their flat white faces as pale as ghosts. Above them, illuminated in flashes by the glowing, darting insects, there appeared to be hundreds and hundreds of tiny dark objects, twitching and twirling as if moved by some invisible breeze.

"Bats!"

They hung upside-down like tiny furled umbrellas – hundreds, maybe thousands, of them, with their skin-draped twiggy arms wrapped around their furry little bodies. But where would bats live in such numbers?

Sometimes, Jamie knew, people complained that a few had got in under their roof, and there had been a small colony in the bell tower of a church near Churnock which had been on the news. The bell-ringers hadn't been able to perform their duties because the bats were a protected species and were not to be disturbed. But the only other place he knew of where bats might hang out was in a cave.

Then he remembered Delving Caves. How, when he was little, their father had taken them inside. How shocked he had been by the darkness – blacker than night except for the light cast by their torch beam – and the chill inside. "Isn't it magnificent?" Mr Wave had cried, holding his arms aloft as if conducting an orchestra. "Like the finest cathedral in the world: better than any palace." And it had been sort of like a church, the same chilly air and musty stone smell, the same yawning void overhead and the shadows that congregated up there, and rows of limestone stalactites which looked just like organ-pipes. ("Remember," his father had told them solemnly, "stalagmites rise from the ground; stalactites drop from the ceiling. It's easy to remember the difference: stalac*tites* have to hold *tight* so that they don't fall down.") Jamie hadn't liked it at all – too dark, too dank. And Cadence? Cadence had screamed her head off and run outside, terrified by the whole experience.

So it made no sense at all that Cadence would be in a cave, let alone what looked as if it might be Delving Caves. It was all very odd. Perhaps the Pearl was mistaken. Even so, he thought he had better look there all the same, when he got back to Cawstocke. If he got back. If he survived Miss Lambent's fury for returning without the Pearl.

The dragon was regarding him curiously, its mesmeric eyes as bright as headlamps.

"Your third question ask now, Jamie Wave."

The question came out before Jamie was ready for it. Indeed, it wasn't even the question he had meant to ask. The question he had been thinking about asking was, *What will Miss Lambent do if she gets her hands on the third magical object?* Because he suspected that if he didn't come back with the Pearl she would find some way of coming for it herself. And that she was likely to become very powerful indeed once she had it in her possession.

But the question that flew out of his mouth came from the heart and was quite different: "Where is my father?"

The dragon cocked its head. "Believe I, at the heart of this whole puzzle that question lies. Look into the Pearl, Jamie Wave, and think of him as you remember him."

And so, seized by a sudden fear, Jamie did just that.

He remembered: a night out at the fairground and how

the bright neon lights from the stalls were reflected in the blackness of his father's eyes like fires.

He remembered: his dad pointing out all the constellations in the night sky with such fervour and accuracy it was as if he had visited each one personally, and how the moonlight burnished his skin with a silver sheen.

He remembered: how his father had made a hide out of cardboard boxes which they took to the park after dark and watched as hedgehogs and cats and foxes made the place their own. And how it had somehow seemed to Jamie as if seeing women pushing prams, or hearing children shouting as they played on the swings, or watching families feeding the ducks in the daytime had been no more than false memories of an entirely other, fictional place. As if the silent night-time world – through which a hedgehog's snort trumpeted like a giant pig's, or a fox's yowl shivered like a banshee's wail – was the true nature of the park. And its cheery daytime façade seemed as false and flimsy as a theatre set.

The Pearl reflected none of this. Between his hands it remained an obstinate deep grey-blue, the colour of twilight falling. Jamie concentrated on it so hard he felt his head would burst. Slowly it offered a background of leaping flames, their light distorting everything it touched. Jamie squinted and turned his head this way and that, trying to see behind the flames where a pair of shadowy figures could just be made out, in some otherwise dark place which seemed to curve over their heads.

There! It was only an instant, but he knew him at once.

Thomas Wave.

Jamie would know that profile anywhere – the long, straight nose, the tight braids, the jut of cheekbone. There was no doubting it was his dad. Though there was something different about him, something odd. As if someone had scribbled on him. He couldn't quite imagine what he meant by that. And beside him, glimpsed fleetingly, was Cadence.

26 AN EXTRAORDINARY GIFT

"They're together! She found him."

Jamie felt a confusion of emotions rush through him. The first was relief – that his father was still alive. The second was jealousy that he and Cadence were together. Then sorrow that he and his mother had been left behind. And how was it that his father had been gone for a year, yet not so far that his sister had been able to find him in less than a day?

There was also the briefest stab of anger that he had wasted a question. If only he had looked just that bit more carefully when the Pearl had shown him his sister. . .

And he still didn't really know where they were.

Tears of frustration pricked Jamie's eyes, and when he took his hands from the Pearl to rub them away he found he couldn't because of the mask. All of a sudden he wanted to take it off and jump on it till it was just a squashed plastic mess, the rubbishy thing that it had seemed to be on the maskmaker's shelves. He wanted to be away from here, away from the dragon and its horrible pearl; away from magic and nonsense. He just wanted his family back the way they used to be before everything in Cawstocke went wrong.

"Time cannot back be turned," the dragon said sadly. "Having existed over three thousand years, that I know. The world turns, then turns again. Only when there is no road left can one feel true despair."

"I haven't the faintest idea what you're on about," Jamie said crossly. "Everything's spoiled. Everything's wrong! And I don't understand any of it!"

"Then you must the cause find. Once you know the cause, the problem you will know. Once the problem you know, the solution you may find."

"I'm just a boy," Jamie said.

"You are a boy. But quite a special boy, think I."

Jamie did not feel special: he felt tired and worried and hopeless. To think that only a few weeks ago he'd thought that Mouth and Michael Rose were the worst problems in his life! The Pearl had raised more questions than it had answered. But at least he had found Jinny and the dragon had said they could leave. That was, at least, a small victory in the face of so much confusion and strangeness. He turned away, head down.

"What are you doing?" the dragon demanded.

"I'm going home."

"Wait!"

He turned back reluctantly, to find the Heavenly Dragon holding out the Pearl.

"This will you need for what you must do next."

Jamie was taken completely by surprise. He stared at the dragon in confusion. "And what is that?"

"Why, save your world," the Heavenly Dragon said, as if it was the only answer there could be. "You see, Jamie, there dual energies at play are. White and black. Day and night. Female and male. Heaven and earth. Yin and yang. These energies at one and the same time complementary are and in opposition to one another. They must in balance be kept, or all is lost."

None of this made much sense to Jamie. He had very little idea what it had to do with trying to get his family back together. He watched as colours swirled in the Pearl until at last just stark black and white came to the surface, forming a symbol that looked to Jamie rather like a black tadpole entwined with its white twin, the pair combining to make a single harmonious circle.

"If closely you look, you will see that each of the energies contains an element or seed of the other."

And indeed when Jamie looked he saw that each

"tadpole" had an eye of the other colour.

"They so closely allied are that one cannot without the other exist; yet sometimes they try to pull apart, and at the worst of times to destroy one another. That cannot be allowed to happen. And perhaps, just perhaps, you are the one in this time and circumstance to prevent it."

"I am?"

The Heavenly Dragon regarded him kindly. "The Pearl tells me you are a bringer of light, a maker of laughter. That the best gift in the world can be. Perspective it gives on life's problems. Tell me one of your jokes, Jamie Wave, and then you may be on your way."

"You want me to tell you a joke?"

Seeing his father with Cadence in the Pearl had rather caused him a sense of humour failure, and the stuff about the balance of energies in the world had taxed him more than most of Mr Hope's science classes. He didn't feel like a maker of laughter at all at the moment.

"No one has told me a joke in over a thousand years," the dragon said sadly. "And even that one not very amusing was."

Jamie tried to think of something – anything – funny, but his usually joke-filled brain was just not being cooperative. The ones that did eventually pop into his head weren't suitable, involving a knowledge of modern idioms and a sense of surrealism he suspected the dragon didn't possess (*I met a Dutch girl with inflatable shoes last week, phoned her up to arrange to go to the cinema, but unfortunately she'd popped her clogs. . . What do bees do if they don't want to drive? Wait at the buzz stop. . .*). What would amuse a three-thousand-year-old dragon? At last, remembering what he'd seen in the Pearl, he thought of something that would have to do.

"All right," he said, taking a deep breath. "There's this vampire bat— Do you know what a vampire bat is?"

The Heavenly Dragon nodded.

"OK. One night this vampire bat comes flying back to his cave after a night of hunting, and he's covered in fresh blood. Worn out, he attaches himself to the roof by his claws, hangs upside-down and tries to get some sleep. But within moments all the other bats smell the blood on him and begin pestering him as to where he got it from. He's completely exhausted. He opens one eye and tells them to shut up and let him sleep. But they just won't stop. They're starving, they say, haven't found anything worth biting all night. They keep on and on hassling him until finally, he gives in. 'Oh, all right,' he says, 'follow me.' So he flies out of the cave and they all fly after him – hundreds and hundreds of vampire bats in a great black cloud. They swoop through the valley, across the plain and into a huge great forest of trees. They fly for miles and miles. At last he slows down and all the other bats flap around him excitedly. 'Do you see that tree over there?' he asks.

"'Yes, yes, yes, we do! We do!' the bats all scream in a frenzy.

"'Well, I didn't.'"

The dragon gazed at Jamie as if expecting more. Then the expression in its eyes changed as understanding dawned and it stuffed its hands over its mouth. Little snuffles and chortles escaped between its claws.

"One should not of others' misfortunes fun make," it said after a long while. "But it hard is not to laugh at such a tale. Now put out your hands."

Jamie did as he was told and the dragon placed the Pearl in them. It was heavier than he had expected. He almost dropped it, and as if it sensed this, the Pearl shrank until it was the size of a cricket ball.

"This I give to you. Do with it what you must."

"I can't just . . . take it."

The Heavenly Dragon yawned and stretched. "It my gift to you is. Or we a loan can call it if it makes you better feel. All these years have I been bothered by thieves who come my pearl to steal. Now I nothing have of value, I need no one fear, and at last I can take my rest." And with that, it lay down and curled its tail around its nose just like a cat about to take a nap. Soon after that, the air of the Chamber of Truth was filled with snores.

Jamie gazed at the Pearl of Wisdom and Everlasting Light. He could not believe the dragon had given it to him. Given it, in exchange for a joke. It hadn't even been *that* good a joke. He could think of loads more now. They were crowding into his head, clamouring to get out. The one about the magician and the parrot, for example. He couldn't help but smile.

"Come on," said a voice behind Jamie. "It's time to go back."

He turned to see a pair of orange eyes regarding him in the gloom. It was Jasper. Jamie stowed the Pearl safely away in a pocket. He had absolutely no idea what he was going to do with it. But he wasn't going to admit that to the cat.

They found Jinny outside by the pillar on which she had stood, transformed by the dragon into a bronze lion. When she saw Jamie coming she rushed over to him and gave him a hug. Their masks knocked together awkwardly and they laughed.

"You came to save me! You are a true friend, Jamie Wave."

"Come on," he said, grabbing her hand. "Let's go home." He turned to look for the cat to lead them out of the lake.

"I know what you've been thinking about me," Jasper

said quietly. "And some of it's true. I was her servant, but I work for another now. You have to trust me: I will explain it all. If we survive."

"If we survive?" Jamie echoed.

"I can't imagine she will be too happy that you're not going to give her the Pearl."

"I'm not?"

Until that moment, Jamie Wave hadn't even realized he'd made a decision. But the cat was right. He wasn't going to give the Pearl of Wisdom and Everlasting Life to Miss Lambent.

Whether it was the magic of the pearl he carried, or the aid of the sleeping dragon, Jamie didn't know: but within moments of wishing that they were back at the willow tree by the edge of the lake whence he and Jasper had entered this world, there they were, and not even wet, which seemed like the oddest thing of all.

The black cat stood beside the tree. "Ready?" he said, and taking a leap, disappeared into nothing.

Jinny gasped. "Where's he gone?"

"Back to the maskmaker's shop. And it's where we're going, too."

"I don't understand." Jinny's voice sounded small and lost from inside the lion mask. "I don't understand any of this. I must be dreaming. It all started as such a logical dream, too. When you didn't turn up at the Pizza Shack I told Mum I was going to the loo and sneaked out to look for you because I found a card for a place called The Maskmaker that fell out of your pocket. It wasn't far to May Street, and I ran all the way, thinking you might have forgotten the time. But when I got there all I found was our art teacher, Miss Lambent, and she stuck something on my head and pushed me through a mirror. And then I fell through dark space and landed in China, and it was hundreds of years ago, and there was a dragon. . . It all sounds mad. . ."

Jamie bit his lip. "It's probably best not to think too much about it."

"One of my aunties went a bit mad. They found her skipping down the dual carriageway in her nightie in the middle of the night and when the police stopped her she said she was off to join the Pied Piper of Hamelin along with all the other children. Madness can be inherited, can't it?"

"Honestly, Jinny, you're the least mad person I know." He got her to stand behind him with her arms around his waist. "Whatever happens, don't let go!"

After a horrible surging, falling sensation that seemed to go on for ever but probably only lasted seconds, they tumbled in a tangle on the carpeted floor of the little room at the back of the maskmaker's shop. Jasper was waiting for them. He looked scared.

"Don't worry," Jamie said. "You don't need to be involved when I tell Miss Lambent she can't have the Pearl."

Even as he said this, he half expected her to leap shrieking through the door, with her toffee-gold eyes sparking and her hands like claws. But there was the silence, until Jasper said very softly:

"I think you'd better come and see this."

27 THE HISTORY OF MAGIC

Jamie could see very little. Then he realized that this was because he was still wearing the stupid lion mask and because night had fallen. They must have been with the Heavenly Dragon a lot longer than he'd thought. He took off the mask and, feeling along the wall, managed to find a light switch.

The bare bulb illuminated a scene of havoc. Masks had been dragged off the shelves and lay in heaps on the floor. Some had been ripped apart, others stamped and crushed; some even appeared to have been bitten. Pieces of them lay scattered everywhere. Jamie saw the cheek and twined ivy of the Green Man mask jutting up against a crushed white Venetian carnival mask. The broken horsehair crest of an Ancient Greek helmet now adorned the head of Cristiano Ronaldo. Elvis Presley had acquired one of Mickey Mouse's ears, while Bart Simpson and Darth Vader had got hopelessly entwined.

The Viking mask he had worn on his quest to bring back the Soulstone was trampled into an irretrievably crumpled mass of metal and plastic. Of the Tuareg *tagelmust* that had transported him to the Sahara there was no sign at all.

Where was Miss Lambent? That was the question. Had she carried out this act of immense destruction herself, in a fit of anger because he had not returned with the Pearl? It seemed unlikely. From everything that she had said to him he had understood that the maskmaker's shop was a refuge for her, her daytime hiding place from the enemy she was trying so hard to avoid. The one of whom she was so greatly afraid.

He looked around at the devastation and took in more alarming details. There appeared to be clumps of fur attached to the mashed remains of a pharaoh. And was that blood smeared on the glass of the door?

Behind him he heard Jinny's voice. "What's happened? Who's done this? Has someone been hurt? And where's Miss Lambent?"

"I don't know," he said, shaking his head. "But I'm going to find out."

"Wherever you go, I'm going with you," Jinny declared firmly. She had taken the Chinese mask off and in the glare of the hundred-watt light bulb looked pale but fierce, her red hair as bright as fire.

"I don't really think that's a good idea."

"You sound like my dad. He seems to think that girls are hopeless in a crisis, but it's always Mum who has to put the spiders out of the house. It makes me so cross! I didn't want to take ballet lessons – I wanted to do kung fu!"

Jamie remembered how she had stood up to Michael Rose. "There are a lot of strange things going on in Cawstocke and they involve magic, and I don't think even kung fu would be much use against them."

"If I'm with you I can face anything," Jinny said. "That's what friends are for."

"It could be dangerous."

Jinny shrugged. "You only live once."

"That's not strictly true," said Jasper.

Jamie regarded the black cat thoughtfully. "It strikes me," he said, "that you know a lot more about what's happening than you're letting on. I think now's the time to tell me what you know, don't you?"

Jinny stared at the black cat, utterly amazed. "It spoke!" she cried.

Jasper's fur ruffled with annoyance. "Of course I spoke. Why do humans think they are the only intelligent life forms in the world?" He turned to Jamie. "If I tell you what I know, she'll skin my kittens. That's what she threatened me with."

"Skin your kittens?" Jinny looked horrified.

"She's got my wife and two little ones somewhere. I can't find them."

"Miss Lambent would never do such a cruel thing," Jinny said.

"Miss Lambent is not what she seems," said Jamie. He stooped to pick up something from amid the detritus on the floor.

To Jinny it looked as pale and floppy as a rubber glove, but when Jamie turned it over she shrieked. It was Miss Lambent's face.

"It's just a mask," Jamie told her quickly. "Underneath it, Miss Lambent doesn't look anything like she does at school: she's an ancient, wizened old woman."

"And a sorceress," added Jasper. "And more. . . Remember what the Heavenly Dragon said."

"You were listening?"

"Information is my job."

"You sound like a spy!" laughed Jinny.

"I am."

"Who *do* you work for?" Jamie demanded.

The black cat sighed. "I will ask you one more time. Will you help me find my wife and kits? Will you ask the Pearl for me?"

"Of course we will," Jinny said at once. "Won't we, Jamie?"

Jamie hesitated. "OK," he said at last. "But if you betray us in any way, you're on your own."

The cat cuffed at the ashes and a few warm flakes drifted up into the air then spun slowly down again, like crow's feathers. "Such glorious times, lost for ever." He sat back and regarded the two children. "Fair enough: it's a deal. We each need the other: you need me to tell you what's going on and you, well, you're the only one who can save the day. Literally." And he gave a small smile, as if he had made a joke just for his own enjoyment.

"This part of the world is much older, and stranger, than you know. Before any of the history you've ever been taught two elemental forces came into existence in the area around Cawstocke, before there even *was* a Cawstocke. These forces were bound together, but always in opposition. I came to know them as the Master and the White Lady. Male and female; darkness and light."

Something was tickling the inside of Jamie's skull: a whisper of a suspicion. He remembered the black-and-white symbol the dragon had shown him, the warring energies it had spoken of. He stared at the cat, willing it to give up the information.

Jasper gazed back at him, unblinking. "All in good time. Let me tell my story and all will become clear.

"For eons the Master and the White Lady lived in

balance. Oh, they had the occasional power struggle, scoring points off each other, as couples often will. You know those hills outside Cawstocke?"

"The Downs?" Jamie narrowed his eyes at him.

"The Downs," Jasper confirmed. "The Master and Mistress created them. They had a fight, a great battle there, around 1642. People took sides, there were many deaths. Historians thought the remains they found came from one of the Civil War battles, but I know better."

"How do you know?" Jinny demanded.

Jasper transferred his mesmerizing gaze to her. "Because I was there." He left a long pause for this information to sink in.

"But you can't have been! That was almost. . ." She tried to do the calculation in her head.

"The best part of four hundred years ago, yes."

Jinny's eyes were as round as saucers. "But how? No cat can live that long. Our neighbour's cat got to twenty-two and everyone said that was the longest they'd ever heard of."

Jasper shrugged. "You'll have to take my word for it. I've come and gone during that time, but I promise you I was there when the Downs took on the shape you know now – all those dips and hollows and scars. There were a lot more stone circles there once, before they were buried for ever.

I watched them fight there, the Master and the White Lady, wielding magic one against the other. It was an awesome, terrifying sight. I think they even scared each other. In the end they called a truce."

"The White Lady. . ." Jinny interrupted. "Is she. . .?"

"Miss Lambent," Jamie said. "Miss Lambent is the White Lady. I told you she was a lot older than she looked."

Jinny shook her head. "No. No, that can't be possible."

Jamie felt sorry for his friend. He understood how confused she was by all this. Everything he believed about the world had been turned upside-down as well, but at least he'd had a bit more time to get used to the idea that a woman who was a lot older than four hundred years old had been alive and well and teaching art at their school. It was like being in a fairy tale.

Jasper went on: "As I said, they called a truce: and they made a pact. They decided not to use their magic against one another any more. Instead, they gathered some of the stones they had uprooted and stored their magic in them. Each watched the other warily, in case of cheating. When they had each stored their magic in those stones they came here" – it waved a paw vaguely – "to this shop. It was just a house then, where the White Lady had a small collection of masks; and the mirror. They cast the stones through the mirror one by one, let them fall at random, into different times and places. Then they shook hands and divided up the day between them, as was only fair. She'd occupy the daylight hours and he'd stick to the night, and that's how it's been ever since. A fragile balance has been kept between them."

"Until now," Jamie said slowly. "She's been collecting up the stones."

Jinny looked sharply at Jamie. "Whatever do you mean?"

Jamie told her about the quests Miss Lambent had sent him on, to fetch the Tiger's Eye from the Sahara and the Soulstone from the Arctic. How the first stone had appeared to flood her with energy; how the Soulstone had made her bones shine through her skin. Then he took the Pearl of Wisdom and Everlasting Truth out of his pocket and put it on the shop's dusty counter, where immediately it grew to its usual size, looking for all the world like a fortune teller's crystal ball.

Jinny's eyes became huge. "Whatever is that?"

"It's called the Pearl of Wisdom and Everlasting Life," Jamie said solemnly. "And if she gets her hands on it she'll be pretty scary, I reckon. But someone else seems to have realized that, too." He gave Jasper a hard stare.

If cats could blush perhaps Jasper would have done so now, but under all that black fur it was impossible to see.

A black cat makes a good spy, for this among many other reasons to do with stealth and general inconspicuousness.

"Yes, I reported to the Master that you were about to fetch the last stone," Jasper admitted.

"You? You're working for him? I thought you worked for Miss Lambent!"

"It's not simple," the black cat acknowledged. "You don't know the half of it yet."

Jamie gritted his teeth. "Go on then, tell me the rest. How did you do it? How did you manage to get away and tell him? You've been with me all the time."

"The owl," Jasper said. "You'll remember the owl that flew over when the dogs were about to attack you?"

Jamie nodded. He'd *known* there was something strange going on.

"It warned the dogs off and I gave it a message to carry back to the Master."

"And just who *is* this Master?"

"Call him what you will," the cat said. "He has many names. The King Under the Hill. Lord of the Dark World. The King of Shadows. None of them are his real name, of course. I'm not sure he remembers that, or even if he has one."

Jamie stared at the cat. Everyone knew about the King of Shadows. How he ruled a faery kingdom under the ground. How, if you stayed out on the Downs after dark, you would find his court dancing in the hollows and around standing stones, their skin glowing aubergine-purple and pearl-white beneath the moon. And if they caught you watching them they would take you away with them, under the hill, and you would never see your friends or family again. How he rode on moonbeams and stole babies from their cots. How you might suddenly find him gazing out at you from the dark reflections of a mirror or a silver teapot – not that Jamie knew anyone who owned a silver teapot – and if your eyes met, you would follow him wherever he went and even forget your own name. The King of Shadows was a fantasy figure: made up and told about in stories. Despite himself, he burst out laughing. "The King of Shadows isn't real."

"He's as real as you or me, and infinitely more frightening. Before all this you didn't believe in magic either; but now you've seen it working with your own eyes. Soon you will see the King of Shadows, too. Do you think all this" – with a paw he indicated the wreckage of the shop – "was an accident? This is the work of his servants. They were probably instructed to destroy the masks – for he understands their significance – when they came for her." He looked away. "Though if I had known they would resort to such violence, I would never have passed on the information that she would be waiting here tonight."

"You knew we would not be back till after dark?" cried Jamie accusingly.

"Ancient China is a very long way away," the cat said, blinking its orange eyes hard.

"You knew where we were going?"

The cat cast a look at the now-empty shelves. "I know every mask here. I have known some of them for centuries. If one moves out of place I know it. There were, I knew, two Chinese lion masks; and when we got back yesterday one of them was missing."

"So you knew where Jinny had gone! We could have gone straight there and saved her from the dragon."

"I had to take that risk," Jasper said. "You have your loved ones: I have mine. I need to find them, before it's too late. I've told you all I know and that was my part of the bargain. Now it's your turn."

28 THE DELVING CAVES

Jamie approached the Pearl and very carefully put his hands on either side of it.

"Please," said Jasper, pawing at his leg. "Ask it where the White Lady has hidden my wife and kittens."

"What are their names?"

"Cressida, Flo and Aurelio."

Those were three words Miss Lambent had hissed at Jasper in the shop, the words that Jamie had taken to be some sort of spell!

Reflected in the Pearl, his lips moved silently. He took a deep breath and asked: "Where has Miss Lambent hidden Jasper's family, Cressida, Flo and Aurelio?"

For long seconds nothing at all happened and Jamie was more convinced than ever that the Pearl must be broken. Or that perhaps it worked only when it was with the dragon. All the Pearl gave back to him was the reflection of his own face, grotesquely magnified. In the vast black pupils of his eyes he saw a smaller image of himself, staring questioningly back, and knew that if he were able to look closer he would see himself reflected in that reflection, again and again, into infinity. Then the interior of the Pearl began to surge and swirl until at last it offered him a night sky scattered with pinpricks of silver light and the edge of a full, white moon. Its focus shifted downwards and suddenly there was movement – something flapping jerkily, tiny and dark; then beneath that figures and animals. He scanned the tableau for the sight of three cats among the melee, but instead he saw silhouetted against the face of the moon a tall, thin person with straggling white hair, being pulled along by means of cords bound around its wrists. Dogs ran along beside the figure, corralling it as they might an errant sheep. Bats and owls flew overhead. The prisoner turned its face towards him for an instant and Jamie recognized the woman behind Miss Lambent's mask, her toffee-gold eyes glowing eerily in the moonlight.

Then the Pearl's vision drew back and he saw that one of the captors pulling her along was his enemy, Mouth, and behind Miss Lambent, carrying a heavy club, was Michael "Rosy" Rose. He gasped.

"What? What have you seen?" the black cat beseeched him.

"I'm sorry." Jamie shook his head. "I haven't seen your

family. But I have found Miss Lambent."

Jinny peered over his shoulder. "That's not Miss Lambent!"

"It's what she looks like under the mask."

"But she's ancient!"

"She looked a whole lot older than that the first time I saw her without her mask," Jamie said. "She's drawn a good deal of power from the stones I brought back for her. They rejuvenated her."

Jinny stared in horror at the woman who had masqueraded as their art teacher; then her expression changed to one of astonishment. "Look!" The Pearl was panning along the hillside to show where the Downs split open into what appeared to be a great red mouth.

Jamie watched with awful fascination. There had never really been any doubt in his mind. Ever since he had seen the vision of his sister and father in that awful place he had known where he would have to go. He knew now that the King of Shadows had taken them prisoner, just as he had all the others who had been plagued by nightmares. Just as he had captured Miss Lambent. And she had taken Jasper's family. Someone had to put an end to it all. To stop the whole awful misuse of magic. To make the world normal again. But how? He had no answer to that rather vital question.

"We'll have to go to the Delving Caves," Jamie declared. "The answer to all of our questions lies there. We'll achieve nothing by staying here."

As if it approved his decision, the Pearl immediately shrank between his hands until it was small enough for him to stash in the pocket of his jeans.

Jasper's eyes radiated misery. "You'll need masks." He sighed. "If you're to hear me."

"You said it was too dangerous to wear them by night."

The cat blinked at him. "It's your choice," it said. "You can go without masks if you'd rather, though it'll be hard to communicate if you lose me in the darkness. Now that he's got what he wants, I doubt very much he'll be using his magic to search for masks. Besides, he thinks they're all broken."

"And he's right," Jamie said flatly.

"I can sense the presence of another entire mask in here somewhere," Jasper said.

He walked to the edge of the debris and with careful paws pulled pieces of broken mask aside, kicking the useless bits away with his back feet. Soon he found what he was looking for. Jamie picked it up. It was a white Venetian carnival mask, one that covered just the eyes and nose, with an elastic string to hold it on the head. He put it on.

"Right, then, let's go." Jasper turned and walked towards the shop's door, his tail held high.

"Wait!" cried Jinny. "I need a mask too!"

"One's quite dangerous enough," the cat said primly.

Jinny caught Jamie's arm. "If we're separated or anything. . ."

Jamie sifted through the wreckage. When he straightened up he had something pink and glittery in his hand. It seemed to be a fairy mask. For a brief surreal moment he felt deeply relieved he hadn't had to wear that one himself.

The Delving Caves were a good eight kilometres outside Cawstocke, and they would have to walk: there were no buses at this late hour. In fact, there appeared to be no traffic on the streets, and no people around at all. More than this, there were no lights on in any of the houses they passed. They walked through the old market square, with its clock tower and war memorial, and it was like walking into an abandoned film set of a townscape. Nothing moved. There was no one at the chip shop, and even the neon sign had been turned off. No one hanging around outside the Miner's Arms for a late-night smoke, no one in the car park opposite, or outside the hospital, where the three ambulances sat silent and unmanned.

"It's weird," Jamie said at last. "As if everyone's been beamed up by alien spaceships, except us."

"Haven't you noticed anything else?" asked Jasper.

They both looked at him.

"It's not just the lack of humans. Not one stray dog? Not a single cat? Not one of the Master's messengers delivering dreams. It's unnerving."

They passed a petrol station closed up for the night, the twenty-four-hour supermarket was dark and nothing was stirring on the industrial estate. But as they passed a row of little shops, something slipped silently across the road in front of them, turning its head for an instant so that the moon reflected in its eyes. Jinny clutched Jamie's arm.

"It's OK," Jasper said. "It's only a fox. They haven't taken sides in this conflict. It's just annoyed that we've disturbed its dinner."

A few paces later they made out an overturned dustbin outside the Indian takeaway. A dozen spicy-smelling tinfoil containers spilled out and lay scattered on the pavement.

Jamie remembered a terrible joke he'd told Cadence only a few weeks ago. "A fox is eating his dinner outside the Raj Tandoori and this dog, who thinks he's a bit of a dog of the world, been around, something of an expert, comes past and says, 'So what's your favourite curry, then?' The fox thinks about this for a moment and then he says, 'Chicken

Tarka Masala.' The dog thinks he must have misheard. 'Chicken Tikka Masala?' he asks. 'No, no,' says the fox, 'it's like Chicken Tikka Masala, but 'otter.'"

Jasper stared at him as if he'd gone mad; but after a moment Jinny started to laugh so hard that her mask fell off and had to be rescued from the gutter. "It's one of my favourite books," she said, but the black cat was none the wiser.

The last houses petered out into the unrelieved dark of the countryside. They came at last to a junction with a signpost. The main, wider, road was signed to Rookford, the right-hand fork to Little Delving.

"It's this way."

Jamie turned right and they walked on in silence and darkness. They passed Jaggard's Farm with its broken fences and its agricultural machinery rusting away in the paddock. There were no lights on in the farmhouse, no sound of cows in the byres or chickens in the coops. It looked like a ghost farm.

They crossed the Churnock River at the ford. Beneath their feet the water lay like a sleeping serpent, the currents coiling and twisting as the river made its way from the uplands down through the winding valleys towards the sea. Here there was a footpath that cut through the woods and up to the Downs, avoiding the village of Little Delving.

Jamie had the sense that if he spoke, the sound would carry for miles, beyond Churnock Woods, into the depths of the Delving Caves which burrowed away below the knotted roots of the trees. In silence, then, they emerged on to the Downs, where the big pale moon hung over them like a lamp, picking them out with beams as bright as a police helicopter's searchlight. Jamie turned, and Jinny flinched, for in that instant the Venetian mask made his face as strange and flat and white as any barn owl's.

"This is where we saw her. Miss Lambent," he whispered. "When we looked in the Pearl. They were marching her along this ridge."

"I hope we're not too late," said Jinny.

"Too late for what?" asked the cat.

Nobody knew the answer to that. Jinny asked Jamie whether he had a plan. "I'm not sure I'd call it a plan, as such. But I've got an idea." He started to take the Pearl out of his pocket.

Instantly Jasper began to hiss and spit, making a noise like water popping on a hot stove. "No! Do you want to alert everyone to our arrival? Magic calls to magic, especially with all these other stones around to amplify it." He waved a paw to where the standing stones formed ancient circles punctuating the sheep-bitten turf all around them. "Perhaps you should stay here, and I'll go alone and see what's happening down there."

Jamie shook his head. "No, we stay together."

Jasper nodded. "There will be sentries in the woods." He indicated the hill a long way ahead of them. "And below that lie the Delving Caves. Follow me, and do what I say, no matter how strange it may seem. Do you understand?"

Jamie looked at Jinny, otherworldly in her fairy mask. Jinny looked back at him steadily. "Ready?" she whispered.

"Ready," said Jamie Wave.

Together they ran across the moorland. They skirted the stone circles and the big sentinel stone that stood on its own. They crossed a stream and picked their way through boggy ground on the other side, the cat leaping lightly from tussock to tussock. They toiled up the steep hill on the other side, a hill that had been created by an ancient battle of magic. At the top giant beech trees stretched their arms into the night skies. Their leaves shut out the harshest light of the moon, their bark glowed pale and smooth. It was easy to walk between them. Very little grew beneath their dense canopy. Beechmast and old leaves crunched underfoot, making Jamie wince. Surely their passage could be heard for miles around?

Indeed, a moment later, a tawny owl drifted overhead,

circled, then flapped urgently back in the direction it had come from.

"Remember, do whatever I say," Jasper said urgently.

Jinny moved closer to Jamie and instinctively slipped her hand in his. He was surprised to find that he clasped it gratefully. They followed, anxious and doubtful.

As they reached the edge of the wood, they paused. And then a howl shivered through the night air. At once more howls joined in, followed by frenzied barking, getting louder and louder. It was a primeval sound, like the cries of a pack of hunting wolves. Jamie wanted to run as fast as he could for safety. But he didn't know whether safety existed in or around Cawstocke any more.

Now they were able to look down into the valley below. In the distant hollow at the base of the hill stood the yawning red mouth seen in the Pearl's vision: the opening to the Delving Caves, filled with a great bonfire. Hundreds of tiny figures milled around, dancing around the flames, disappearing into the shadows. But closer, much closer, came the immediate danger – a band of dogs tearing up the hillside, their panting breath making pale clouds in the dark air.

A low moan escaped Jinny.

"They won't hurt you," the cat said. "He'll have sent them to see who you are."

The lead dog bounded up the last stretch of hill, eating the ground up effortlessly, and Jamie recognized it as the big Alsatian that had led the pack of dogs at the recreation ground.

It came to an abrupt halt a few feet away from them. "You again, little spy!" it growled at Jasper. "And what are these creatures you have with you? Filthy, stinking little mask-wearers! You've got a nerve bringing them on to the Master's territory!"

The rest of the pack now stood glaring at them with drool dripping from their panting jaws. Moonlight shone silver in their eyes. They looked like ghost dogs.

Jasper hissed, "Back off, Turk! And keep your minions at bay. I bring two prizes for the King of Shadows. Prizes he will be pleased to receive. If you damage them in any way, he will make you pay with as much pain as you can bear before expiring. You know this to be true."

The Alsatian curled its great black lip to show off the length and quality of its ivory fangs and the degree of contempt in which it held its species-enemy. "He will not like the masks. Perhaps it is you who will pay."

Turk turned to his followers. "I could fancy a bite of roast cat tonight, boys. What do you say?"

Growls and wheezing laughter greeted this remark, but they kept their distance.

The Alsatian took another step forward, sniffing the air. "I know you," he said to Jamie. "We have met before."

Jamie tried not to let the creature see his fear. "Yes, you and your mongrels disturbed me once on my way home."

"Who are you calling a mongrel?" an odd-looking cur barked out, its wide, square head seeming far too big for its slender yellow body.

"We should have killed the boy when we had the chance."

"We would have, if it wasn't for that sneak of an owl."

"Owls and cats, they are no more than vermin. We are the Master's true slaves. We cry his name in the dark hours, and he gives us the night."

"Enough!" cried Jasper, arching his back. "I am taking my prisoners to the Master. You may accompany us if you wish, but you will not prevent me."

"We could kill the cat," suggested a sly-looking whippet, "and eat it here and now. No one would know."

"Then we could claim *we* found the prisoners. He will reward us," agreed a poodle. It had clearly not been groomed in a long while, though it had obviously once been a pet, for there were still tufts of fur on its tail and legs which showed how it had once been clipped like an ornamental hedge.

"If you do anything to the cat I will tell the King of

Shadows that you attacked his servant and he will punish you!" Jinny's voice rang out clear and true in the night air without the least trace of the tremble Jamie could feel running through her.

"You are very bold for prisoners," Turk said suspiciously. "You smell of fear, but not fear of your captor. This seems most odd to me."

"What do dogs know?" Jasper hissed. "Little more than to bite and bark and slaver. These are the White Lady's servants, so beware."

"There is not much to beware about the White Lady," Turk returned contemptuously. "She hardly put up any sort of fight when we took her." Even so, he turned back to his troops. "Guard on either side!" he barked. "If any of them does anything that looks magical, bite their legs, right?"

"Rrrrright!"

So saying, he marched them down the hill towards the entrance to the Delving Caves, with his vanguard capering hungrily on either side of them.

29 THE KING OF SHADOWS

As they drew closer to the caves, they could see that the bonfire was enormous. Its flames shot seven or more metres into the air. There were hundreds of people gathered around it, their faces lit orange and red by its feral light. Some of them were dancing in an odd, uncoordinated fashion, waving their arms in the air and hopping from foot to foot, but though they danced, there seemed to be no music. They looked like savages, Jamie thought, wild people from another age and culture. They could have been Plains Indians, cavemen or anything, except for the way they were dressed.

Jeans, sweatshirts, dresses, suits – they all wore modern clothing. Though one or two seemed to have come in their nightwear. He glimpsed – or thought he did – Mr Reynolds, their maths teacher, with his shirt loose and his tie tied around his head, dancing as if he was very drunk.

Jinny nudged him. "It's. . ."

He nodded. "And look, over there, it's Mrs Horne, Angela's mother."

Mrs Horne had been an exotic dancer in her youth, Angela boasted, but if that had ever been true since then she had run to fat and lost any sense of rhythm. She danced with her arms around a tall, thin man who was just about to lose his spectacles in the fire.

"It's Mr Martin!" Jinny whispered, appalled. Mr Martin was their history teacher, and was completely terrifying. He didn't look very terrifying at the moment, though, wearing a dressing gown and a pair of frayed old slippers, with Mrs Horne draped all over him.

As they looked at the gathered crowd, more and more familiar faces appeared. Jamie's cadaverous neighbour, Mrs Rosberg. Archie, the caretaker of their building. Kylie Morris, whom everyone thought had run away to London. Mr Jones, who sold building materials and drove a truck with fire painted over its wheel arches; Mr Russell, Helen Russell's stuck-up father, looking utterly incongruous in a three-piece suit. Mrs Russell in a flimsy white nightie. There was Mr Patel, who ran the shop, flailing his arms around in a random fashion, as if they no longer belonged to him. And there was his daughter, in a brightly coloured sari, with a large-eyed baby slung across her back.

Jinny's fingers suddenly dug painfully into his arm. "It is!" she wailed. "It's Mum!"

Jamie followed her gaze, and there, leaping wildly, was Mrs Briggs, her face stretched in an inane grin, as if she had lost her mind. As if she had totally forgotten that the day before her daughter had gone missing and she'd been mad with worry trying to find her.

"Mum!" Jinny shouted, but if her mother heard she gave no sign of it, instead grabbing hold of the next person in the circle by the waistband of his trousers and whirling him around to dance with her.

It was Mr Jellicoe, their headmaster. Jinny's face went crimson with shame. "What is she doing?" She turned the glittering fairy mask to Jamie. "Are we dreaming? This is horrible!"

Jamie Wave shook his head slowly. "No, we're not dreaming, but I think they might be."

And then he saw Cadence.

She was twirling round and round, her head back so that her long yellow hair hung to her waist, being held up by the arms of some tall, thin red-haired boy. It was Mouth! Never in a million years would his sister have anything to do with such a creep. He couldn't believe what he was seeing.

"Cadence!" he yelled. Just for a moment her head came

up and twisted around to follow the sound of his cry, and he saw that while her mouth was stretched in a rictus of a grin, her eyes were fearful. She looked to Jamie like someone desperate to escape but unable to do anything but dance and dance and dance.

"There's something really weird going on here."

"I know," said Jinny. "Mum would never dance with Mr Jellicoe. She can't stand him. She says he's a pompous ass."

Jamie had the incongruous image of his headmaster adorned with a pair of long, grey donkey's ears. At that moment, even if Mr Jellicoe had sprouted them out of the top of his big bald head it wouldn't have surprised him. Jamie thought nothing would surprise him ever again.

The dogs stopped just beyond the bonfire, and as Jamie took a step forward, Turk growled, "Stay! The spy will announce us. It does not do to surprise the King of Shadows."

The King of Shadows. He was in there, just out of sight. They were really going to see him. It didn't seem possible that such a person could exist, let alone that he and Jinny Briggs – two friends from Cawstocke High, where they should be doing double maths and geography tomorrow morning – should now be walking into his presence, into the realm of mythology and make-believe. He touched the

Pearl furtively, suddenly terrified by what he must do. Under his fingers, the Pearl vibrated like a living thing, sending little warm tremors up his arm, into the bones of his shoulders and down into his ribcage. For a moment Jamie suddenly felt reassured. For a second – just a second – he knew that everything was going to be all right. More than all right. It was going to be the way it should always have been, before, before—

"Bring the boy to His Majesty, now!" barked a tall grey deerhound from the mouth of the caves.

"What about the girl?" asked Turk.

"The girl is nothing. You can do with her what you will."

Hungry dogs began to growl appreciatively at this, but Jamie Wave stepped forward. "I'm not going anywhere without her."

The deerhound gave a non-committal shrug. "As you will."

Together, they stepped into the Delving Caves. In front of them, upon a convolution of stalactites and stalagmites which formed a grand throne, sat the King of Shadows. Before him, bound to a column of limestone, her toffee-gold eyes flaring defiantly in the light of the bonfire, was the White Lady, Miss Lambent. Two vast Dobermanns sat on either side of her, their ears pricked, their sharp teeth gleaming. At the foot of the throne, collapsed in the shadows, was Jamie's mother.

"Mum!" Jamie called, but she did not raise her head. He couldn't believe it. Whatever was she doing here? How had she worked out where Cadence had gone? Had she found his father, too? He looked around.

"I believe you have brought me a gift," said the voice above him. It echoed off the walls of the cave, bouncing and reverberating so that it sounded as if a hundred kings had spoken.

Jamie squinted up into the semi-darkness. He was surprised to see that the speaker had on what looked like a pair of ripped black jeans and a dark pullover, which was not at all what he had imagined a faery king might wear. He had bare feet. Wide, dark feet just like. . . Jamie peered into the darkness to make out the king's face, but the jumping light of the bonfire threw shadows across it, instead illuminating a horde of tiny bats that flitted around his head, this way and that, making a sort of glittering dark halo. Then he saw that Jasper was seated on the King of Shadow's knee.

"My excellent spy here tells me you have brought me a gift – a magical gift, no less. The Pearl of Truth and Everlasting Life!"

"No!" Miss Lambent's howl shivered through the air. "The Pearl is mine! The boy fetched it for me!"

"Shut up, witch! Shut up or you'll burn as all your kind have burned down the centuries!" the King of Shadow's voice boomed out, and its hundred echoes swamped the retreating echoes of Miss Lambent's cry.

Jamie stared at the cat in horror. "I can't believe you told him."

"I did warn you not to trust anyone," Jasper said softly. "Unfortunately, that advice included me."

Jamie remembered how he'd disliked the beast at first sight. He should have trusted his own instincts and nothing else. He'd taken the creature into their home; he'd let it sleep on his bed, and it had betrayed him. But yet . . . he remembered also how it had saved him from the dogs in the park; and brought the polar bears to save him from the shaman. . .

"Why?" he cried out plaintively.

The cat's orange eyes burned with shame. "I have to know where my family is. My master will ask the Pearl."

"*I* asked the Pearl!"

"You did not know them: I realize now that the Pearl could not find them because you could not imagine them. My master, however, knows them well."

"Little turncoat!" spat Miss Lambent from her stake of limestone. "I never trusted you. Cats are too sly and selfish ever to make good servants. Well, you'll have your just deserts in the end, and so will your wife and children." She gave the cat a stare that brimmed with malice.

Above her, on the throne, the King of Shadows made a strange, high sound and suddenly all the bats that had been flying around his head swooped down and flew at Miss Lambent, flapping their leathery wings in her face and tangling their tiny claws in her hair until her shrieks filled the cavern.

"Now then," the king said. "I think I'll have my gift, and then we shall burn the witch and day and night shall both be mine, for ever!" And he threw Jasper lightly down to the cave floor and came down off his throne and into the light.

Jamie tried to say something, but it was as if every word he had ever known suddenly clotted together to form a hard knot in his throat. He felt as if he had been eviscerated, turned inside-out, so that his heart was beating on the outside of his ribs. He felt that everything he was and had ever been had been scoured out and left hanging in cold air for this . . . *being* to inspect.

The King of Shadows was his father.

Thomas Wave.

And yet, at the same time, a complete stranger.

Images shuttled back and forth through his mind – all the cherished memories and longings and wishes that he had gathered in the twelve years of his life. His father decking the Christmas tree with lights. Sleeping on the sofa during the day after another night shift at the mine. Setting off fireworks in the park on Bonfire Night. On the dodgems at the Fair. Laughing at some comedy programme on TV. How could his father possibly be this terrifying being known by others as the King of Shadows? Jamie Wave's dad was flesh and blood. Thomas Wave watched the news and ate baked beans and went to the loo and sang (badly) in the shower.

But a little grain of doubt had embedded itself in Jamie's soul. Now that he thought about it, had he ever seen his father in the full light of day? He couldn't, now he really concentrated on it, think of a single instance of it. He was at work all day long, and at weekends he often pulled another shift, and he often disappeared at night. Which was why his parents had rowed so much. Even now he could hear his mother's words, her constant mantra during their final year together: "You've changed, Tom! You're not the man I married." Even at weekends his father would stay in the living room, which had no window on the outside world, lounging on the sofa, asleep, or watching TV. All of his outdoor memories of his father began with twilight or were in full darkness. He remembered now that his mum had told him how they'd met – in a nightclub. . .

All of which was very odd.

He didn't know what to do. He felt like running at top speed out of the Delving Caves, all the way back to Cawstocke and home to his bedroom and into bed, where he would pull the covers over his head and pray that when he woke up all this weirdness would have gone away. But what he did instead was to take off the Venetian mask.

"Hello, Dad," he said. "I wondered where you'd been all this time."

The King of Shadows regarded him with an unreadable expression on his dark, narrow face. His black eyes glittered. Were those tears Jamie saw there, or just a trick of the light? Then he ran a hand through the intricate little braids on his head, just like the ones Jamie remembered his mother plaiting for him as his father sat on the floor at her feet. "I'd rather you didn't call me that."

Jamie stared at him, dumbfounded. Was it really so dark in here that his own father didn't recognize him? He cast about wildly. Perhaps he'd had an accident and banged his head and forgotten all about his former life and come wandering here to the caves a year and more ago. And perhaps he'd woken up thinking he was the King of Shadows. And the dogs and other things believed him. That seemed like a good theory. Jamie was quite proud of himself for thinking it up. But then his father did something very odd indeed. He snapped his fingers and said a couple of words and everything stopped. The dancers, the black cat, the dogs, the bats, even the leaping of the bonfire's flames. They all stopped. Stock-still. Suddenly, it was like standing in a photograph.

Then a single raucous sound rang out. The White Lady barked out a bitter little laugh. "That old trick!" she said contemptuously. "Release me and I'll show you a better one."

The King of Shadows stalked over to her and stared at her with loathing. "Never. Not now I've finally got you right where I want you."

"We could make an accord, like the agreement we used to have." Her voice was soft and wheedling.

"What, I am confined to the hours of darkness and you get all the day? Do you know what it's been like all this time, stuck here in these chilly caves, having to steal a body from time to time just to keep my powers alive? Still, I did well with this latest one, don't you think?"

He paraded this way and that, swinging his hips like a fashion model. Jamie's father had been tall and rangy, with finely chiselled features and a ready smile. The King of Shadows had all the ranginess, but none of the grace or humour of his father. Something essential was missing.

"I had to tunnel my way into the wretched silver mine

to get this one. No one comes into the caves by night any more. And even then, I was so weak I had to bargain with him, had to explain the entire ridiculous situation. He would only let me borrow the body at first for a day or two at a time, fought me all the way. Me – the King of Darkness – reduced to pleading with a mortal! I got stronger day by day, hour by hour, but still he struggled, refusing to give up and come to me until his son – or should I say 'our' son! – started at Cawstocke School. I think he thought you'd watch over him, my dear!"

Jamie began to feel sick.

The King of Shadows laughed. "And do you know, even after that he fought me. It's taken me the best part of a year to fully subdue him. He still struggles a bit even now, which is hopeless because it wears us both out. He won't last for ever, and I'm sick of being confined to darkness. Even sending my nightmares out to plague people has begun to bore me. It was interesting for a while, learning of their disturbed sleep and their bad tempers in the day, knowing that the whole town was getting run-down as a result. Even enticing them here had its charms. But the novelty has really rather worn off. Once I've worn them down sufficiently to get them here they don't really do anything, just cry and wail and try to escape. It's very annoying; very dull. I've got them dancing, but they're no good at it. No, I've a fancy to take back the light as well as the dark hours, have a proper life again. Just think of the havoc I could wreak with the whole day at my mercy. No one and nothing could escape me."

Miss Lambent smiled. "Oh, I don't think that will work at all." She turned her head towards Jamie. "Your mortal father came to see me once, did you know? Before my brother here took him, body and soul."

"Your b-brother?"

"So you see, in a way I'm your aunt. Isn't that lovely?" She gave a twisted smile. "We're twins, actually. Born of the same mother, at the same time. Well, actually, I emerged first. My brother has never forgiven me for being the elder. That would be . . . remind me, my dear . . . over a thousand years ago?"

The King of Shadows shrugged. "Who knows? Who cares? It was long ago, too long, and I'm bored with it all. Now I'm just going to have to burn you and take the Pearl from the boy and then I shall live and rule for ever." He lifted his hand to snap his fingers and bring the world back to life, but Jamie said hurriedly, "No, wait! Do you remember when you brought me and Cadence here, to Delving Caves, and showed us how the stalactites and stalagmites were formed? We threw pebbles into the deep pool and listened and counted while they fell. . ." He closed his eyes and relived the moment, hand outstretched as if he were dropping his pebble even now. "One and two and three and four. . ." He opened his eyes. "Do you remember teaching us how to count the seconds properly, to work out how far the stone fell?"

The King of Shadows lowered his hand and gazed at Jamie curiously. "No," he said. "I don't."

"Or when you made that huge Jamaican curry for dinner?" Jamie recalled it vividly, how the vapour had wreathed around his dad's face. "It was way too spicy to eat, do you remember? Really, really hot! It made our faces sweat after just one mouthful! You ate half of yours and then drank about a gallon of water. In the end Mum made us all baked beans on toast instead!"

Something twitched in the King of Shadows' face, a little muscle in his cheek. Was some part of his father still in there, Jamie wondered, like a cat trapped in the cellar of an abandoned house?

"Well done, Jamie," Miss Lambent whispered encouragingly. "That's the way. Keep going. Make him remember, that part of him that's still your father. It's our best chance!"

"Remember when Grandma came over for dinner and when she'd finished stuffing herself with pudding she made a huge farting noise and you made us laugh by walking around behind her for the rest of the night making faces at us and waving your hand in front of your nose?" Jamie couldn't help but grin at the memory, and when he looked up he found that the King of Shadows had a strange sort of half-smile on his face.

"Or when you braided Cadence's hair, and Mum had a complete fit? Or when I gave you a mug I'd made in pottery class for your birthday and the first time you used it the handle fell off and your tea went all over the white rug, and how Mum was practically in tears worrying about the stain and you and I were rolling around the floor giggling?"

The King of Shadows became very still. "Jamie. . ." he said suddenly, and it was as if the king had a second voice, a voice Jamie remembered, a voice that sent a wave of warmth through him. "Jamie, my lad. . ."

Then the muscles of his face twitched again, and the king was back in control, furious. "No you don't! I know your game and it won't work!"

"A joke," prompted Miss Lambent. "Think of your father's favourite joke."

Jamie trawled desperately through his recalcitrant brain. His dad had loved his jokes, the sillier the better. But there had been one. . . One that he made Jamie tell him again and again, each time embellishing it with a bit more detail. "There w-was this p-pirate ship," he started. "A really big one with loads of sails and a Jolly Roger flag. And the captain was a man called Black Jones, and he wore only black. He wore a black hat and a black coat and black breeches and one black boot. And his wooden leg was black, too. In fact the only thing about Black Jones that wasn't black was his parrot, Blue. And it was orange. And green."

The King of Shadows snorted, but whether it was with contempt or with humour, Jamie didn't know. He went on quickly:

"The ship had a huge crew, and every time they raided a village or overhauled another vessel, more people joined them until the ship was completely stuffed. Now, some of the voyages they went on were very long and the crew often got bored, so Black Jones decided to employ a magician to keep them entertained and make sure they didn't mutiny. Except that he was rather mean, Black Jones, so the magician he took on was a bit rubbish. It was clear to everyone, including the parrot, how he did his feeble tricks. Indeed, the parrot took to calling out what he was doing in the middle of the tricks. He'd say, 'It's up his sleeve!' or 'It's in his shoe!' or 'Look, it's not even the same hat!' and other handy tips, until the poor old magician was at his wit's end. Until the day they hit an iceberg, right in the middle of his act."

The King of Shadows was grinning now. His eyes had a sheen they hadn't had before.

"Black Jones and most of his crew drowned and, as fate would have it, the magician and the parrot are left clinging to the same bit of wreckage in the middle of the ocean. The parrot keeps staring at the magician with absolute hatred and puzzlement. At last, on the third day of floating out there in the sea, the parrot can bear it no longer—"

And then the King of Shadows interrupted him. "'OK,' the parrot croaks, 'I give up. What did you do with the ship?'" And then he burst into peals of laughter.

Jamie gazed at the man he had known as his father in delight. He was there, in front of him; he was present. He was back! Out of the corner of his eye he became aware of movement. Some of the dancers were no longer statues, frozen in time, but had slumped to the ground and were looking around, bemused and bewildered, as if they had no idea where they were or how they had got there. Some of the dogs were whining. The bats drifted back to their roosts in the roof of the caves. The owls flapped silently towards Churnock Woods. Even the bonfire seemed less lively, as if the spirit had gone out of it. It was as if the King of Shadows' magical grip had somehow loosened, if only for a moment.

And in that moment something else moved, too. Maybe

it had been the magic that had bound the White Lady to the pillar of limestone, or maybe her bonds had not been efficiently tied, but suddenly she was free!

30 THE WHITE LADY

The White Lady looked from Jamie to the King of Shadows and back again.

"How touching!" she sneered. "Father and son, together again at last. How mortified I am to have to break up this little family gathering, but *c'est la vie*." She advanced upon Jamie with her right hand held high. Between her fingers there glowed an unearthly green light.

It was the Soulstone!

"I thought we searched you thoroughly," gasped the King of Shadows.

She gave him a withering look. "I'm a *witch*. Isn't that what you called me? Don't you think we *witches* have a trick or two up our sleeves?" She glared at Jamie. "I knew you would come here, you see. You were bound to look in the Pearl and see him at the Caves, your dear departed dad. Did you really think I was so feeble I could be taken prisoner so easily?" She laughed scornfully. "Well, I suppose I helped to give you that impression."

"B-but, they've destroyed everything," Jamie said. "All the masks . . . everything."

"Masks." She clicked her fingers dismissively. "I can always make more masks. But once I've dealt with this little . . . situation, I'll have no need to hide any more, shall I? Give me the Pearl."

Jamie shook his head slowly. "I-I d-don't think so."

"Give it to me or" – she aimed the stone's light so that it beamed upon the handsome dark face of the King of Shadows – "I will send my beloved brother, and whatever is left of the soul of your father, straight to Hell!"

Jamie might have been mistaken but he could have sworn that a tremor of fear passed across the king's face, and suddenly he knew what he had to do. "What will you do if I give you the Pearl?" he asked her carefully.

"What will I do with the Pearl? Why, I shall take the power it offers me: I shall live for ever. I will be immortal!"

"And what will you do with that immortality?"

The White Lady regarded him slyly. "I shall use the gift for the good of others, of course, for the good of all."

Very slowly, Jamie Wave took the Pearl of Truth and Everlasting Life from his pocket. In his hands it instantly swelled to its usual size. He could feel the gazes of the King of Shadows and his pale twin upon it. It held their attention as honey traps flies.

"Pearl," Jamie said softly, "if the White Lady gets hold of you, what will she do?"

Quick as a flash the Pearl gave back its vision. An endless vista of light. A line of slaves toiling under a blistering sun. The White Lady, ethereally beautiful, enthroned on a mountain of gold and ivory so that she might watch the progress of the construction that was under way. Sweating, bleeding slaves driven on by whip-bearing overseers were tearing down the walls of the last buildings in Cawstocke, levelling the ground. Down went houses, schools, the hospital, churches; down went the football ground. Down went Little Delving and the outlying villages, down went all the trees in Churnock Woods and up went walls and towers and guard posts until a gilded palace complex covered the ground in every direction as far as the eye could see. The ancient standing stones and stone circles that had graced the Downs since the dawn of human time were gone. In their place were raised enormous statues of the White Lady, presiding over the entire landscape. Below them, white-robed women made ritual chants, while men in strange masks slaughtered a variety of pleading animals, whose red blood splashed obscenely over the ground. . .

The White Lady seemed mesmerized. "Ah," she breathed, seduced by the vision in the Pearl. "Aaahh. How beautiful. Yes!" And then she launched herself at Jamie.

He saw the Soulstone coming for him. For the briefest second he was paralysed with terror. Time seemed to slow – or perhaps it really did slow. Perhaps this was the parting gesture of the King of Shadows. For in that moment, he lunged. Pushing Jamie aside, he raised the Pearl of Truth and Everlasting Life so that the gleaming orb met the full force of the Soulstone.

There was a great roaring noise; a whoosh; a quake. The shockwave passed through him, shaking every atom of Jamie's being. He felt as if he were being torn apart, disassembled by a giant intelligence, the shards scattered wide and then drawn back together. The light of the blast tore through him. It was like being pierced by a million brilliant rays, and when it ended Jamie couldn't see a thing. He rocked where he stood.

Somebody took his hand. "Jamie? Jamie Wave? Are you all right?"

He blinked and something – someone – came into focus. Someone not quite as tall as him, and with bright red hair.

"Jinny?"

She was so relieved she couldn't speak. Instead, she just smiled and smiled and smiled.

Jamie let his eyes adjust to the new light. Dawn was just announcing itself over Churnock Woods, the dark trees standing out clearly against the tinge of reddened cloud. He looked around. Of the White Lady, whom he had known as Miss Lambent, there was no sign. The King of Shadows – or was it his father? – lay unmoving on the ground. Jamie's mother was bent over him, running her fingers through his tangled braids in a gesture that was infinitely tender.

"Thomas," she said, over and over. "Come back, come back to us."

Thomas Wave stirred and blinked. He caught his wife's hand in his own and brought it to his lips. "Jemima," he whispered. "Is it really you?"

At the moment of her father's awakening, Cadence Wave appeared in the entrance to the cave, her hair tousled, her eyes sleepy. She looked as if she had just woken up after a long weekend's partying. Perhaps she had. She caught Jamie's eye and stared at him, puzzled. Then she grinned. "Crikey O'Reilly!" she exclaimed. "That was a dream and a half!" She transferred her gaze to the ground in front of Jamie. "What's that?"

Jamie looked down. Something pale lay in a heap of cinders at his feet. He poked at it curiously and it fell to one side.

"Aaaagh!" He leapt back, horrified.

Jinny Briggs caught his arm. "What is it?"

Amongst the blackened charcoal, the skeleton of what had been Miss Lambent's right hand stood out white and gleaming, the delicate finger bones still grasping the Soulstone. All the green malice had gone out of the stone. It looked as the Tiger's Eye had looked after she had drained it of its magic – lifeless and harmless at last.

"Where's the rest of her?" Jinny asked in awe.

Jamie shook his head slowly. "I really don't think I want to know."

Beside the gruesome remnant of their one-time art teacher lay the Pearl of Truth and Everlasting Life, apparently untouched. Jamie knelt and picked it up. He nearly dropped it instantly as something moved inside it. Somehow, he remained holding on to it in grim fascination, watching as something drew closer, and closer, and closer. Something dark and shiny, a swirling purple and black. He couldn't drag his gaze away from it, could feel himself going woozy as he looked at it. He remembered a similar sensation. . .

The colours coalesced and a long vertical line of black suddenly split the sphere of the Pearl from top to bottom. And then . . . it blinked. It was like shutters coming across from the sides of the sphere, rather than from top and bottom like any normal eye. Dread gripped him.

"Hello, Jamie Wave."

He knew instinctively that the voice didn't come from behind him, in the shadows of the caves. But he couldn't help himself from looking around, because he couldn't believe what his instinct was telling him. There was his father, sitting up and touching his head gingerly as if he had banged it and he wasn't sure how. There was his mother, beaming in a way Jamie hadn't seen for the best part of two years; and Cadence, crying and laughing at the same time. None of them were looking in his direction, and it certainly hadn't been Jinny who had spoken. He stared at the Pearl.

"Yes, I'm here."

The eye drew back, then acquired a surrounding of delicate green-gold scales, a long muzzle, a horn, an ear; a bit of shoulder and a wing.

"Hello, Heavenly Dragon," Jamie said uncertainly. "I don't understand. Are you actually *in* the Pearl?"

"Of course. It is a part of me just as I am a part of it. Always has been, ever since it came to me. Paradox though that is."

"Then why did you give it to me?"

"I did say it was a loan."

Jamie, who knew he could be surprised by nothing any more, said, "Um, how do I give it back to you? I mean, to China, and all?"

China was a very long way away, and even if he'd had the money for the air fare he was pretty sure the dragon didn't live in a China that existed now. He wondered whether the mirror and the lion mask would still work now that the Maskmaker was dead. . .

"Don't worry about any of that," said the Heavenly Dragon. "But before I take back my Pearl, I want to say, well done. You were very brave."

"I didn't feel brave."

"That's the bravest thing of all. You can only really be brave if you're scared, but still you stand your ground. And you stood your ground, Jamie Wave. Because of you the magic that had rooted itself in those who fought over the dark and the light has cancelled itself out. Such battles are going on all over the world, all the time, in a thousand different ways, but it is good to see that in this small corner of the world balance has been restored once more. You can be proud of yourself for that. Now the people of your tribe will be able to get on with their lives in safety, free to make their own choices and mistakes, their own chances of happiness. I must go now, and I doubt we will ever meet again, but I am proud to have made your acquaintance." It paused. "And I enjoyed your joke about the magician and the ship."

"You were listening?"

The eye gazed at him solemnly. Then it winked. Then something broke the surface of the Pearl in just the same manner that the Heavenly Dragon had broken the surface of Tianshan Lake. It was a single scaly talon, followed by another, and another and another, till it seemed that the Pearl of Truth and Everlasting Life was grasped by a great claw attached to an invisible arm.

"Meeearrrow!"

The black cat was at his feet. In its mouth it held the white Venetian half-mask. Jamie stared at it, not sure what to do. The cat had betrayed him, betrayed them all. He wasn't sure how he felt about that. But it looked so desperate that he sat down on the ground beside it and put the mask on, one-handed, being careful not to drop the Pearl and its semi-invisible occupant. "I'm not sure this is going to work any more," he told the cat.

"Please," Jasper implored, "I need to know what the witch did with my wife and kittens."

One by one, the talons disappeared back into the Pearl.

"Place a paw on the Pearl and ask your question," the dragon intoned, and Jasper touched the pad of his front foot to the gleaming surface.

"Where are Cressida, Flo and Aurelio?"

A crack of light appeared in the sphere and both Jamie and Jasper saw, low down, as if from a cat's eye view, a vast and terrible machine roaring slowly down a road. It stopped, and a door in its side opened. A figure in neon overalls clambered out and walked around to the rear of the monster. The figure disappeared from view for a few moments, then reappeared hauling two giant green wheelie bins. These he attached to a metal brace and the machine whined and shrieked and lifted the bins high before inverting them so that their contents spilled into its ever-hungry maw. Then a cage came down and something inside the machine bore down upon the new arrivals, crushing and crushing and crushing.

"It's the binmen," breathed Jamie Wave.

Now the Pearl offered a view of a sleepy-eyed man in the driver's seat, pressing buttons and pulling levers. Then the lorry drew slowly away, causing the second man in the depleted crew to run after it and jump on to the footplate at the back of the vehicle.

The vista changed again, whirling through the streets of Cawstocke until it came to rest on a building Jamie knew well. It was the back of his school, behind the kitchens, where they kept the rubbish bins. Quite distinctly, a mewing sound could be heard coming from one of the bins.

Jinny gasped. "They're in the bin! They'll be crushed!"

At once, Jasper's paw came off the Pearl. He turned panicked eyes to them. "We've got to go!" he cried. "Now!"

Jamie hesitated. He looked towards his family, then back at the Pearl.

"Go," said the dragon. "They'll be at home waiting for you. The cat let you down, but he did it for the best of reasons. The only reason that really counts, in the end. Go on, Jamie. Be a hero one more time."

And then the Pearl . . . disappeared, with a faint popping sound. Just like that. As if the very air of the cave had swallowed it up.

Jamie Wave looked at Jinny.

"Don't you dare go without me!" she said fiercely.

Jamie catches her by the hand and together they follow the black cat, up the hill, through the woods and across the Downs as the sun rises into the morning sky. It's a long hard run all the way back to Cawstocke School, but for some reason they feel full of energy, and full of hope.

EPILOGUE

It's a Saturday morning and the sun is shining down on May Street. It shines on gleaming glass and the gloss of newly painted window frames. It shines on the window boxes overflowing with bright red and pink geraniums. It shines on the cobbles, now free of weeds and rubbish; it shines on repaired roofs and brass door-knockers.

We pass an antique shop, outside which a pretty flowered sofa has been placed. Sitting on it, a girl with long blonde hair sips coffee from a polystyrene cup and laughs with a man with intricate braids and flashing dark eyes. He ruffles her hair affectionately; she pokes him in the stomach and a mock-fight ensues, but it is not very serious: the girl doesn't want to spill her coffee.

Opposite, there is a costume shop, and a woman in the shopfront is putting the finishing touches to the stiff white ruff on a figure of Queen Elizabeth I, complete with massive farthingaled skirt and curly red wig. Next to her is the mannequin of a pirate, looking just like Captain Jack Sparrow, down to the eyeliner and slouch hat. *Got a fancy-dress party to go to?* reads a large card in the window. *We've got everything from gorilla suits to spacesuits!*

The fancy dress shop is doing well. There have been a lot of parties in Cawstocke in the past few months, for people seem to have plenty to celebrate. There have been Christmas and birthday parties, office parties and weddings – and parties just because people feel like having a party. People are working again in Cawstocke, and working hard. New businesses have started up; the council has dedicated money to regenerating the run-down areas, like May Street. They have even given out grants to local people to start up new shops and cafés and smarten up the town. Money is flowing around the system again; even the football team has struck winning form at last. It looks as if they may even be promoted this season, after all. Cawstocke School is thriving, especially in art. The new art teacher has inspired his pupils, bringing a whole new cultural perspective to their studies. His name is Mr Long. He says in Chinese his name means something very specific, but no one has managed to discover what it is yet. He's told them all about the lucky properties of the colour red and he has told them amazing stories about the battles between gods and heroes and magical dragons.

The woman in the shopfront stands back now to admire her handiwork, then turns and grins at the couple opposite. It is Jemima Wave.

Her daughter, Cadence, waves back; Cadence's father gets up from the flowered sofa and slips across the road and into the costume shop, where he whips the wig off poor old Gloriana, leaving her mannequin as bald and vulnerable as she was in life, and jams it over his braids, and Mrs Wave laughs at her husband, and laughs, and laughs. And then the door opens and a bell rings and two more customers come in.

The adjoining shopfront still boasts its original, ancient sign.

The Maskmaker

it says, in its ancient, flowing script, now repainted gold and bright against its glossy wooden background.

We push open its heavy old door. Inside we find it is connected to the costume shop next door by a wide double door. Through it Thomas and Jemima Wave can be seen encouraging a pair of customers in fake medieval knight outfits to flourish their plastic swords at one another.

In this part of the shop, though, as the name promises,

there are masks everywhere. All sorts of masks. Masks for fancy-dress parties, masks of famous singers and footballers, actors and politicians. Monster masks for horror and Halloween. Elegant eye-masks and Venetian masks ready to be worn to a midnight ball. Superheroes and cartoon characters. Masks from ancient civilizations, Indian, African, Maori and Aztec; the head of an Ancient Egyptian pharaoh and a Native American chieftain complete with feather headdress. A Viking mask sits next to one of Darth Vader. The wizard Gandalf and the famous swordsman Zorro. And a number of handmade masks made from papier mâché and plaster of Paris: of fanciful beings all pink and sparkly, sequinned and feathered; of unicorns and dragons, and one particularly handsome tiger painted in shades of rusty orange and black and white, with a ruff of fake white fur, a nose of dusky pink, and sharp teeth showing between its black lips.

A couple of people are already in the shop: a girl with long curly red hair and a good-looking, dark-skinned boy. They are kneeling on the floor, playing with a fabric mouse attached to a length of wool and a pair of handsome tabby cats.

"Oh, Flo!" cries the girl as the female cat snags the mouse yet again. "Do give Aurelio a chance."

But Aurelio is bored by the game already: he is too old for this sort of nonsense. Now, if it were a *real* mouse, things would be quite different. Then he would be like the tiger on the shelf above. He would be a mighty hunter, ripping his prey to shreds. And he would share none of it with his sister at all.

Above them, on the counter, sits a smart black cat with penetrating orange eyes and a rather elegant striped cat. Their tails are entwined to form an infinity symbol, like a sideways figure of eight.

As the door opens they all look up. "Hello, Michael," the girl says.

The first of the boys who has just come in smiles sheepishly. "Um, hello, Jinny." He blushes.

The second visitor is not so shy. He has a face like a weasel, narrow black eyes and lips like a pair of chipolata sausages.

The lad who was playing with the cats stands up. "Hello, Mouth," he says warily.

"I'd rather you called me Freddie," the other boy says, looking awkward. "We, er. . ." He looks to his friend for support. "We, um, well, we heard you sell 'adventures' here."

Jamie Wave grins widely. "Ah, adventures. Yes, we do. Adventures can be hard to come by in the modern world.

Real adventures, that is. But everyone should have one." He makes an expansive gesture, one that takes in all the hundreds of creations populating the polished shelves.

"Choose a mask," he says.